W9-CGL-652

DARK MOUNTAIN

DAVID WOLF BOOK 10

JEFF CARSON

CROSS ATLANTIC PUBLISHING

"FREAKING CRAZY. The next morning, I was on the ground by the plant in the living room and my pants were around my ankles." Deputy Thomas Rachette of the Sluice–Byron County Sheriff's Department adjusted the vent so that the vanilla-scented air fluttered across his closely shaved hair.

Pat Xander laughed and slapped the steering wheel. "Man, I'm telling you, it's that kind of stuff that made me quit drinking. You should give it a try."

"You know what? I think you're right," Rachette said, meaning zero of the words he'd just said. "I tell you what, though. That plant was the healthiest in my apartment."

"You talking about that decrepit one that leaned against the wall over by the window?"

"Yeah."

"Wasn't that the only plant you had?"

"Yeah, so?"

Smiling wider, Pat shook his head and switched the radio dial to 90.3.

With the local NPR station providing an acoustic instrumental as his soundtrack, Rachette leaned back and let the washboard dirt road massage his body through the passenger seat.

The forest flitted by the window, gilded by a half-moon hovering in a sea of stars. Another flash lit the landscape, coming from the encroaching storm behind them.

"Gonna be a big one," Rachette said. "You'd better be careful on the way home. Last night, it rained so hard it almost washed away the doghouse."

"You're gonna be in the doghouse tonight."

Rachette smiled and eyed the dash clock, which read 11:10 p.m. "Nah. Char won't care."

The truth was, he was proud of himself for cutting short this Thursday-evening trip to the bar. Usually he would've downed at least three more, which would've put him over the edge. Drinking only seven beers, and not nine or ten, meant he'd sleep well tonight and wake up feeling decent.

He had tomorrow off work, but being hungover for the appointment would've been a bad move. Charlotte would've been pissed and probably read something too deep into the fact that he was pie-eyed for their latest look at the baby's progress on ultrasound.

His wife needed to be calm, which was Rachette's sole mission in life these days. Stress was how miscarriages happened.

"You guys pregnant yet?" Pat asked, apparently a phenom mind-reader.

"No, not yet," Rachette lied. Because that's how miscarriages happened, too. You talked about it too early to people and jinxed your luck. He knew that from last time.

Charlotte was past her first trimester, which was usually the go-ahead to start blurting out baby names and posting ultrasound pictures on the internet, but they were playing it safe this time around.

"You still trying?"

Rachette made a noncommittal noise.

"Ahhhh ... never mind. I get it."

Rachette pinched an eye and looked at his designated Thursday-night Uber-driver.

Pat turned up the music a notch and tapped a beat on the gear shift.

The man was more than a driver. He was a likeable, rock-solid guy and Rachette considered him a friend. Since Rachette now lived in the boonies, he paid twenty bucks for the ride. Probably a little overpriced considering it took about thirty minutes, round trip, but Pat was a night owl and never failed to show up, which couldn't be said for the other flaky bastards who drove in Rocky Points.

"Thanks again for picking me up, brother," Rachette said.

"Yep."

Leaning back again, he gazed out the windshield and down the straight road gouged through the virgin forest. Tall mountains cut the east and west sky, striped with snow tendrils glowing in the moonlight.

Since their marriage last year, Rachette and Charlotte had purchased a small place on five acres, northeast of town. Staring at the darkened woods, he smiled to himself with satisfaction at their decision to buy out here, where few others lived.

To move into the sticks was ballsy, but to wake up on his own chunk of raw land every day brought back memories of growing up on the farm in Nebraska. He and his sister had been raised by mother nature as much as their parents, and now he and Charlotte could recreate that experience with their own family.

"What's happening here?"

Rachette blinked out of his reverie and saw Pat leaned toward the windshield.

A beat-up Ford truck with a raised hood was parked along the right shoulder. A man poked his head out from the engine, then walked out, wiping both his hands on a rag.

"Damn," Rachette said. "Broke down out here in the middle

of the night with a storm rolling in. Better stop and see what's the haps."

"Yeah, plus this guy might get killed by the crazy people living up here," Pat said, slowing to a crawl.

"Funny."

They were nearing Rachette's house, no more than a few miles up road.

Pat flicked his lights back to normal and pulled up behind the truck. It had New Mexico plates and was a mid-eighties model Ford F-150 painted black with a white stripe, speckled with rust and dented more than a few times.

"Wow, who's this guy?" Rachette asked, unbuckling his seatbelt.

Still holding his hands cocooned in a rag, the man stood motionless in the headlights. His head tilted downward and his glimmering eyes peeked out from under a prominent brow covered with hair.

"Frickin' Neanderthal looking ..." Rachette opened the door. "I'll check it out. Stay in here."

"I'm pretty good with engines," Pat said.

"Okay. Well, keep your ass in the truck for now."

Rachette shut the door, hitched up his jeans, and walked around the front of Pat's car and through dust swirling in the headlights. The night was brisk and the air smelled like pine and the approaching rain.

The guy's beady eyes tracked Rachette, but the angle of his head remained unmoved, which made the headlights paint a long shadow over his brow.

"How's it going?" Rachette asked.

Big lips parted and glistened with saliva, but the guy said nothing. His out-of-order expression remained until he flinched as a flash of lightning lit up the sky.

"It's coming in," Rachette said. "What's happening with the truck? Broke down, eh?"

No response.

The man wore jeans and a black zip-up jacket. His sweatshirt-rag was clean, which Rachette thought odd since he'd been digging under the hood. He scanned the man's waistline and saw no bulges, but decided the jacket was bulky enough to hide a weapon tucked underneath.

Rachette had seven beers pumping in his veins, but buzz or not, he was a cop and had a bad feeling about this guy.

"I asked how it's going," Rachette said.

The man closed his lips.

Had he blinked yet? Rachette didn't think so.

"Well, what happened?" Pat asked out his window. "You broke down?"

The man squinted toward Pat's voice.

His scalp was shorn close, and Rachette saw a long scar running around his head. Perhaps he'd been injured in one of the wars. Now Rachette felt disgusted with himself for judging this guy.

"Pat, why don't you get out here and give it a look?"

Pat's door squeaked open and he walked into the light. "Hey there. I'm Pat. Your name?"

The guy blinked and took a step back from Pat's outstretched hand.

"Uh ... right." Pat gave Rachette a sidelong glance and made for the truck. "So, can I take a look under the hood?"

The man's eyes darted towards something behind them.

The uneasy feeling in Rachette boiled up again, and that's when the silence was shattered by two shotgun slides racking back and forth, followed by a cocking pistol hammer.

His stomach quickened and his muscles tensed.

Flashlight beams danced across Rachette and Pat as crunching footsteps approached behind them.

"Freeze right where you are, gentlemen." The voice was deep and forceful.

Rachette raised his hands and Pat followed suit.

"What the hell is going on here?" Rachette asked, anger fueling his voice. They'd been duped into this, and now, rather than pity the man who'd flagged them down, he wanted to beat him to a pulp. "Who are you guys? Show yourselves." He turned to look over his shoulder and in the same instant felt a blow to the back of his head.

CHAPTER 2

"OH MY GOD."

The exasperation in the woman's voice two tables over made Chief Detective David Wolf lower his forkful of eggs and hash browns. Most eyes in the Sunnyside Café swiveled to the windows, so he twisted to the glass next to him and scanned the parking lot for himself.

Outside, two men stood chest to chest, poking one another, each balling a fist by his side.

"Shit." Wolf dropped his fork and slid off the linoleum booth bench.

"Go get 'em, Dave!" a woman's voice called after him as he pushed through the entrance door.

"Hey!" he said, marching through the parking lot.

"She came home with me, bro. So why don't you just get back in your piece-of-shit car and drive away?"

"She's my girlfriend. Go get your own and get the hell out of here. Crystal! What are you doing?"

Wolf stood between them. "Gentlemen, please. Calm down."

A woman, a young boy pulled next to her, watched from across the parking lot. She seemed torn between getting back in her car and going into the restaurant.

"Go away, Jed!" a muffled woman's voice screamed out of an old Saturn sedan. Crystal, apparently.

"Who are you, asshole?" one of the men asked Wolf. "Mind your own business."

Wolf recognized one man as Matt Whitsom but couldn't put a name to the guy asking the question. Facing the stranger, he put a hand on the paddle-holstered Glock tucked into the waistband of his jeans. Next to the gun, a Sluice–Byron County SD badge hung from his belt.

"I said beat it, asshole." The man stared into Wolf's eyes with a practiced psychotic glare.

Being a detective, Wolf had no set dress code so he usually donned a pair of jeans and button-up patterned shirt, like he wore now. He also drove an unmarked SUV. The drawback of the first privilege was playing out.

"It is my business," Wolf said, tilting up his badge. "Now why don't you lower your voice and stop cussing. There're kids out here in the parking lot. There're families watching you guys through the windows of the restaurant."

The man remained oblivious. "Move it!"

He grabbed for Wolf's shoulder and Wolf blocked him, connecting hard with the man's forearm bone.

With lightning speed, the man threw a left jab and hit Wolf's forehead.

Wolf leaned his head back, seeing stars for an instant, then leveled his gaze on the man.

"Oh, shit." The man backed away and threw up his hands for mercy. "Sorry, I didn't see the badge until just now! I didn't know. I didn't know."

Wolf fought back the urge to charge. Noticing the alcohol stench in the air for the first time only fueled his fury.

"Hey! That's the sheriff, you asshole!" Matt Whitsom said behind him, which wasn't true—Wolf was now chief detective—

but the statement had a horrifying effect on the other man. "Aw, you're screwed!"

An SBCSD siren chirped and a department SUV sped into the lot.

"Sorry, sir! I didn't know! Please!"

"Yeah, bro! You're going to get it. This is David Wolf!"

Wolf turned to Matt Whitsom and held up a finger. "Please be—"

Matt had been jumping up and down close behind Wolf, and as Wolf turned, Matt accidentally head-butted him in the temple.

"Ah ..." Wolf grabbed his head and bared his teeth. Hot pain spread to the back of his neck.

"Shit ... sorry." Matt backed away with the same mercy gesture but received none as Deputy Nelson parked, flew out of his car, and tackled him to the pavement like an NFL linebacker.

More sounds of flesh and bone bouncing off the parking lot came from behind, and Wolf turned to see the other man face down with Undersheriff Wilson straddling his back.

"You all right?" Wilson asked.

Wolf nodded, regretting the gesture immediately.

"Stay down!" Deputy Nelson pushed Matt Whitsom's head into the ground.

Without having to turn, Wolf knew that a crowd of cellphone owners had gathered to watch the action.

"Deputy," he said.

Nelson caught Wolf's tone and let up. "On your feet."

"Nearest unit to assist an 11-24 up on County Road 18." The radios on their hips squawked with the voice of their dispatcher, Tammy Granger, letting them know about an abandoned vehicle.

Wolf watched with a throbbing head as Wilson cuffed the mystery man and Nelson followed suit with Matt Whitsom. A crowd spilled outside the front door of the Sunnyside.

Wilson looked up at Wolf. "Uh ... you want to take that? Or this?"

CHAPTER 3

COUNTY ROAD 18 was a heavily forested gravel road that Wolf was recently familiar with. Months ago, Tom Rachette, Wolf's detective, had moved into an area along the route known as Ponderosa Gulch, a rare section of the Chautauqua Valley that had yet to be overrun with homes.

Wolf had yet to reach Rachette's new place when he saw Deputy Yates's SUV parked on the shoulder. He slowed to a stop behind the vehicle and checked his forehead in the rearview mirror. An angry welt rose above and between his eyebrows as if his skull was birthing a golf ball.

The scent of pine filled his nose as he stepped outside. He heard water rushing somewhere in the trees below. What would normally have been a trickling stream was howling with melt-season runoff from the thirteen-thousand-foot peaks lining the east side of the valley.

He walked around the SUV's bumper and went to the edge of the shoulder.

Yates stood next to a Chevy sedan in the trees down the slope.

"Hey!" Wolf called down to him.

"Hey!"

The vehicle had done a Price-Is-Right Plinko-chip impression down the side of the mountain, side-swiping trees before slamming head-on into a ponderosa. The tree trunk had snapped at the base and fallen onto the car's roof, which explained the overpowering pine smell.

"Whatcha got here?" Wolf asked.

Yates shrugged. "Apparently, we got an anonymous call about this thing a couple of hours ago. I just got down here. Watch your step. It's muddy."

Studying the scrape marks Yates had left, Wolf took the warning to heart as he stepped over the edge and skidded down on his heels.

After a brisk descent, he entered a cloud of Yates's cologne.

Deputy Yates was in his mid-forties, fit and muscular from a religious workout ethic. He wore an SBCSD baseball cap shading a nose like a hawk's beak and bulging blue eyes. He pointed at Wolf. "What happened to you?"

"Zit."

Yates frowned and studied his head closer.

"Anonymous call, you said?" Wolf steered the attention back to the mangled Chevy sedan.

"Some guy. Didn't leave a name. Tammy says it didn't hit."

Meaning the phone number wasn't associated with a known person in the dispatch computer system. The people in and around Rocky Points and its surrounding Rocky Mountain boonies often carried prepaid anonymous phones.

The vehicle's interior looked empty and clean through the windows. The only anomaly was the dent in the felted ceiling from the hundreds of pounds of tree lying on it.

"What do you think?" Yates asked.

Wolf shrugged. "I think it's a strange place to park your car."

He studied the slope above. His and Yates's fresh tracks gouged the hillside. Otherwise, last night's rain had carved a web of erosion channels into the ground, erasing any other clues.

"Doesn't look like anyone climbed up," Yates said, following

Wolf's gaze. "But it rained like shit last night so it could've erased the footprints. When I was pulling over up there, my SUV almost slid over the edge." Yates turned downhill. "That water's really flowing. The driver could've walked down, I guess."

"You see any blood inside?" Wolf asked, donning some latex gloves.

Yates lifted his cap and wiped his forehead with his sleeve. "None that I can see. Registration and insurance in the glove compartment show the vehicle belonging to Pat Xander, with an X."

"How about the trunk?"

"It's jammed shut. Big dent in the side where it hit a tree so I couldn't get it open. And that's as far as I've gotten. Now you're here."

Wolf lifted the handle on the rear door. It swung open, bouncing hard on its hinges, and he caught the scent of vanilla, along with something much less pleasant.

"You smell that?" Wolf wrinkled his nose.

"The vanilla? No shit, the guy has three air fresheners around his stick shift."

Wolf leaned in and reached behind the headrest of the rear seat. He found a button and pushed, but it was locked.

"No keys?" Wolf eyed the steering-wheel column.

"Nope."

The smell had become a stench now.

"Geez. You step in dog shit?" Yates asked.

"We have to open this."

"Why? What?"

Wolf ducked out and gave Yates a grim look.

Yates took his hands off the car door and stumbled back. "Oh shit. Are you kidding me?"

Wolf dug his toes into the slope and began to climb. He slipped immediately on some mud and landed on his knee. Using his hands, he continued upward at a fast clip, muddying his gloves in the process.

By the time he'd clawed his way to the top and reached his SUV door, he was breathing heavily. Not because he was out of shape; rather, it had been a steep climb.

Lately, he'd been proud of his fitness level. He was no Yates but he'd been hiking regularly with Lauren and Ella, and his trips to the department gym had become a three-day-per-week habit. He'd flex his muscles for Ella and the seven-year-old would gawk in awe. Or at least she'd pretend to. She was easily readable, though, and he believed she was sincere. He'd also flex them for Lauren, who openly pretended.

Wolf popped the SUV's hatch, dumped his muddy gloves inside, and pocketed some new ones. Then he unzipped a backpack—a waterproof design filled with extra cold-weather clothing, protein bars, water, lighters, a flint, multitool, and other necessary accoutrements in case of emergency.

He fished around inside the pack and pulled out a jackknife pick set. Designed like a pocket knife, the tool had seven tempered stainless steel picks and could open many basic locks.

He pocketed it, then closed the door and skidded back down the slope.

Yates was well away from the sedan now and looking pale.

Wolf ducked back inside and inserted a pick. He tried to open it, then switched to the next one in line.

Yates shuffled closer and watched.

After a minute of jiggling and twisting inside the lock, the seat flopped open onto Wolf's knee.

Daylight bore into the darkened space behind the seat, illuminating brown, neatly combed hair, along with bone, gray matter, and blood.

Wolf held his breath, his eyes fixed on the sickening display. When his lungs screamed, he backed outside the door.

"What?" Yates stumbled out of the way. "What's in there?"

"Dead male." Wolf turned to the trees and sucked in mountain air. "Shot in the head."

Yates snuck a peek and then walked away from the vehicle, looking like he might be sick. "Shit. Can't un-see that."

CHAPTER 4

"PAT XANDER." Sheriff MacLean spat on the shoulder of County Road 18. He glazed his steel-gray eyes and shifted the Copenhagen snuff to the other side of his bottom lip. "I know the guy's mother. Mary Xander. Owns that vitamin shop in town."

Wolf nodded. He'd met her before.

Another vehicle rolled down the road behind them and parked, adding to the line of trucks from multiple county agencies.

Down the slope, Dr. Lorber, the county medical examiner, and his team of white-clad crime-scene investigators swarmed the vehicle below. A camera flashed inside Pat Xander's trunk, which had since been pried open with crow bars.

"He's a driver," Undersheriff Wilson said. "One of those Uber guys."

MacLean looked up at his undersheriff like the man had spoken Mandarin Chinese.

Wilson was tall and muscular underneath a thick padding of perpetual winter weight. Though much bigger than MacLean, he looked down at his boss like he might get punched. "Uber? The car-ride service?"

MacLean blinked. "Yeah, I've heard of it. Normal people

giving taxi rides with their own cars. Uses an app on the phone." He frowned. "You think I live in a box?"

"Yes. Of course you've heard of it, sir."

MacLean turned his gaze toward the vehicle below and petted his goatee. "Looks like Pat picked up a psycho last night."

"We can check easily enough." As if taking a cue from his boss, Wilson stroked his own facial hair, a thick blond cop mustache. "Soon as Lorber gets the phone back to the station."

Sheriff MacLean looked at Wolf. "Get on that."

Wolf nodded.

"Shit. I'm beginning to think this town's pipes are made of lead." MacLean spat again and raised his eyes to the waves of blue mountains above the trees. "I'll head into town and tell his mother."

Wolf was somewhat taken aback, assuming the sheriff would've pawned that terrible deed on one of the two men standing next to him. Sheriff MacLean delegated well and often.

Wilson seemed equally surprised and flicked a glance at Wolf.

"On another note." MacLean turned to Wolf. "You have the go-ahead to hire. It's official. I was going to tell you when you came in this morning. So, now's a good a time as any to pull the trigger on that stack of résumés. Looks like you're gonna need the help."

Wolf raised his eyebrows and nodded. There had been a hiring freeze after last year's Van Gogh Killer case. The sick-minded culprit had become official county personnel, which had spooked the council and elected officials. For months, they'd been vetting every step of every department's hiring practices to make sure it never happened again.

Wolf's best detective, Heather Patterson, had quit the department to go work for a law firm. Wolf and Rachette were the entire detective squad now.

"So cram that into your schedule and smoke it," MacLean said.

"Right," Wolf said, not enjoying the thought of picking one of ten underqualified potential hires that had put their names in the hat.

Down the slope, the body was still in the trunk and Lorber reached inside to take some samples. Standing at six foot seven inches tall, the medical examiner towered over his team when he straightened up to his full height. After doling out orders to the man holding the camera, he turned and waved a long arm at Wolf.

Wolf raised a hand in greeting and hooked a thumb on his belt.

"This is going to be a bomb." MacLean took off his cowboy hat and rubbed his forehead. Turning on his boot heels, he walked down the road, uttering obscenities.

Wolf and Wilson followed silently.

A dozen people from various county departments spoke in hushed tones. Vehicles lined the opposite shoulder and squawked with radio noise.

"All right, I'm heading out." MacLean walked to his SUV, climbed in, and fired it up.

"He spends a couple of hundred bucks a month on vitamins from Mary Xander," Wilson said.

"Aha."

"He's always trying to get me in that shop. Won't shut up about the regularity of his bowels."

Wolf blew air from his nose. Watching the receding SUV, he didn't envy the man his duty. Wolf'd had the unenviable job of telling parents that their children were dead, and he could scarcely think of anything worse.

"Forehead's looking normal," Wilson said.

"Yeah? Good. What happened with those two?"

"Apparently, they were fighting over some broad in the car."

"Crystal," Wolf said.

"You know her?"

"Nope."

Wilson gave him a puzzled look. "Anyway, I know what it's like to be her. Women are always fighting over me."

Wolf smiled. Wilson had three kids and was happily married. He'd never seen the guy out in a social setting without the whole family in tow.

Gazing up the road, Wolf pulled out his cellphone. "Well, looks like Rachette will have to work through a hangover."

"God knows it won't be his first time," Wilson said. "See you in a bit." The undersheriff melted into the crowd.

Wolf dialed and checked his watch—9:38 a.m. At this time, there was a chance Rachette was still asleep. His detective tended to drink enough alcohol to kill an elephant on Thursday nights, then sleep like a teenager on Fridays while Charlotte went to work.

The phone rang until it went to voicemail. Music filled Wolf's ear: Rick Astley's "Never Gonna Give You Up." Rachette spoke loudly over the soundtrack. "Hey, you've reached Thomas Reginald Rachette. I can't get to the phone right now because I'm probably screening you. Leave a message and I'll consider calling you back."

Wolf hit the call-end button, knowing a note strapped to a pigeon's leg had a better chance of reaching Rachette than a voicemail.

Staring at the screen, Wolf remembered the last time he'd seen Pat Xander alive. Wolf had been with Rachette inside the coffee shop on Main, and the two men had acted like more than acquaintances. Hangover or not, his detective would want to know about this sooner rather than later.

He started tapping out a text message, then decided a personal wakeup call might be better.

CHAPTER 5

RACHETTE'S new Chevy Colorado pickup was parked in the driveway and gleamed in the overcast morning light.

Sparky, his black Lab, barked incessantly in the backyard at Wolf's arrival. That the dog could make such a racket without a scolding told Wolf that nobody was home, but he went to the door and knocked anyway.

Knee-high wildflowers and grass swayed in the breeze in front of the house. Apparently, Rachette had yet to buy that riding lawnmower he'd talked about.

Wolf took a step back from the front porch and appraised the paint job Rachette had been bragging about for two weeks. A house that had once been covered in flaking forest green was now gray with white trim.

When Wolf had first seen the one-story structure, it had looked droopy and sad. Now shorn up and sturdy-looking, it was a perfect place to raise a family, which he knew was Charlotte and Tom's precise intention.

He knocked a few more times and got no response, then remembered Rachette mentioning that Charlotte had a doctor's appointment this morning. He'd thought it probably had to do with the pregnancy he wasn't supposed to know about.

After her morning rounds at County Hospital one day, Lauren had stopped in to visit her friend in pre-natal when she saw Charlotte emerging from the ultrasound room. It took a second for the nurse to figure out what was going on, and Charlotte had admitted she was pregnant and asked her to not tell anyone. Which meant, of course, that Lauren had told Wolf at dinner that night.

Rachette had been silent about it for more than a month after that incident; and under threat from Lauren, Wolf had been playing dumb ever since.

He stepped off the front porch and pulled out his cellphone. After deciding against another call, he shot off a message to Rachette, telling him there was an emergency and that he needed to talk to him right away.

Sparky barked harder than ever, so Wolf walked around the house to the back and stuck a hand through the fence. The dog wagged its tail and eagerly received a scratch behind the ear.

"Tell your dad to call me," he said.

Sparky barked again and ran away at full speed, then returned with a tennis ball.

Wolf smiled and pulled the sopping-wet ball through the wire, then tossed it back into the yard.

"I'm leaving," he said, walking back to his SUV.

CHAPTER 6

HEATHER PATTERSON KNELT on the damp ground inside the trees flanking the multi-million-dollar mansion. Aspen leaves ruffled on the breeze, casting a green glow on the forest floor.

The house she was staking out stood like a metal-and-glass sculpture. Nestled in Aspen's southeastern hills, it wasn't far from where she'd grown up. But this homecoming was a job and she felt little nostalgic. With that thought in mind, she shifted to the next aspen tree over, getting a better view through the forest to her target's windows.

She'd already photographed the cherry-red Porsche approaching the property, the woman parking and getting out, her picking a wedgie—which surprised her as she'd assumed that such an occasion would merit going commando—and then some more photos of the woman walking up to the giant wooden front door.

Patterson had held down her breakfast, though only barely, as Chandler Mustaine's fat, hairy, gold-adorned form opened the door and wasted no time grabbing the woman's breasts with both hands.

Squealing in delight, the woman had laughed as she was reeled inside nipples-first.

Of course, Patterson had clicked off at least a dozen pictures of that little gem of a moment.

Now she put her eye to the Nikon D7100 and twisted the 300 mm zoom lens, pulling Chandler's bedroom bay windows into focus.

She steeled herself for worse, certain she'd need electro-shock therapy to scrub her memory after this morning's mission was done.

Chandler Mustaine, the owner of this house, thirteen other properties around the world, a movie distribution company, two television production companies, one music label, and a warehouse full of vintage cars—as well as a few hundred million dollars in other assets—stood on the other side of the floor-to-ceiling bedroom-window glass.

Standing side-on in his underwear, his silk boxer shorts tented underneath a gut that hung off him like he'd swallowed a medicine ball. Curly black hair, dense as a Christmas sweater, covered his chest and back.

Mistress Three, as they were calling her in the firm, was already naked, kneeling, and looking ready to go spelunking underneath that belly at any moment.

"Aaaaand there it is," Heather said to herself as Mistress Three pulled off Mustaine's boxer shorts.

Heather clicked away as Mistress Three went to town. Could one feel sick to their soul? They could, she decided, because that's what she felt.

Her cellphone buzzed in her pocket, indicating a text message. She lowered the camera and ducked around the tree, taking the opportunity to catch her mental breath.

As she leaned against the smooth bark, movement drew her eye to a deer standing a short distance away. Adrenaline shot through her system, and the next thing she knew she was crouched in a tactical fighting position.

The deer twisted an ear and continued walking.

"Jesus. Take it easy, Heather."

She propped herself against the tree again and normalized her breathing.

Ten months ago, she'd been bested in hand-to-hand combat, drugged, stuffed into a trunk, driven up into the mountains, and almost become the next victim in a long line of murders.

Days after her physical recovery from the ordeal, she'd begun a higher-intensity training regimen with Sensei Masterson, determined never to be put in that situation again.

The training had kept her sharp, just in case. And the time spent at the dojo seemed to be the only thing that could fight the bad memories.

Her new routine had worked out fine for seven months, until Sensei Masterson had refused to train with her anymore. He'd told her she was running from something and that the dojo was in the wrong direction; moreover, she needed to stop fleeing and breathe.

Of course, he'd been right. She was skittish, there was no denying it. And, it seemed, there was no stopping it. But she'd be damned if she was going to sit on a couch and talk things out with a head shrink. Speaking to a notebook-scribbler was not her idea of working through a problem.

Sometimes she wondered what would've happened if she'd stayed with the department. Maybe things would've worked themselves out and her mind would've been at rest by now. Assignments like these, not homecomings to Aspen, stirred nostalgia within.

She reminded herself that she no longer worked shifts and could see her son, Tommy, every night. She was making a comfortable six figures and, after this, she'd be done with work for the rest of the day and could spend the afternoon with him.

Of course, Tommy napped in the afternoon. He would be asleep at one thirty, which was right about when she'd be back after the long drive from Aspen. He'd wake up at four or five, the way he'd been sleeping lately.

In actuality, the afternoon would be spent catching up on emails, then probably reading for a couple of hours on the back deck.

But ... she would still be seeing Tommy right when he woke up.

That was something.

Now she was snapping photos of fat rich-guy stiffies.

That was something else.

She was photographing sex. Other people who did that were called pornographers. Moreover, she knew that her client, Chandler Mustaine's wife, was no saint. This was far from a noble cause mission. That perfume-doused low-life wench screwed other men by the busload. But she wanted her payday, and she was shrewder than her idiot husband, who hadn't asked for that prenuptial agreement when they tied the knot eleven months earlier, despite his stable of lawyers' insistence. And now Mr. Mustaine was in for a serious surprise, all thanks to Heather Patterson's brilliant detective work ... detective work that could've been pulled off by her two-year-old son.

She gave herself a mental slap on the cheek, stood up, and dared a peek around the tree.

"Oh God."

Mistress Three was mashed up against the window, fogging the glass with frantic breaths.

Heather snapped two photos and ducked back.

Her phone vibrated again, reminding her of the new text message, so she pulled it out and looked.

The 970 area code told her that the number was northern Colorado. She entered her PIN and a picture flashed up onscreen. Initially, she was desensitized to the graphic photo on her phone, her eyes having just endured the horror on the other side of the tree.

Then she stood up straight as she realized what she was looking at. And when she read the message underneath the picture she began running. In her haste, she collided with a tree, scraping her arm and bashing the two-thousand-dollar camera.

As she swerved through the trees, memories came flooding back—a needle jabbing into her skin, her captor's smile, a dark car trunk, the realization that the heat beneath her was from another human being ...

She stopped and leaned up against a tree. Sensei Masterson was right; she needed to breathe.

So, she did.

She scrolled through her phone contacts, looking for a familiar name.

The sound of knocking on glass pulled her attention toward two naked people staring at her from the window. Chandler pointed at her, miming a gun with his thumb and index finger, then disappeared into the house.

"Shit."

She pocketed her phone, took the camera off her neck, and ran as hard as she could.

CHAPTER 7

WOLF PARKED in the station lot and walked around the building to Main Street.

Traffic was heavy for a Friday morning in June and he knew it would get progressively worse as the day wore on.

From a real-estate developer's point of view, they were living in the next gold-rush era. Put a for-sale sign in dog poop and it went for twenty grand over asking. To Wolf, Rocky Points was becoming claustrophobic.

Or maybe the dead body up on County 18 still lingered in his nostrils.

He crossed at the four-way stop and hung a left, then jogged the block and a half to Wind Shade Bliss, a gallery showcasing local and state artists. This weekend's exhibit featured the works of a hot new up-and-comer named Lauren Coulter.

The artist's black Audi Q7 was parked in front of the building with the hatchback raised, revealing cloth-wrapped paintings inside stacked like books on a shelf.

A young girl skipped out of the gallery doorway toward the car.

"Hey," Wolf said.

Ella Coulter, Lauren's seven-year-old daughter, gave him a double take and stopped. "Hey, Dave!"

Wolf suspected this girl's smile had something to do with the Earth's recent climate change. She had green eyes and her mother's squint, long auburn hair, and a toothless grin.

She slammed into him and wrapped his torso in a hug.

It had been under a year since Ella and her mother had moved into his ranch house. He'd spent months trying to bond with the girl, which had been surprisingly difficult. For the better part of the winter, Ella had been quiet and shy.

But their relationship had risen to the next level one afternoon when she'd twisted her ankle. Lauren, a nurse at County Hospital and a far more qualified candidate to handle the situation, had been out and Wolf had taken over, bandaging her injury and soothing her with hugs and ice cream.

Then there was the incident of the bonked forehead on the tree branch, which he'd handled masterfully, taping the wound shut and making her laugh even as blood gushed down her face.

He and Ella had gotten close over the months that followed, and now she was like a daughter to him. But times like these reminded him she was not. She hadn't yelled "Daddy!" She'd called him Dave.

He and Ella's mother weren't married, and Wolf often pulled back from getting too close. Because the last thing he ever wanted to do was disappoint this little girl.

She scurried away to the car and grabbed a painting.

"Careful, honey," a man's voice said from the gallery doorway. He was tall and lean, wearing yellow-framed Italian-style glasses perched on a handsome face. His hair glistened and was styled appropriately for a fashion photo-shoot, and his wardrobe said he was someone who defined style where others followed it.

The man stopped on a dime, his shoes clicking on the sidewalk, and turned back toward the doorway. "So I said to him, forget it. I'll pull the exhibit."

Lauren came out wearing jeans and a Gibson guitars T-shirt, both fitting her trim figure snugly. Her red hair was pulled back in a ponytail and her green eyes narrowed as she smiled. And right now, she was smiling at the man, her face painted with a certain awe that she normally reserved for Wolf.

"Are you serious?" she asked.

"Yeah." The guy looked at Wolf and stopped. "Hi."

"Hey."

Lauren gave him a double take. "Hey, there you are. I ... you've met Baron, haven't you?"

Wolf shook his head.

"This is David?" Baron asked, his lips curling into a smile.

No man's smile had ever dazzled Wolf. Until now. Baron's teeth were white and straight, his lips symmetrical and wide. He had a diamond stud earring that added to the effect. His slicked-back hair shimmered in the outdoor light and he was young and fit. Handsome, too, at least five years Wolf's junior, and could probably bench press Wolf a dozen times. Otherwise, a real loser.

"Hi." He shook Baron's hand, noting the strong grip.

"I've heard so much about you. Ella won't stop about the great David."

Lauren cleared her throat and put her arm around Wolf. "I talk about him, too, Baron."

"You do?" Baron held a straight face and smiled. "I'm kidding —she's always talking about you too."

Baron looked at Lauren and shook his head. "My goodness, David. You are a lucky man. What a beautiful, talented woman you've found yourself." He stared a beat too long at Lauren's torso.

Wolf wondered what it would sound like to punch this guy on the forehead.

"It's a little early for lunch, isn't it?" Lauren asked.

"I'll just keep going with the paintings," Baron said. "Nice to meet you, David."

"Yeah." Wolf pasted on a fake smile and watched the man grunt while he picked up a giant canvas.

"Oh, geez, Baron. Here, David can help you."

"He's got it."

She looked at him, appalled.

"Hey, yeah. Let me help you with that."

"No, no, no. I have it." Baron whisked away inside.

Lauren studied him and smiled. "What's going on? You jealous?" she asked, pulling him into a hug.

"Me? No. But he is."

"Whatever." She laid her head on his chest.

Wolf's phone vibrated in his pocket.

"Whoa, what's that?"

Smiling, he pulled out his phone and paused.

"Who is it?" Lauren asked.

He pressed the call-end button and pocketed the phone. "Heather Patterson ... I'll call her back later. How's the show coming?"

"Oh, good. I'm so nervous."

"Nervous? You know everyone already loves your paintings. What are you nervous about?"

"I know you love my paintings." She narrowed her eyes and looked at him suspiciously. "Or you say you do. But these people are, like ... real ..."

Wolf lowered his voice. "Assholes?"

Lauren rolled her eyes. "Real influential critics in the art scene."

"Yeah, like I said."

Ella came skipping outside and went to the hatchback. Wolf went over and helped her pull out a painting.

"Did you know Baron lives, like, right next to the Empire State Building?" Ella asked.

"Uh, no, I didn't."

"Yeah."

"Can you take this big one?" Lauren pointed at a tall painting wrapped in brown paper.

Wolf recognized its shape. "Ah, the sunset one."

He grabbed it and followed Ella inside the building. The old wood floor creaked under Wolf's weight. The interior smelled like scented candles. Floor speakers standing in the corner streamed New Age music.

"Hey, David." Kitty Pickering, the art-gallery owner, tended to a hanging wire on the back of a frame. She wore a canvas apron over a floral dress and white blouse. As she moved, the silver adornments draped around her neck tinkled.

"Hi."

Baron was up on a ladder, hammering a hanger in the wall. "I want that one over here." He pointed at the painting Wolf had just put down.

Wolf eyed Lauren and brought it to the base of the ladder.

"Lift it up to me."

Wolf raised the painting.

"Hey, is there something happening with you guys today?" Kitty asked. "I saw a bunch of vehicles peeling out of the parking lot earlier."

He pulled the corners of his mouth down, brainstorming vague responses. "I'm not sure."

"Do you have a bruise on your forehead?" Standing on her toes to look, Lauren ran her fingers over his forehead. "You do. What happened?"

"Nothing. Just a stupid thing."

She stared at him suspiciously and then walked back outside.

"Can you get that bubble wrap off the bottom?" Baron held down a painting to Wolf.

"Sure, Baron." He pulled off the plastic and shoved it in his pocket. "Anything else?"

Baron shrugged. "No."

Wolf watched Baron hang up one of Wolf's favorites: the sage-covered landscape north of town at sunset after a cleansing rain.

"She really is a gifted artist, isn't she?" Kitty gazed up at the painting.

Wolf nodded. "Yeah."

Kitty flicked a glance behind him and he stood straight at the sight of a familiar man talking to Lauren outside.

First Baron, now him? Wolf went out the door to the sidewalk.

"Everything okay?" he asked.

Greg Barker, former SBCSD deputy, stood with crossed arms, smiling and nodding at Lauren.

Lauren looked up at Wolf with a strained expression. "Yeah. You?"

Ella came trotting outside again. She became shy at the sight of the tall, red-headed man and sidled up next to Wolf's leg. "Hi."

"Hey there." Barker unfolded his arms and hitched his thumbs on his jeans. His muscles had gotten bigger since he'd been summarily fired from the department.

"Can I help you?" Wolf asked, letting his voice frost at the edges. Watching Baron ogle his girlfriend was one thing, but watching this man stand within a block of his girlfriend and her daughter was another.

"Ah, no. I was just ... I saw Lauren had her paintings and I was just asking about the exhibit this weekend. Sounds exciting."

Wolf said nothing.

"Anyway ... I hear there's an opening in the department for detective."

Barker and his father were still connected to the back rooms of the government buildings, it seemed. Which said a lot about the people running things.

Wolf cracked a smile at the incredulous suggestion.

Barker kicked an imaginary rock on the ground. "Anyway. I

happened to be stopping by to officially put my name in the hat." He looked up at Wolf. "I'm a changed man, Chief."

Wolf nodded. "Okay. Hardly the place or time, Greg. See you around."

"Yeah. Right. Anyway, good luck tonight, Lauren." Barker walked away.

They stood in silence for a full minute until he'd disappeared around the corner.

"I need a shower after talking to him," Lauren said, looking pale.

Ella had been kidnapped a couple of years previously, and although Greg Barker hadn't done it, his actions within the department had, arguably, set off the events.

"Who was that guy?" Ella asked.

"Just someone I used to work with."

"Why did he say he was a changed man?"

"Oh ..." Wolf looked down at Ella. He recognized the look of a seven-year-old who was going to beat an explanation out of him.

"He once did something bad to David, honey," Lauren said.

"What did he do?" she asked.

He falsified a report, saying I was derelict in my duty to help a drowning man in his upturned vehicle in the river. He tried to make me look bad to undermine the entire department so that he could get me and the sheriff fired and a different candidate could come in, take over the department, and hire him into my position.

Wolf said, "He called me a doo-doo face."

Ella giggled. "That's bad."

"Dang right it is."

Lauren passed Wolf a small painting and he handed it to Ella. "Can you take this one in? I have to talk to your mommy."

Ella grabbed it and walked inside.

"What's happening?" She studied his face. "Something's wrong, isn't it?"

"There's a ..." He looked over both shoulders. "... situation happening this morning. I'm not going to be able to make lunch."

"Okay. Yeah, no problem. Sounds ... situationy." She turned and pulled another painting out of her Audi. "Are you going to be able to make tonight?"

He nodded. "It shouldn't be a problem."

Her eyebrows peaked.

"I'll try my best."

"Be right back." She walked away and into the shop, then materialized a few seconds later with Ella on her heels.

"Sorry," he said, sensing she was upset now.

She stood in front of him and rolled her eyes. "Don't worry about it. Like I said, I'm just nervous. But I can handle these people, right?"

"There's nothing to handle. Just watch them gawk at your paintings."

"No, but like ... the interviews. There's that woman from *Vanity Fair*, for Pete's sake. The pictures and all that."

"Yeah." Guilt stabbed him now. "Listen, I'm going to try and be here."

"Okay." She stretched up and kissed him.

Her lips tasted like strawberry lip gloss.

"Can we have ice cream today, mommy?" Ella stared at the shop two doors down and licked her lips.

"It's going to be tough today with the show ... maybe Baron can take you."

"Or could you take me?" she asked Wolf.

"David has to go back to work today, honey."

"What about tomorrow? Or the next day?"

Lauren shrugged at Wolf. "It's hard to say no to a seven-year-old."

"Impossible. And, of course, I would never want to. Yeah, sure. I'll take you."

"Yesssssss." She ran back into the gallery building.

Wolf smiled after her, then watched an SBCSD vehicle drive past.

"Okay," she said. "Go take care of your situation. Call me, okay?"

"Okay."

They kissed again, and as he walked away he glanced inside and saw Baron's head swiveling back to whatever he was pretending to do.

"Later, Baron," he said to himself.

CHAPTER 8

WOLF TWISTED open his office window blinds, letting in light to warm the frigid air hissing out of the floor vents.

From the department's third-floor perch, the western windows offered an unobstructed view of the ski resort, which was verdant from bottom to tree line. Snow still webbed the crags of the twin granite spire-like outcroppings known as Rocky Points.

His phone vibrated again, reminding him of his voicemail. He pulled it out and slapped it on the desk, then collapsed into the leather swivel chair and fired up his computer.

While the PC woke up he pressed the phone to his ear, awaiting Heather Patterson's voice.

She'd once been his best detective, but after a particularly nasty encounter with a serial killer, ending with her getting acquainted with the trunk of the killer's car, she'd quit the department to devote more time to her young son, Tommy.

The last time he'd spoken to her was three weeks previously when she'd showed up at the station—something to do with a case she was working for Leary, Crouch, and Shift, one of the largest criminal defense and family law firms in the Colorado Rockies, and her new employer.

He'd detected no regret that she'd quit. Her stories involved her family now, and that was good. Bad for him. She was impossible to replace, as the stack of résumés piled next to his computer monitor reminded him.

"... help ... message ..." Wolf checked his phone and saw he had full reception. "... as soon as possible. I'm coming over there now. I'll be there in an hour or so. Shit. I'll call you back."

He tried to listen to the voicemail again and got the same result. The poor reception had jumbled what she'd said, but the angst in her voice had been loud and clear.

He called her back and it went straight to voicemail.

The computer screen flickered to life and he swiveled to continue his battle with technology, this time with the ever-updating PC that pre-dated Chautauqua Valley's first inhabitants.

After a few seconds, he was inside his email. He scrolled down the screen, passing over three requests for meetings, some paperwork attachments for him to print and sign, a message from MacLean with the subject "New hire candidates," and other headache-inducing reads that he could put off until later.

He almost shut down the computer, but decided to check the junk-mail folder just in case. More than once, that oldest trick in the book had caused him to miss a vital document.

The top message caught his eye and reeled him in close.

Farewell, David Wolf.

The subject line could have been crafted by an evil-doer on a different continent wanting his credit-card number, but his heart jumped when he read the name.

Paul Womack.

He hadn't thought of that name for years. The email contained a video link so he clicked on it, but the software wouldn't let him open junk so he dragged the file over to his inbox and waited.

Paul Womack had been sentenced to eighteen years in Leavenworth, and in the federal prison the maximum sentence reduction for good behavior was fifteen percent. That would've left him with just over fifteen years to serve, assuming he'd been a model inmate.

Wolf finished the math and put his release at this year.

He clicked the link and the computer motor revved up. The still shot showed Paul sitting at a table. His mouth was open and his eyes were half closed, as if in mid-sentence.

He still had the same haircut—a spiky flattop and shaved around the sides, making his head look like a toothbrush. He was just as Wolf remembered him—blond and blue-eyed with a confident air—but he was skinnier in the neck and shoulders and his receding hairline put his huge forehead even more on display.

His huge forehead, Wolf remembered with a snort. They used to call him "Fivehead" because of that thing.

His smile evaporated as he spotted a Beretta M9 service pistol lying on the table near Paul's folded hands.

Wolf hesitated, then pressed the play button.

"You—witness. Wolf. It's ... your fault. Wolf. It's ... your fault."

Pulling his eyebrows together, Wolf stopped the video, pulled back the slider and played it again.

"You—witness. Wolf. It's ... your fault. Wolf. It's ... your fault."

Paul's face and posture transformed with inhuman speed. His tone rose and fell in pitch unnaturally.

Wolf had been confused the first time around, but now he realized that the words had been carefully edited—clipped and put back together to relay the message.

This time he let the video play its course.

On the screen, Paul stared at the gun in front of him.

If not for the hissing static coming out of the speakers, Wolf would've thought the video had stopped or paused.

Finally, with deliberate slowness, Paul Womack unfolded his hands and grabbed the M9.

With each second that Wolf watched, the room shrank

around him. He scrolled the mouse cursor to the stop icon and hovered his finger over the button.

Hesitating, Paul lowered the gun and looked into the camera.

"You—witness. Wolf. It's … your fault. Wolf. It's … your fault."

The screen went black, but the video was unfinished. Because a second later the sound of a gunshot came from the speakers.

CHAPTER 9

WOLF STOOD up from the chair. Behind him, the metal blinds clanged. He couldn't recall having pushed away from the desk.

His lungs pumped air as if he'd just finished a sprint.

"What the hell?"

Frozen in place, he took deep breaths and stared at the black video window.

There was a knock on the door.

"Not now!"

Footsteps receded into nothing.

Sweat beaded on his forehead and under his arms. He sat on the edge of the desk and breathed some more. He shut his eyes, thinking about the sound.

Pop.

It had been a pistol shot, no doubt. There'd even been a rustling afterwards, and Wolf tried to blank his mind rather than think about Paul's dead body sinking to the table.

He stood up and grabbed a half-full bottle of water off the bookshelf and drank it down.

Slowly, he eased himself onto the loveseat against the side wall and stared at the floor. Drifting inwards, he pushed past the video to fainter memories from a distant time and place.

"It's on now, bitch!"

The C-17 Globemaster's engines muted all sounds inside the cargo hold, but Wolf lip read PFC Gunderson's catchphrase to the squad members nearest him.

Turning his head to the Ranger sitting next to him, Wolf met SPC Paul Womack's steady gaze. Wolf always drew strength from that blue-eyed perma-frost look his friend had before action, and he'd told him so on many occasions after a dozen beers.

Womack smiled.

Due to their last names being so close alphabetically, he and Womack had been lined up in formation next to each other in the Ranger Indoctrination Program. Three years later, the two men were still shoulder-to-shoulder along the wall of this latest C-17, taking them to the next mission in over a hundred they'd endured together.

"It's on now, bitch!" Womack screamed in his ear.

Wolf smiled. Closing his eyes, he leaned against his pack and let the bouncing aircraft lull him into meditation, thinking of nothing but the sensation of breathing. He'd read about the technique for dealing with high-stress situations on a few websites after the nightmares had started to take over his life.

A short time later, their stomachs lifted as the plane descended. Minutes after that they were rolling on sand as they landed at the forward operating base.

When the aircraft jarred to a halt the loadmaster lowered the cargo ramp and they streamed out into the cold early-morning air.

The stars rivaled the clearest nights back in the mountains of Colorado, with the Milky Way painting a swath across the sky. The kumbaya moment was short-lived because they walked directly to a ready Blackhawk helicopter, piled inside, and lifted back into the air.

There was little conversation. No "It's on now, bitch!" Gunderson knew when to shut up.

During the daytime, the brown terrain of Afghanistan's Helmand Province looked to Wolf like northern Utah or southern Wyoming. Now, with no moon, the landscape was dark and what few lights twinkled below were like lone ships in a black sea.

Their mission was to secure a cluster of buildings—mud huts —on a hill somewhere out there. Intel reported a high-worth target among the population of the small compound and the objective was to capture him, or them. As far as missions went, this was no more special than any others they'd been tapped for. Of course, there was always the possibility that this would be Wolf's last.

That would be special.

Inhale. Exhale.

Then they were back on the ground, off the helicopter, and moving under the blanket of stars again.

An hour later, Wolf's NVGs revealed a cluster of huts perched on a hill and surrounded by a rock-and-mud wall, growing larger with each crunching boot fall.

Wolf's adrenaline spiked as they reached the wall and slipped inside an opening without hesitation.

The air inside smelled like goat dung and smoldering wood fires. There was no sound but Wolf's breathing, and then Sergeant Henning's order in his earpiece.

"Team One, engage."

Wolf stood against a building and watched the action unfold a dozen yards away on the other side of a packed dirt road. Team One entered with muted speed and ferocity. There was a clipped scream of a woman, followed by another, and then nothing.

Womack was next to Wolf, and just like Wolf he scanned the buildings up ahead with his M4 carbine.

Painted green by Wolf's night-vision goggles, huts made from rock, mud, and ancient wood leaned against one another, looking like they'd been built countless generations previously.

He felt like they were a team from the future that had transported back to biblical times. Except for a wheelbarrow with a rubber tire leaning against a wall, he mused, this place hadn't changed in two millennia.

A goat tethered to a pole bleated nearby.

"Clear. Team Two, go."

Pushing off the wall, Wolf entered the doorway to his right with Womack a half-step behind. He kicked the rudimentary door inside and it fell on the dirt floor.

He was hyper-focused now, scanning the room for a weapon pointed in his direction. At least a dozen people slept, covered in brown blankets and lying on thin mattresses.

One blanket stirred and a scruffy-headed child poked her head out to look. With eyes shining like a cat's in Wolf's NVG display, she opened her mouth and screamed.

The room burst to life.

"Freeze! Freeze!" Gunderson said in Pashto. Then he ordered the occupants to huddle against the back wall.

Gunderson kept talking, telling two men in their thirties to get up.

The two men complied, walked over, and then when Gunderson asked them more questions they competed to have their stories heard as they pointed outside.

Gunderson spoke some more, and again they pointed. Then they put their hands together as if pleading, motioning to the terrified women and children behind them.

Gunderson turned to Wolf. "They say there're two men, two doors down on the right side. They killed an elder two days ago and they're taking what they want. Threatening violence. Terrorizing everyone."

"Two doors down on the right?" Wolf clarified.

Gunderson nodded.

Wolf nodded to PFC Maystone. "Stay here. Keep them under guard."

Wolf, Womack, Harilek, and Gunderson went outside. Henning had gathered six women wearing blankets and expressions of mild shock.

Team One ushered the women across the road and into the building under Maystone's guard, and Wolf relayed what they had learned to Sergeant Henning.

Without hesitation, they made their way down the row of houses.

Wolf's aimed M4 flicked between hut openings. They'd come in without firing so far, but compared to the relative silence of the night they probably sounded like a freight train to anyone awake.

The next building was a pen housing the goat. When it bleated, it was all Wolf could do to not shoot the animal on the spot.

Their target hut's windows were a mere few yards away, covered with fabric.

Silently Wolf's fire team made their way to the building and huddled near the openings, Wolf nearest the front door.

"Go," he said under his breath. He kicked down the wood propped in the doorway and followed it inside, his M4 leading the way.

Wolf was no more than a half-step inside when his NVGs flashed and a gunshot rang out in front and to his right. The blow to his chest felt like a major league batter had swung into him. He stumbled back and a fellow Ranger quickly pulled him out of the doorway.

As the hut erupted in gunfire, he rolled on the cold ground outside. The action was over as quickly as it had begun, and he found himself dazed, staring at the stars again.

Womack appeared over him and patted him down. "You hit? You hit?"

"Yeah." Wolf struggled to speak; he couldn't breathe. He

convulsed, writhing side to side as he tried to inhale. His vision darkened around the edges, and the Milky Way began to disappear.

Finally, with agonizing slowness, his lungs opened and he sucked in a stream of air. He coughed, choking on the cloud of gunpowder smoke flowing from the hut.

"I'm okay." The pain in his ribs beneath his collar bone told him otherwise.

"Clear!" Harilek announced.

Womack pressed on the exact spot Wolf had been shot. "Hit your armor."

"Good." Wolf struggled to his feet and shrugged away Womack's supportive arm.

Walking inside the hut, he joined the line of somber soldiers looking down on two men shot to death in their beds. One slumped against a red-splattered wall, a pistol in his hand. The other occupant's blanket had been ripped aside, revealing an AK-47 lying next to his steadily bleeding corpse.

He turned to Womack. "Thanks."

Womack ignored him and continued down to the final two huts that made up the tiny township, the team in tow.

Wolf tried to follow but Sergeant Henning slapped a hand on his shoulder. "Get back to the hut and help Maystone watch the non-combatants."

"Yes, sir." Wolf hurried back to the hut. The short walk felt like the length of a football field. His legs seemed to move in slow motion, as if they were filled with sand.

He thought of the green muzzle flash again, the pop of the gun. He'd felt bullets graze his flesh before, but had never been hit point-blank in his armor.

He winced through the pain of breathing and thought of Sarah's smile, then of Jack, their two-year-old son, waving at him on the computer screen, calling him Dah.

The hut's doorway yawned black, then Maystone's head appeared. "What happened?"

Wolf tried to talk but felt a sharp pain and stumbled inside.

"Hey." Maystone looked at him. "You okay? What happened? You hit?"

Wolf shook his head. "Hit my armor."

Maystone eyed him, then put a finger through the hole in Wolf's BDU. "Jesus."

Wolf sank to the ground and sat against the hut wall.

Sometime later, Womack came inside. "All clear. We're supposed to keep them in here until the dust settles."

Womack looked at Wolf with renewed concern. "You okay?"

"You want a kick in the face? Ask me if I'm okay again." Talking felt like getting run over by a truck.

"I guess that's a yes." Womack took off his helmet. "Hot as shit in here."

A collective murmur rose from the women. They huddled around their children and pleaded with Gunderson.

"What's going on?" Womack asked.

"They're ... they think you're going to do something to them." Gunderson narrowed his eyes and shook his head. "I think they think you're going to rape them. They're talking about your blond hair."

Womack looked self-conscious and ran a hand over his head.

"Remember who was here last," Wolf said.

"What do you mean? Wait. They think I'm a Russian? They think we're Russians?" Womack pulled off his pack and put it on the ground. "Jesus, what did those commie bastards do to these people?" He unzipped a side pocket and produced a huge bag of candy.

Mounds bars, Snickers, and Tangy Taffy in hand, Womack smiled and inched forward.

The children looked unsure and the women even more so as they held them back.

But an older girl escaped her mother's clutches and snatched the Snickers. It took a few seconds for her to figure out how to open it, but she managed, and then took a bite. The smile on her face was infectious and melted the tension in the room. Then the floodgates opened as every child stood up and grabbed the treasure from Womack's bag.

Wolf's eyelids were like lead, fluttering open and shut. The last thing he saw before he succumbed to sleep that night was a hut full of smiles.

Three knocks on the door ripped Wolf from his memories.

"Yeah?"

Wolf's office door opened and Lorber poked his head inside. "Hey ... Jesus, you okay? You look green."

Wolf stood. "Yeah. What's happening?" He walked around his desk to his computer. Lines danced across the screen so he left the computer in sleep mode.

"You're bathed in sweat."

"What can I help you with, Doc?"

The light in the room had dimmed with the skies outside the window. A storm was flowing over the ski resort, descending into town.

How long had he been daydreaming? His wall clock said eleven forty-five.

Lorber stood staring at Wolf.

"What?" Agitation sharpened Wolf's tone.

"We have a serious problem."

CHAPTER 10

WOLF'S SUV crested a rise and Pat Xander's crime scene came into view in the distance. Two SBCSD vehicles were still parked on the side of the road.

"It's gonna be the crime scene." Lorber pointed at the GPS coordinates on the mobile computer and checked them against the paper in his hand. As they neared the vehicles he nodded. "This is it."

Wolf pulled over and shut off the engine. He stepped outside into the familiar pine-scented air, which felt electrically charged from the approaching storm.

Deputy Nelson climbed out of his car and walked toward them. "Hey, what's going—"

"Shhh," Lorber said, putting a thin finger to his lips.

"Yeah, all right."

Wolf called Rachette's phone and cocked an ear to the forest.

His detective would not be picking up. The seven unanswered calls he'd tried today told him as much. They were listening for Rachette's ditched phone, which, according to Summit Wireless Services, was somewhere within fifty yards of their current position.

They stood back here at the crime scene because of a set of

fresh prints found on the interior door handle of Pat Xander's vehicle—prints matching Rachette's.

Lorber's next move had been to call Rachette to see why. When there'd been no answer, the situation had darkened a shade.

When calls to Charlotte revealed that her husband hadn't returned home the night before, things looked ... Wolf left the thought unfinished. And after triangulating his cellphone, they were here, and Wolf tried to figure out plausible reasons for why his detective's phone would be ditched near a crime scene where they'd found a man shot in the head and stuffed in a trunk. Given those circumstances, none of the reasons could be good.

Thunder rumbled from the southwest and the clouds blocked the sun, cooling the air.

"Better find this thing fast," Lorber said. "Gonna pour."

A wall of rain hung like a curtain off the front of the clouds. Behind it, lightning flickered.

"You looking for Rachette's phone?" Nelson asked.

"Yeah, now be quiet and listen for it," Lorber said.

Wolf walked away from the sounds of the SUV's cooling engine and called again. Lorber went in the opposite direction and Nelson took the other side of the road.

"He always has his phone on silent–vibrate mode," Wolf said. "So we're going to have to find it."

"Perfect," Lorber said.

After four more calls and continuous walking, Wolf had climbed a slight rise in the road to a spot that he estimated to be fifty paces from where Pat Xander's car had gone over the slope. Which meant he was at the edge of the circle surrounding Lorber's phone-trace coordinates.

As he stopped and turned around, something pinged at his feet. "Hey, I have shell casings here!"

He slipped on a latex glove and picked one up.

Lorber and Nelson jogged to him with crunching feet. When

the ME arrived, he had an evidence bag open and ready to receive.

".45 ACP. Two shells." Wolf dropped them into the bag.

"Good bet we'll find that's what killed Pat Xander," Lorber said.

Wolf studied the ground, focusing on a spot behind him. Last night's rain had been a deluge, but even so, a stain in the dirt remained. "Blood."

"Shit." Lorber stepped over. "Watch it. Jesus, we had two dozen people up here two hours ago and none of them saw this?" The ME started taking samples.

Tire scrape marks bore into the ground a short distance down the road—the first vehicle in a line that had extended back toward the crime scene. Apparently, no one had been this far.

The forest off the side of the road was flat, on the same level as the road. The drop-off where they'd found Pat Xander was fifty paces down a slight hill.

"This is quite a ways from Pat Xander's car."

"Maybe they pushed it down this hill and it finally dumped off the edge of the road and into the trees down there," Nelson said.

"Somebody shot him here," Lorber said. "This is blood, no doubt."

"You find any other prints in that car besides Pat's and Rachette's?" Wolf asked. "On the driver's side? The keys were missing. They could've driven it down there and dumped it. Taken the keys before pushing it off the road."

Lorber shrugged. "Team's still processing the car."

Wolf nodded.

"Way I see it," Lorber said, twisting the cap on a sample container, "this is good news."

"How is this good news?" Wolf asked, dialing Rachette's phone again and scanning the trees.

"Well, good news for Rachette. Two shells. Two holes in Xander. All the shots are accounted for. One bloodstain."

Thunder shook the air and rolled down the valley.

"It's gonna rain." Lorber quickened his pace taking a sample.

Despite the midday hour, the sky was dark as dusk and the hairs were standing up on Wolf's arms.

His phone rang and his adrenal glands fired. When Patterson's number flashed onscreen he pressed the call-end button and called Rachette again.

A dollop of rain hit him in the shoulder and another slapped his ear.

"Shit," Lorber said. "I'd rather we find a dry phone."

Wolf stepped off the shoulder and stared down the road. Keeping his eyes unfocused and still, he tried Rachette's number again, willing himself to catch the light of the phone screen.

Lightning flickered and a crack of thunder followed seconds later.

The encroaching storm injected more tension than they needed, but the darkening skies ended up revealing Rachette's phone. If it had been a bright and sunny day, there would've been little chance of Wolf seeing the glow in his peripheral vision. "There!"

He ran over and picked up the cell with his gloved hand and put it in a plastic bag just as the rain let loose and soaked his shirt to his back.

CHAPTER 11

"SHIT!" Heather Patterson lowered the cellphone to her lap and looked out the windshield.

At first, she'd been parked along the front of the county building, but now she sat in the rear lot. Clearly something was going on today. She'd worked here long enough to pick up on the general vibe, and the two SUVs she'd just watched enter the lot came in at faster-than-normal speed.

Then there was the tow truck delivering a Chevy sedan into the parking garage. It had been dented and scraped like it had gotten in a fight with the forest and lost. Since they were towing it here, and not to Viper's impound lot, she knew it was evidence.

Worse, she thought she recognized the vehicle. Familiar hippy-stickers coated the back window, and when she remembered that a man named Pat Xander drove the car her blood pressure doubled. Rachette had once introduced Pat Xander to her as his Uber guy.

What did Pat Xander have to do with this? Was he the one who sent her the message? He'd not seemed like the psycho type, but few psycho people look psycho until they go psycho.

Times like these brought forth her memories of being stuffed in a trunk. That guy had been crazy and she'd never suspected him.

Rain drops started smacking her SUV, then marble-sized hailstones that sounded like rocks.

"Shit," she said again.

Watching a deputy jog across the lot toward the rear doors, she got out and ran, timing it perfectly to arrive behind him.

The deputy must've worked in the jail in the basement because she failed to recognize him. He looked at her, and she made a show of fishing for her own card inside her purse, like they were now in a race for the honor of slapping their magnetic card on the reader before the big rain hit.

He won. The doors hissed open and the deputy eyed her again.

She smiled and held up her hands. "Thank God you're here. I'll probably find it halfway up the elevator ... I hope."

The man looked less than fooled but walked in anyway, pulling out his phone and tapping on the screen as he disappeared into the building.

Idiot. She could have been a gun-wielding maniac walking in off the street.

The doors hissed shut behind her, and she felt like she'd stepped into a walk-in freezer. Someone needed to take their palm off the thermostat in this place.

Contemplating whether to ride up the elevators or go talk to Tammy, she opted for the reception area at the front of the building and found a familiar woman behind the glass.

The receptionist and dispatcher talked into her headset, furiously tapping keys on her computer. "Yes, ma'am. We'll send a deputy over this afternoon to speak to him ... you're welcome. Have a good day."

Tammy gave Patterson a double take as she took off her headset.

"What's going on today?" Patterson leaned her elbows on the counter.

Tammy looked like she wanted to speak but couldn't, which was technically exactly what was happening.

She was no longer Detective Heather Patterson. She was a civilian walking in off the streets.

"Not much," Tammy said.

"I saw Pat Xander's car being towed into the garage just now." Patterson narrowed an eye. "Why?"

"I can't tell you, Heather. Come on, you know that." Tammy stood up and walked away. A few seconds later, the door in the wall opened and she came out. "Come here and give me a hug."

Tammy was a bear of a woman and had a hug to match. "I've missed you. I hear about you coming in every once in a while, but you never come say hi." Tammy let her go. "Which is a crap-shoot, because I'm the receptionist."

Patterson smiled. "Yeah, sorry. I usually come in the normal way. Through the back, on the heels of someone and their key card."

Tammy's eyes glazed over, then she locked eyes with Patterson.

"What?"

"Nothing. You'll have to talk to somebody upstairs."

"About Pat Xander's car?"

Tammy hesitated, then nodded.

"I'll talk to Wolf. Is he up there?"

"No. But he's on his way back in with Dr. Lorber." Tammy flourished her hand toward the elevator banks. "Third floor, Mrs. Patterson."

"It's technically Patterson-Reed."

"Right." Tammy peaked her eyebrows. "You look good, honey. How's Tommy doing?"

She smiled. "Great. He's doing great."

"I saw him at the playground the other day. Kid's growing up so fast already. All right. I'll let you go. Come in more often and say hi to me."

Patterson nodded and made for the elevator bank.

Stepping inside the elevator was like slipping on an old pair of boots. How many times had she rushed in here with her morning coffee and stabbed that third-floor button? Stared at these God-awful green tiles on the floor, looked up at the fish-eye camera lens in the corner?

The bell chimed and the door swished open. The terrazzo hallway gleamed like ice after a Zamboni had passed over.

She stepped out and considered her options. The hall was empty, but at the end of it excitement echoed from the squad room. Sheriff MacLean paced inside his aquarium office, talking excitedly on the phone.

Squeaking footsteps rose in volume and a deputy strode out of the squad room and into the hallway, straight toward her. She froze at the sight of her friend Charlotte approaching.

There were hundreds of people in this building and Charlotte was the last person she wanted to see.

Charlotte wiped her nose as if she was crying. Studying the floor in front of her, she failed to see Patterson and darted side-ways into the women's bathroom.

Not waiting another second, Patterson moved, making straight for the second office on the right. She knocked on Wolf's door, and when there was no answer she twisted the knob. Relieved that it was unlocked, she pushed the door open and entered.

Now she was trespassing, and an inner voice screamed at her to get out, but she had nowhere else to go.

Ducking inside, she shut the door and stood in the dim office.

The room was almost silent. Despite the monsoon outside, the rain was a mere whisper against the triple-paned glass. A flicker of lightning lit the office and a low rumble shook the building.

It smelled like cheap soap and aftershave. Classic Wolf.

She considered flicking on the light, but decided against it. Somebody might walk by and peek inside to say hello.

The window blinds were pinched between his office chair and the glass, as if he'd left in a hurry.

She walked to the chair and ran her fingers over the empty desktop, then swiveled the chair back into its position at his desk. It bumped the wood and the computer screen flickered to life.

Breaking into his office was one thing. Breaking in and snooping on his computer raised her sense of betrayal to another level so she walked to the loveseat against the wall and sat.

But the glowing screen beckoned and gave her an idea. She pulled out her phone and emailed the photo she'd received to herself. She looked out at the rain. My God, she thought. Was he getting rained on right now? She needed a better look at that photo.

And who was she kidding? Wolf would understand.

She walked to the desk, pulled back the chair, and sat down.

Wolf had a video open onscreen. Deciding she would minimize her violation of Wolf's space, she steered the cursor to the close button without looking at it. She clicked once and when it failed to close she flicked a glance inside the video window. She couldn't help noticing a man sitting with a pistol lying on the table in front of him, which froze her in her tracks.

Was this something to do with Rachette? Had Wolf gotten the same message she had? Probably not ... he would've answered her calls during the past couple of hours, not screened them.

What was this?

She pressed play.

CHAPTER 12

WOLF AND LORBER arrived at the station during the height of the downpour and ran through the lot to the automatic doors. Once inside, they made straight for the first-floor forensics lab.

Lorber led the way in, supremely at home among the modern microscopes, fume and particle extractors, chromatographs, and spectrometers perched on clean white counter tops. He made a circle, all the while clicking on devices, and pointed at Wolf.

"Hit the lights, please."

Wolf turned and flicked a switch, and the overhead lighting blazed on.

"Team must be out in the garage with the sedan," Lorber said.

Wolf watched the tall ME don a pair of blue latex gloves and approach a boxy-looking machine no larger than a toaster oven. He swung a glass door open, fished out a shell casing from the bag, and placed it inside.

"This is called CERA," Lorber said, bending his lanky frame over the machine as he pressed some buttons. "Cartridge Electro-static Recovery Analysis. You know how futile getting a latent off a spent cartridge can be. Firing temps vaporize and break down the skin oils left on the shells prior to firing. Of course, this baby uses a high-voltage static charge along with some graphite spheres to show the prints that would've otherwise been invisible."

"Let me know when you're finished." Wolf paced across the white-tiled floor, thinking about the Paul Womack video and Pat Xander's body in the trunk. And now his detective was gone. All indications that Rachette was in major trouble.

He needed to know Paul Womack's fate.

The video had gone black and there'd been a shot. If Paul Womack had shot himself, as the video suggested, then who sent the video? Or had Wolf missed something? Had Paul shot someone else?

"Hey." Lorber stared at him expectantly.

"What?"

"I said I got a print." Lorber walked to a desktop computer and sat down. "This is a good one. If it's in the system, we'll get a hit."

"There's still Rachette's phone, too." Wolf picked up the plastic bag with the cell in it. "Might be a clue in the data here. The calls he made, his texts. Maybe that's why it was in the woods. Maybe he threw it there for us to find."

Lorber nodded absently, then tapped the keyboard with some finality. "Okay. Now we wait on this."

"How long?"

Lorber shrugged. "You know the drill. Average wait time is twenty-seven minutes. Could be more. Could be less. Meanwhile," he snatched the bag from Wolf's hand and poured out the device onto his hand, "let's look at the phone. Shit. Locked with a PIN."

"1-2-3-4," Wolf said.

"Seriously?" Lorber tapped in the code. "Apparently, you are. Looks like he messaged Charlotte at 7:05 p.m. Here ..." He leaned forward for Wolf to see.

Rachette: *Hey baby, I'm at Goggles. Tipping a few with the boys.*

Charlotte: *Okay. Remember I have the doctor's appointment tomorrow.*

Rachette: *You do? For what?*

Charlotte: *(Emoticon of a middle finger.)*

Rachette: *I'll be up bright and early ready for action.*

Charlotte: *Just try and cap it at six tonight, huh?*

Rachette: *Bright and early.*

Charlotte: *I miss drinking.*

Rachette: *Me too. Wait ... here's my beer. Ah. Tastes good.*

Charlotte: *(Emoticon of middle finger.)*

Rachette: *I love you, baby. You'll be sipping your wine chillers again in a few short months.*

Charlotte: *Love u 2. Later.*

Lorber looked up from the phone. "She misses drinking? Doctor's appointment? Is she pregnant?"

Wolf shrugged. "Looks like it."

"Come to think of it, I've noticed." Lorber blinked behind his John Lennon-style glasses and tapped the screen. "Okay, that's it for last night's messages. He made a call at 11:09 p.m. to Pat Xander for a duration of thirty-four seconds. Nothing after that."

"And prior?" Wolf asked.

"Charlotte in the afternoon ... 3:32 p.m. Looks like he called you at 1:43 p.m. ..."

"Scroll further."

"Nothing out of the ordinary. Yates ... Charlotte ... Charlotte ... you ..." Lorber raised his eyebrows and held out the phone. "Gloves are over there."

Wolf put on some latex gloves and grabbed the phone. Scrolling through the messages and recent-calls list, he agreed.

"All right."

He handed back the phone and trashed the gloves, then took off his damp SBCSD baseball cap and ran a hand over his hair.

You robbed me. It's ... your fault.

"... and check the phone, too."

He looked at Lorber. "What's that?"

"You seem rather preoccupied. I know that look. You're not telling me something."

Wolf shook his head. "Let me know the second you get a hit on any prints. You're checking the phone, too, right?"

Lorber took off his glasses. "That's what I just told you."

"Right." Wolf left the lab and went upstairs.

CHAPTER 13

PATTERSON WATCHED with growing anxiety as the man in the video grabbed the pistol.

"You—witness. Wolf. It's ... your fault. Wolf. It's ... your fault."

The screen went black.

Pop.

"My God." She stood up and wiped the sweat off her forehead, noting the shake in her hand. She sucked in a breath, then exhaled and closed her eyes, trying to blank her mind.

The door flew open and the light came on.

She turned around, involuntarily glancing at the computer and the still twisting computer chair. "I ... hi, sir."

"What are you doing?" Wolf's eyes bulged. "Get away from that."

Patterson stepped out from behind his desk. "I'm so sorry. I was just ..."

"You were what?" Wolf pushed her aside and went to the computer. He moved the mouse, saw what she'd been looking at, and froze.

Patterson said nothing. She felt like she'd been caught stealing from his wallet, but after the text message she'd received earlier, she'd had an unshakeable resolve. And now there was this video. "What is that?"

Wolf let go of the mouse and turned to her. "You watched it."

"Yes. What the hell is it? What's it supposed to be? A suicide video? Is that noise him shooting himself or ... who's this guy? The email address has the name Paul Womack in it. Is that his name?"

Wolf ignored her, stoking her anger.

"I called you three times this morning," she said. "I had to talk to you. Didn't you get my messages?"

"I did. Well, it broke up and I couldn't understand what you were saying. And I've been a little busy this morning, so I couldn't talk."

Her former boss turned and stared out the window.

She took out her cellphone and pulled up the text messages. Ignoring the four missed ones from her new boss, she tapped the screen and held out the phone.

"I have to show you something."

"I have to tell you something."

They spoke at the same time.

She pushed the phone closer. "Here. Look."

His face went through a series of expressions—incomprehension, annoyance, confusion as to why she'd showed him a picture of a naked man. Then he blinked and there was surprise as he realized the naked man was Tom Rachette. Then he grabbed the phone out of her hand and his face dropped as he studied the finer features of the photo—the bound hands, the pile of straw underneath, the blood-caked hair ... the closed eyes.

"Where did you get this?" He stood up.

"From the number provided." Her voice cracked. "I called you."

"That's a Colorado phone number." Wolf sounded surprised.

"Yeah," she said. "I can tell that from the area code. Why are you pointing that out?"

Wolf raised his watch. "It's one fourteen."

"I know," she said. "We have two hours and forty-five minutes until they call."

The message she'd received this morning had come in two parts—a photograph of Rachette, naked and hogtied on a bed of straw, bloodied and beaten, and then a text message immediately after telling her: *Get to David Wolf. Both of you answer the next call at four p.m. or he dies. Tell nobody else or he dies.*

"That's all you got?" Wolf scrolled the screen.

"That's it. I just got the picture and then the message. What's happening this morning? I saw Pat Xander's car being towed into the garage. Everyone's running around like something's going on. And I get this text message." She gestured to the computer. "And what was that video you were watching? The guy said, 'It's your fault, it's your fault.' What's your fault?"

Wolf handed back the phone. Running his hand across his face stubble he turned back to his computer. "We have to check on Paul Womack. That's why I came in here."

"The guy in the video."

"Yeah, the guy in the video."

Wolf sat down at the computer and pulled up a New Mexico State website. He clicked through to the Sheriff's Department website for Taos, New Mexico.

"Taos, New Mexico?" she asked.

He was on a mission and ignored her. He found a number, dialed it on his phone, and sat straight.

"Hello, this is Chief Detective David Wolf from the Sluice–Byron County Sheriff's Department up in Colorado. I need to speak to your sheriff, please ... okay ..."

She paced the office and listened to Wolf try to figure out the fate of the man in the video. Another text message from her boss came in for her. He wanted the photos. He'd have to wait.

Pocketing her phone, she stared out the window. It still

poured and the thought of Rachette lying naked on a bed of straw made her shiver.

"Paul Womack ... W-o-m-a-c-k. Is he in your morgue right now?"

Pacing some more, she punched out a message to her boss.

I got your messages. I'll be in touch soon.

Bad move. Her phone vibrated and rang immediately.

Hesitating, she answered it. "Hello, Bryce."

"Where the hell have you been?"

"Aspen."

"And?"

"And I got the photos."

"So why aren't you here?"

"When's your meeting with her?"

"Three hours."

Frustration mounted inside of her, threatening to materialize into a stream of cuss words. "You'll have your photos in time for the meeting."

"I'd better have."

"Bye, Bryce." She hung up just as Wolf did. "What's the news?" she asked.

"Taos SD has no reports of anything when it comes to Paul Womack. No John Does in their morgue. So they're sending over a unit to his house. They'll be in touch." He leaned back and rubbed his temples.

"Look," she said, "I need to know everything that's going on. I feel anything but up to speed on all this. Pat Xander's car being towed into the garage earlier—what was that? It looked beat up, like it'd crashed in the trees."

Wolf stood. "This morning we found Pat Xander's car in the trees off County 18. Pat's body was in the trunk, shot twice. Once in the head and another in the back."

Her face dropped. "Jesus. County 18. Rachette's new place is on County 18."

"I called Rachette right after we found Pat's body. It's Rachette's day off but I knew that he knew Pat and would want to know what had happened. But he didn't answer. And then Lorber found his fresh prints in the passenger side of Xander's car, so we triangulated Rachette's phone and found it alongside County 18 next to the crime scene. Along with two spent cartridges and what looks like blood."

"Pat Xander's blood and the two shots that killed him," Patterson said.

He nodded.

"And there's this video," she said.

"Which I'm not sure what to make of." Wolf made to pass her. "He was at Beer Goggles last night. I'm going to talk to them, see what I can find out."

She put a hand on his chest and stepped in front of him. "Wait a second. What about this guy, Paul Womack? He's from New Mexico? How do you know him?"

Wolf dismissed the question at first, then stood and rubbed a hand over his stubble again. "He's an old army buddy."

Patterson waited for more explanation but none came. "This number that texted me his photo—was there anything from this number on Rachette's phone?"

Wolf shook his head. "No."

She crossed her arms and chewed her bottom lip.

"There was nothing out of the ordinary," Wolf said. "He talked to Charlotte and Yates, and called Pat Xander for a ride home just after eleven last night."

"Latents on the shell casings you found?"

"Lorber found prints. He's running them in the database now."

"DNA match on the blood?"

"He's on it."

"Prints on the car? His phone?"

Wolf blinked.

Patterson nodded. "Sorry ... Paul Womack. I need to know more."

He lowered his gaze. "He was recently let out of Leavenworth for something that happened in Afghanistan."

"What happened?"

"He killed some people. Civilians."

Patterson nodded, trying to fit the pieces together. "When did you get the email?"

"This morning."

"A dead man couldn't have sent that video," she said. "And the way it's edited suggests somebody besides Paul sent it. Otherwise, this Womack guy would've said what he wanted to say and not done a cut-and-paste job on the video."

Wolf stared at the floor.

"Which means he's dead, right?"

He nodded.

"So somebody's mad that he's dead. Somebody found the video and they're blaming you."

Wolf rubbed a hand over his stubble and turned to the window.

Two knocks hit the door and it opened. "Hey, DNA match shows it's Pat Xander's blood. And I got a match ..." Lorber gave Patterson a double take. "What are you doing here?"

She noted the hostility in the medical examiner's voice and decided to ignore him.

"Uh, I got the other match," Lorber said.

"The shell-casing prints?

"Yes."

"So tell me."

"With her in here?"

Patterson got the sense Lorber had stopped himself short of spitting on the floor. Lorber had taken her under his considerable wingspan when she'd joined the department years ago. She'd gotten the sense that she was the daughter he'd never had, and her leaving had hit the man hard.

Like a pouting child, he'd been hostile every time they'd interacted since. At first, she'd felt touched that he'd been hurt so deeply by her absence, perhaps even a little guilty for leaving him high and dry, but right now she couldn't have cared less.

"Yeah," Patterson said. "With me in here. Wolf told me everything, so why don't you tell us whose prints are on those shell casings?"

Lorber's eyes flared, then he looked at Wolf for confirmation.

Wolf nodded. "Whose are they?"

"Guy named Ethan Womack. Found his prints on the driver's-side door handle, too."

Patterson watched Wolf's eyes turn to glass.

Volleying glances between them, Lorber folded his arms. "What? You know him?"

Patterson opened her mouth to mention the video, then decided Wolf was being silent for a reason and closed it.

"Well ... anyway, it's about time we brief MacLean on this, right?" Lorber hitched a thumb over his shoulder.

"We'll be right there," Wolf said.

Lorber stared at them for a few moments and then left.

"You didn't tell him about the video," she said. "You don't want to tell anyone?"

"The text message said, 'Tell nobody else or he dies.'"

"Technically it said tell nobody about Rachette being kidnapped and hogtied. About the call at four p.m. Not this video."

Wolf shook his head. "They're tied. I'm not telling MacLean about this until we know more."

"But ..." The sentence never came out, because she understood. The SBCSD was filled with well-intentioned men and women, but given the proper situation, and especially under the leadership of Sheriff MacLean, the group could turn into an over-reactive beast.

"Never mind," she said, following him out into the hall.

CHAPTER 14

WOLF OPENED the door to Sheriff MacLean's office without knocking.

The sheriff had a semi-steadfast rule of leaving his window blinds cracked open so the entire squad room could see into his aquarium-like office, so he'd seen Wolf, Patterson, and Lorber coming.

The man had had his own thermostat installed to counteract the building's arctic temperatures and walking into MacLean's office was like entering a sauna.

"Sir," Wolf said.

MacLean leaned back in his chair, eyeing Heather Patterson. "What's going on? Why's she here? And ... oh, yeah, hello, Patterson. Or is it Patterson-Reed? What are you calling yourself out in the civilian world nowadays?"

"Heather." She smiled. "But you can call me Patterson, sir."

"What are you doing here?"

"Sir." Wolf cleared his throat. "Tom Rachette's missing."

"What?"

Wolf looked at Lorber.

Lorber said, "We found a set of fresh fingerprints on the

passenger-side door of Pat Xander's sedan. The prints match Tom Rachette's."

MacLean stroked his mustache with thumb and forefinger.

"And Rachette's not answering his phone," Wolf said.

"Triangulate it," MacLean said.

"We did. And Dr. Lorber and I found it a short distance from Pat Xander's car. Up the road, fifty yards. We also found two shell casings and blood matching Pat Xander's."

MacLean eyed Lorber. "You get any latents on the shells with that new doohickey?"

Lorber nodded. "A man named Ethan Womack. The same prints were on Rachette's phone and on Pat's driver's-side door."

"Who's Ethan Womack?" MacLean asked the room.

Wolf and Patterson exchanged glances.

Lorber looked at Wolf, who remained silent. "The system has him living in Taos, New Mexico. Has aggravated assault on his rap sheet."

MacLean swiveled to the windows and stood up. "Shit. So, what are we making of all this?"

"Rachette drank at the Beer Goggles last night," Wolf said. "Looks like he called Pat Xander at eleven p.m. They must have been forced off the road or something, and this guy Ethan Womack shot Pat Xander."

"And where's Rachette?"

"That's what we have to find out, sir," Wolf said.

The sheriff petted his mustache some more and looked at Patterson. "Shit. Okay, answer me now. Why's she here?"

"I called her in," Wolf said.

Patterson lifted her chin.

"I want her help on this. I need her. You should deputize her, sir."

"Heather Patterson, I deputize thee." MacLean flourished a hand toward her, then looked at Wolf. "Satisfied? If you need any more help, I have a room full of actual Sluice–Byron County Sheriff's deputies on the other side of that glass. Now what's our next move?"

"Rachette drank at the Beer Goggles Bar and Grill last night," Wolf said. "We need to go there."

"And we should get Taos police to go to Ethan Womack's house," Lorber said. "Check into him, too. Where he works. Get his cellphone number ASAP and get a location on him. All of it."

MacLean nodded. "I'll make the call to the Taos SD. I know the sheriff."

Wolf ignored Patterson's glance. "I called them a few minutes ago and requested they go to his house ... but you calling and lighting a fire under their asses for all the rest wouldn't hurt."

"Okay, I will." The sheriff leaned over and looked past them through the windows and into the squad room. "Who's going to tell her?"

They followed the sheriff's eyes to Charlotte Munford, who sat with her back to them at her desk.

Then the gazes of the three men retracted back to Patterson.

Patterson looked like a cornered cat. "I don't know whether everyone's aware of this, but she's pregnant."

"So?" MacLean asked.

"So she's in a sensitive state."

Lorber nodded. "She had a doctor's appointment for it this morning."

Patterson looked up at him and her face dropped. "Shit."

"What?"

"She's had a miscarriage before." Patterson shook her head. "I saw her crying earlier. What if she ..."

"What if she what?" MacLean's impatience was cranked to ten.

"What if she received bad news again at the doctor's, you know, about the baby. And that's why she was crying?"

They collectively exhaled.

"Well, we have to tell her, right?" Lorber folded his arms. "You can't just leave her in the dark in this. It's gonna get out."

They looked at Patterson again.

MacLean raised his eyebrows. "Deputy?"

CHAPTER 15

PATTERSON FELT DETACHED from her legs as she approached Charlotte's desk.

"Hey, Char."

Charlotte stopped typing on her keyboard and turned. "Hey, I saw you in MacLean's office with Wolf and Lorber." She stood up and hugged her with a big smile.

She was happy, not someone who'd received devastating news this morning.

"What's happening?" Patterson asked.

"Oh ..." Charlotte lowered her eyes. "Not much. Just another day."

She glanced down at Charlotte's stomach, and Charlotte saw it.

Looking side to side, Charlotte's eyes beamed. "Went to the doctor today, actually."

"You did?" Heather swallowed. "Oh ... and?"

Charlotte turned and opened a drawer, then turned back and thrust a curly ultrasound photograph into Patterson's hand. "It's a boy. A healthy boy."

Emotion flooded through Patterson and a tear ran down her cheek. "Oh ... great. That's so good to hear, Charlotte."

They hugged and Charlotte spoke as she clutched onto her. "We were going to tell everyone ... but Tom's a dickhead."

"What do you mean?"

Charlotte let go of her and stood back. "I mean he never came home last night after drinking. He knew I had a doctor's appointment this morning." She wiped the corner of her eyes. "Whatever. It's Tom. This is what he does. When the going gets tough, he runs away and leaves me alone to pick up the pieces. I don't care." There was real anger in her eyes. "I really don't. I'm done. I'm going to raise this kid by myself. He's not fit to—"

"Charlotte."

"—raise a child anyway. He's a child himself."

"Charlotte."

Patterson's tone stopped her.

"What?"

Glancing back down at Charlotte's stomach, she said, "Sit down, please."

"What?" Charlotte's face collapsed. "Oh, shit. What? What's happened?" She looked past her.

Wolf walked up to join them.

"What's going on?" Charlotte asked him.

"Tom's in trouble," Wolf said point-blank.

"What do you mean? Is he hurt?"

"We don't think so," Wolf said. "But ... we don't know. Pat Xander gave him a ride home last night, and we found Pat's body this morning."

Charlotte collapsed into her chair, landing hard on the armrest.

Patterson and Wolf leapt forward to help her sit.

Lorber came rushing over with Sheriff MacLean.

Charlotte's face was white and she breathed like she was hyperventilating.

"Listen, Charlotte," Wolf said. "He's okay. He's alive and we're going to find him."

Lorber and MacLean took up positions behind Charlotte and shot glares at Wolf.

"He's fine? What do you mean? But Pat Xander's dead? He's the body found in the trunk this morning on 18? So what's happened to Tom? How do you know he's fine?"

"We believe he's been taken by someone," Wolf said.

Lorber and MacLean looked uneasy. Like they could barely contain their confusion at Wolf's leap in logic. And who could blame them? They hadn't seen the picture on Patterson's phone.

Wolf stared into Charlotte's eyes. "We'll get him back, Charlotte."

At that moment, Patterson believed her former boss's words. "Yeah, Charlotte. We'll get him back." Her voice sounded a lot less sure than Wolf's had.

Wolf grabbed Patterson by the arm. "Now we have to go and get him."

"I'll ..." Patterson back-pedaled. "Sorry, Charlotte. We'll get him."

She had to turn away from Charlotte's shock before she broke down herself.

As they rounded the corner outside the squad room, Patterson turned to Wolf and shook her head. "Damn, that was bad. We can't just spring news on her like that and leave, can we?"

Wolf looked at his watch. "We have two and a half hours until we get a call from that number. We don't have time to be thoroughly sympathetic."

"Beer Goggles?"

"Yep."

She followed, jogging to keep up. Everything seemed to be going so fast. Too fast. "Wait a minute."

"What?" He pushed through the stairway doors and started down the steps, two at a time.

"I have something at work that'll help us. Let's stop there first."

CHAPTER 16

TOM RACHETTE LAY PARALYZED on a pile of red ants that were biting him from head to toe. He'd been wandering the Gobi Desert for days without food or water, searching continuously without luck.

But now the search was over because his legs were twisted and useless. Why they were immobile was another question. He failed to remember falling or getting mauled by an animal.

The ants kept coming. He felt them crawling underneath him. Why was he here? He needed to get up.

A flash of light seared his retinas and the sound of a gunshot woke him.

Opening his eyes, he sucked in a breath and a piece of something dry and scratchy went down his throat. He coughed and thrashed, trying to sit upright, but he was stuck.

He remembered the hell he was in.

Ropes were still fastened to his wrists, which pulled against loops around his ankles.

The unfathomable itching was the result of being naked on a bed of straw.

But there was light now, and he was warmer. That was different. Heavy blankets had been draped over his body, and though they felt like steel wool, they were keeping him toasty.

The last time he'd been conscious he'd been shivering uncontrollably, wet to the bone, and pre-hypothermic. His captors must've wanted him alive if they were covering him. The thought gave him hope.

He heard a shuffling noise and looked over the edge of the blankets.

The unibrow guy from last night stood staring down at him. In the different light, with his alcohol buzz worn off, the man looked even weirder than before. Those eyeballs were like holes in paper.

Behind him, a full bottle of water stood on a workbench.

Rachette could only turn his head so far and for so long before the pressure on his neck made him collapse back onto the hay, but the image of the water bottle was seared onto his eyeballs. On any normal day after a night of drinking he would've been dehydrated. Now every swallow felt like choking down dust.

"Water," he croaked.

Rachette stared at the dry straw in front of his face and waited for a reply that never came.

He remembered the guy standing on the side of the road—the strange way he folded his hands in front of him and the same blank look that he wore now. He recalled the man's head scars and wondering whether he'd been injured in the war.

He remembered his friend.

"Where's Pat?"

No answer.

Beyond the hay in front of Rachette's eyes, dust danced in slivers of sunlight lancing through cracks in the wood of the shack. Where the hay ended, dirt covered in animal hoof tracks began, something he hadn't noticed the previous night, what with the blow to the head and his drunken stupor.

He squirmed and the hay beneath him scratched his skin like a bed of knives.

Taking a steely breath, he cranked his neck again.

Rachette ignored the creepy way Unibrow stared at him, like he was a specimen, and noticed the water bottle missing from the workbench.

The pain was too much so he collapsed back to the hay, catching just a glimpse of the bottle hanging in the man's hand.

"Can I have some of that water?"

He remembered stepping out of the car, and then the flashlight beams and the sound of a shotgun slide-action freezing him in his tracks. And then a blow to the head, which still throbbed with every heartbeat.

"Fine, asshole, keep your water. Where's Pat?" he asked again. Rage swirled inside of him and he sat up, digging the ropes harder into his wrists. "Where's Pat, you piece of ..."

He let his sentence die, because outside a car engine grew to a roar. Brakes squealed and tires crunched to a stop on what sounded like dirt and rocks. A door thumped and footsteps approached.

Dropping his head back onto the hay, he relaxed and waited.

Daylight exploded inside as the door opened and a man with long blond hair and beard of matching color walked inside. He gave Unibrow a look, saying nothing, and then loomed in the doorway, his attention landing on Rachette.

"You up yet, ya drunk bastard?" The guy's voice was gravel, the accent Irish. His silhouette showed him to be overweight but he walked over to Rachette with athletic speed.

"Who the fuck are you?" Rachette said.

He craned a finger toward Unibrow. "Give me that," he said and then knelt in front of Rachette with the bottle of water.

Beads of sweat ran down the plastic and Rachette licked his lips. "Yes."

The man put a cold, callused hand that smelled like cigarettes on Rachette's forehead, then gripped his mouth and twisted his face this way and that, as if examining an animal.

A star-shaped earring dangled from his right ear and Rachette decided he would call this guy Lucky Charms. He appeared to be in his late fifties and had weathered red skin and beady blue eyes. The hair around his mouth was stained yellow by nicotine.

"What's going on?" he asked, feeling violated by the guy's cold, calculating demeanor.

Without warning, he gripped Rachette's neck and yanked him upright.

A cross between a cry and a gurgling noise escaped Rachette's lips. The ropes dug into his wrists and ankles and his limbs felt like they were being stabbed by a million needles.

"Drink." Lucky Charms put the bottle to his lips and tilted it back.

Rachette was unprepared and coughed as the water poured down his throat like a waterfall. Mucus and water spewed from his nostrils, but the guy kept the bottle tilted up.

The ice-cold liquid ran down his chin, over his bare chest, and down to his crotch.

"Drink!"

Rachette turned his head and took a full breath. The icy water splashed into his ear and down the center of his back.

Ignoring the shock, he turned back and sucked greedily on the bottle. In the end, he stomached only a few ounces and bathed in the rest.

Lucky Charms pushed him down onto the hay and poured the last trickle of water on his shoulders. "Piece of shite."

Now Rachette was thirsty and back to pre-hypothermic.

The man hurled the plastic bottle at his head. It bounced off his skull and skittered onto the dirt.

"Easy! What the hell's your problem?"

Lucky Charms bent down and stared at him. "You don't recognize me?"

Rachette squinted. "Nope. And I'm pretty sure I'd remember a shit-stained mouth like that."

The man turned around and walked out the door.

"What did you do to Pat?"

Cold air billowed inside and Rachette was almost sure they were at altitude. It felt like being on top of the Rocky Points Resort and his Nebraska lungs had to strain to get oxygen.

Unibrow shuffled into Rachette's periphery.

"What happened to Pat?" he asked again.

Unibrow backed away quickly as Lucky Charms came inside again, this time holding a toolbox.

Though he was determined to show no weakness, Rachette shivered uncontrollably. "Hey, I have to take a piss."

Lucky Charms set down the toolbox on the workbench. With back turned, he rummaged around inside, setting aside a hammer, then a screw-driver.

"What are you doing over there?" Rachette asked.

"Aha." Lucky Charms packed up the tools and put the box on the floor near the doorway. Then he approached Rachette, holding tin snips.

"Hey, what are you doing?" Rachette trembled harder now. Ropes tore into his skin as he tried to roll to his stomach. When that failed, he tried to curl into a ball to protect his manhood. "What the fuck are you doing?"

Lucky kicked the blanket away.

"Stop!" Rachette yelled. "What do you want? What are you doing?"

Lucky Charms smiled and laughed, sounding like a wounded bear. With eyes wide he asked, "You want to be just like little Davey Wolf, don't you?"

"What? I—"

"Answer the question!"

"I ... I ..."

"Answer!"

"Yeah, sure!"

"Good." Lucky Charms's expression became serious and he reached behind Rachette.

The ropes tightened on his wrists and he realized that the man was cutting him free.

But the relief was short-lived as he felt the cold iron of the tin snips on his pinkie finger, and now the crazy man's question made sense. David Wolf had lost his pinkie two years previously, blown off by a nine-millimeter bullet fired at point-blank range.

Rachette's mouth opened in soundless horror as the snips severed his finger from his left hand.

And then, again, darkness overtook him.

CHAPTER 17

THE PARKING LOT FOR LEARY, Crouch, and Shift was a stable for luxury-model SUVs.

Wolf parked next to Patterson's new Acura MDX and a top-of-the-line Land Rover and climbed out.

The rain had stopped and the sun was out. The air was moist and smelled of pine. The storm, now a midnight-black smear in the northeastern sky, bellowed on its way up and out of the valley.

Still on the phone, Patterson climbed out of her car. "... okay, see you. Thanks so much. And there's a new bag of chicken nuggets in the freezer ... I'll call you later. Bye." Patterson pocketed her phone and reached into the back seat. She pulled out a leather bag and shouldered it. "This way."

Patterson was undersized, but given the proper motivation she moved fast. Right now, Wolf had to jog to keep up.

The modest-sized, box-shaped building was painted white and trimmed with brown wood. The name of Patterson's employing law firm was etched on a metal sign on the façade. Though a new building, the architects had given it a mid-1800s look, a seemingly popular trick of the trade in Rocky Points that had never grown old.

"We have offices in twenty-seven towns up and down the

Rockies," she said, following Wolf's eyes. "Bozeman is the farthest north, and Taos the furthest south. None in the major cities. We say we do criminal law but it's mostly real-estate deals and divorce."

It seemed as if she talked for something to do besides think about Rachette.

He understood. On the drive over, his jaw had been clenched for most of the morning and he'd had to concentrate on breathing deep to counteract the tension.

Inhale. Exhale.

Patterson walked silently around the side of the building to the heavily wooded rear. "We'll take the back entrance and try and keep away from any action on the way to my office."

She put the key card on a pad and the door clicked. She pulled it open and waited for Wolf to follow, then went inside.

Patterson led him down a carpeted hallway, past closed doors with names on them, to a metal stairway door. They climbed to the fourth floor and she pulled the door open slowly, sneaking a peek before she stepped out into the hallway that ran left and right.

She hung a left and Wolf followed. They'd not traveled a few feet before a deep voice bellowed from behind them.

"Heather, there you are."

Patterson raised her eyes to the ceiling, then turned around and pasted on a fake smile. "Hello, Bryce."

Wolf turned to meet a man dressed in a tight, blue, and very shiny suit with lightning-yellow tie. He was tall and good-looking, probably early forties, with a haircut suitable for someone twenty years his junior—shaved on the sides and slicked back in the middle.

Bryce walked to them, ignoring Wolf's presence. "Where have you been?"

"Yeah, sorry," Patterson said. "I was ... detained."

The man held out a hand to Wolf, still keeping his eyes on Patterson. "Bryce Duplessis, regional partner."

Wolf grabbed the manicured hand and shook it, finding a handful of platinum rings in the process.

"You're David Wolf," Bryce declared, still not looking at him. "Chief Detective of the Sheriff's Department. Heather Patterson speaks of you like a long-lost brother she adores."

Heather raised her eyebrows and blinked rapidly. "Can I help you, Bryce?"

"The photos."

"Right. Like I said, I did get the pictures and I'm on my way to upload them now."

Bryce held out his hand. "I can upload them myself."

"Yes." She pulled out a camera with a zoom lens from her bag, ejected a memory card, and handed it over. "Thank you. That would be much better for me."

Bryce grabbed the memory card and then snatched the camera out of her hands. With expert speed, he re-inserted the card, flipped around the camera, and pressed some buttons. "Oh … yeah." He shook his head, his eyebrows dancing while he studied the display screen. With a smile he said, "Once again, Heather Patterson delivers the goods."

Patterson tapped Wolf's shoulder and walked away down the hall. "Don't disturb us," she said.

"Yes, ma'am." Bryce chuckled and walked in the opposite direction.

Wolf followed her around a bend to an office door with a name plate that read *Heather Patterson—Investigation.*

She unlocked it and walked inside, and Wolf paused in the entryway, taking in the space. Shelves lined the right wall, packed with books and pictures of Heather, Scott, and Tommy.

She dropped her bag on one of two plush leather chairs, then rounded a dark-wood desk and sat in a high-topped swivel chair.

Behind her were two windows with vertical blinds pulled open to display Rocky Points and the Chautauqua Valley beyond.

"Can you please shut the door?" She pulled herself into her desk and started typing on a MacBook. "Take a seat."

He shut the door and sat down. "Now can you tell me why we're here?"

She sat ramrod straight in her chair and her fingers were a blur on the keyboard. A few seconds later, she clucked her tongue and shook her head. "Damn it."

"What?"

"Just a second." She typed some more and waited.

He stood up and walked around the desk. Her computer screen looked like how he envisioned an NSA mainframe. In the center window, he recognized a street map of Rocky Points.

"What's this?"

"Cellphone location and tracking software."

Letting the information sink in, he sat on the edge of her desk. "You mean you can track where a phone is by entering the number?"

"Something like that."

"Without the consent of the wireless carrier, or the user," he said.

She kept her eyes on the screen.

"The Sluice–Byron County Sheriff's Office doesn't have access to something like this," he said.

She shrugged. "Neither do I."

"Because something like that ... this ... is illegal."

"I know." She clicked on the screen and typed some more.

Wolf blinked. "What about the number that texted Rachette's picture? Can you locate it?"

"That's what I'm looking at now."

The screen had a logo in the center that kept spinning.

She shook her head. "It's turned off. And there's no name to the number. According to the IMEI number, it's a burner purchased at a Walmart down in Ashland."

"I can't believe I'm asking you this, but can you figure out who purchased it?"

She shook her head. "No."

"How about Ethan Womack's cellphone? Does he have one? Can we trace it?"

She typed again. "Checking ... putting it in my reverse-lookup software."

This wasn't the first time in his career he'd felt like an accomplice while working with Heather Patterson.

"Okay. I got his number. I'll trace it."

"What are you guys doing with this software?"

Her gaze slid to his. "This is my personal computer. It's my software running on an encrypted VPN. Nobody else in this law firm has any knowledge of this."

He held up a hand. "Whatever you say."

The logo spun in the center of the screen again.

"No luck?" Wolf asked.

"Dang it. His phone is off."

"Any way to check a location history?"

She shook her head. "Not without prior planting of a device or piece of software on his phone. Or using the usual, legal means of serving a warrant to his wireless provider, which the department is already doing." Pushing back from her desk, she said, "That's all I have. Sorry I just wasted twenty minutes we don't have, but I thought we might get something."

"Good try," he said.

She swallowed and flicked a look back to her computer. "You going to put me in jail for this?"

He allowed one side of his mouth to lift. "Let's find Rachette ... and then we'll talk."

She pointed down. "We have to be here for that text message

at four o'clock. When we receive a call, I can enter the number and this software will pinpoint it in milliseconds."

"And if it's a text message?"

Shrugging, she said, "It's more difficult. But doable."

He checked his watch again. "Two fifteen. Let's go."

CHAPTER 18

"WHY ARE you guys in here asking questions? Did something happen last night?"

Wolf knocked a knuckle on the bar counter. "Just answer the question, Jerry. Who was in here last night?"

Jerry Blackman, the owner of the Beer Goggles Bar and Grill, looked between Wolf and Patterson with a mixed expression of suspicion and marijuana-induced paranoia. "I swear this place is like a vortex of evil or something. I think I need to sell it."

"Jerry," Patterson said.

"Yeah. Uh, let's see. I have a stack of receipts right here." Jerry picked up the pile from behind the bar. "John Grayson ... Matt Repplinger ... Matt Whitsom ..."

"Matt Whitsom?" Wolf asked, rubbing a tender spot on his temple where the man had accidentally head-butted him earlier that morning.

Jerry nodded. "Yeah. He's in here quite a bit."

"Go on."

"Let's see ... Tom Rachette ... Tyler Eggleston ..."

A man at the end of the bar raised his hand. "That's me." He wiped his mouth with his napkin.

Tyler Eggleston was a middle-aged man with a straight brown

beard who trimmed trees in town and did handiwork for many of Margaret Hitchens's rental properties.

"Hi, Tyler."

"What's going on?"

Patterson edged a few barstools closer toward him. "Hi, Tyler."

"Hi, Heather. Long time no see. How's Scott?"

She nodded. "We're just trying to get a sense of who was here last night, you know? Who drank with whom?"

Tyler Eggleston swallowed and flicked a glance at Wolf. "Why? What happened?"

Wolf held his hand out to Jerry. "Could I see that stack of receipts?"

Jerry hesitated, like he was considering mentioning warrants or rights violations, or maybe contemplating the vastness of the galaxy, then handed them over and wiped the bar top.

Wolf flipped through them one by one, looking for Ethan Womack's name. "Do you guys remember a man named Ethan in here?"

Jerry and Tyler furrowed their brows.

"No," Jerry said.

"Nope."

"Anyone you didn't recognize?" Wolf asked them.

Tyler shrugged. "Thursday nights are pretty busy. I sat here, watching the game." He pointed to a television above the back of the bar. "Don't really pay attention to who comes and goes, except for the locals I guess."

"Can you tell us who Tom was with?" Patterson asked.

"Rachette?" Tyler chomped on a French fry. "Let's see. I hung out with him, if you count sitting here listening to him spout off pointless movie trivia and jokes I've heard twenty times as hanging out."

"Is there another way to hang out with him?" Patterson asked, drawing a laugh from Tyler and Jerry.

"So I was here, Tom, Yates, Repplinger ... and—"

"Deputy Yates was here?" Wolf asked.

"Yeah." Tyler paused, looking between them. "That's how Tom got here, and why he got a ride home later from X. Because Yates left earlier."

"X, as in Xander?" Patterson asked.

"Yep. That's his go-to guy for a ride home. Won't let any one of us use him."

Wolf thought about Pat Xander's head and focused his attention back on the stack of receipts in his hand. Rachette's came next. "Says you closed out Tom at 11:06 p.m. Did he leave right after that?"

"Yeah," Jerry said.

"And there're no doubts about that?" Wolf asked, looking at Tyler.

Tyler shrugged. "Yeah. Left right after he paid."

"I've been meaning to ask you guys for years now ..." Jerry leaned across the bar and winked at Wolf. "You guys want some suds?"

"No, thanks."

"You know, back in your dad's day, those deputies down at the old station used to stop in here looking for a cold one. Burton'd come in, and without saying anything he'd give me a nod. I'd push a glass to the bar and he'd down it in a single gulp. Sometimes I'd push another glass. And another. Things aren't like they used to be, eh?" Jerry slapped his neck and studied his hand. "Damn it. Mosquitos are thick already."

Wolf nodded at Patterson. "Ready?"

Jerry wiped his neck with the bleached rag.

Patterson nodded. "Yeah."

They said their goodbyes and walked out into the parking lot.

"What do you think?" Patterson asked, stepping over a puddle.

Wolf and Patterson reached Wolf's SUV and got inside. They'd left Patterson's Acura back at her office.

"I don't know," he said finally.

"Why the hesitation?"

"I'm just wondering about the difficulty of one man handling Rachette, shooting and killing Pat Xander, picking up his one hundred and ninety pounds of dead weight and stuffing him in the trunk, and dumping the car over the edge of the road. Then ... he'd have to get Rachette into his own car. Hogtie him ... I don't know."

Patterson nodded in thought. "Seems difficult, especially with Rachette's tenacity, but I don't know who this Ethan Womack guy is. Rachette looked pretty beat up. Could have clobbered him with a baseball bat."

Wolf shook his head. "Yeah, I guess."

"Ethan Womack's a brazen son of a bitch," she said. "He leaves his fingerprints on Pat's car, the shells next to the blood, prints on Rachette's phone. Either that or he's stupid. We need to get a trace on his phone as soon as possible."

Wolf pushed the ignition button and shifted into reverse."

"Or he's not very worried about what happens *after* whatever he has planned," Patterson said.

Wolf shifted back into park. "I forgot."

"Forgot what?"

Wolf held up a finger and dialed a number on his phone.

"Hello?" Tammy Granger answered.

"Tammy, it's Wolf."

"I know. What's up?"

"I need you to read me a phone number, please."

Patterson took an unspoken cue and dug out her cell to enter the number as Wolf read it.

Tammy read it off and Wolf repeated it to Patterson, who tapped her screen with her finger. When they were done, they looked at one another.

"Thanks, Tammy."

"Sure thing."

Patterson's forehead crinkled. "What was that all about?"

"I forgot to tell you that we found Pat Xander's car this morning via an anonymous tip. That's the number that called us."

"It's the same cell that sent the message."

Wolf backed out of the parking spot and they bounced down the potholed dirt lot, then over the bridge spanning the Chautauqua River.

"So, he called it in?" she asked. "Why? To lead us to the car, the body, the shells, the fingerprints everywhere?"

He turned onto Highway 734 with the roof lights flashing and pressed the gas.

"That's not brazen," she said. "That's strange."

"Yeah."

CHAPTER 19

WOLF AND PATTERSON made it to the station in three minutes. Another minute of running later and they were up the stairs, down the hallway, and into the lecture hall-like situation room.

Deputy Yates, Dr. Lorber, Undersheriff Wilson, and Sheriff MacLean were standing down on the front floor, their attention locked on the roll-down screen.

MacLean turned at their arrival. "There you are."

Patterson couldn't help but notice that the comment had been directed squarely at Wolf. Wilson and Yates only gave her a passing glance and nod, and Lorber pointedly ignored her. What did she expect? This was not a reunion party.

"We have a live link to the Taos Sheriff's Department," Lorber said, gesturing to the projected video.

"What's that?" A tinny voice came scratching out of a set of speakers next to a laptop perched on the table.

The onscreen video flipped in a swirl of images and then a man dressed in a khaki Sheriff's Department uniform and cowboy hat filled the view.

"Uh, nothing!" MacLean was just short of shouting. "Our chief detective just joined us. And ... his assistant."

Lorber leaned closer to Wolf and nodded toward the technical setup. "We can see what they see as they walk around inside Ethan Womack's place."

Patterson put a hand on Lorber's arm. "You guys have live-linking capabilities with their department? What are you using?"

Lorber ignored her for a second, then said, "Facebook. Ever heard of it?"

"Facebook?"

The ME rolled his eyes and leaned down to her with a lowered voice. "Facebook Live, a laptop and a smart phone, and we're in the building with them. I came up with the idea."

"Shut up, you two," MacLean said. "Deputy Miller, can you please go back out to the body so my detective can see it?"

"Yeah, okay," the voice said. The picture on the screen jostled and swirled.

Patterson thought Deputy Miller of the Taos SD had little talent as a cameraman. The images bounced and jiggled with each step, and he kept covering and uncovering the microphone hole on his phone, which rattled the speakers.

Springs creaked as he opened a door, then the display went white as he stepped outside. Footsteps crunched through the speakers and finally the jostling stopped.

"Here he is."

"Shit." Patterson breathed as the overexposed image darkened to the clear picture of a dead man lying face down on the ground. Her eyes were drawn to the hole in his head, exposing brain tissue and bone illuminated by the sun.

She immediately recognized the clothing and hair as the man in Wolf's video. Paul Womack.

She glanced at Wolf. He was frozen, staring at the screen, just like the rest of them.

Deputy Miller's camera skills improved, and he gave them various close-ups and angles of Womack's corpse.

"Blood's dry underneath him. Very dry, and the insects have already done a number," Lorber said with a raised voice. "Their initial estimation of time of death is seventy-two hours, and I concur based on what I'm seeing in the video here. Looks like a self-inflicted wound. You can see the gun in his right hand still. Powder burns on one temple, the other temple ... clean gone."

The pictures onscreen followed Lorber's voice prompts as if Miller was now Lorber's symbiotic extension.

"Gunshot residue on his right hand," Lorber said.

The camera zoomed into Womack's dead hand resting on a Beretta pistol lying in the dirt.

"His name is Paul Womack." MacLean said, now looking at Wolf. "Ethan Womack's older brother. Guy served fifteen of an eighteen-year sentence in Leavenworth for murdering a woman and child in Afghanistan."

Wolf kept his gaze on the screen.

"We're working on getting a full history on him," MacLean continued. "This house was owned by Paul and Ethan Womack's mother, who died two years ago of ovarian cancer and left it to the two men. Can I get a shot of the area, please?"

The image went white again, then darkened to show a rolling landscape covered in small shrubs. Miller swung in a slow circle that showed the house, a weathered off-white one-story building with a boarded-up window. Rotating further, a small detached garage or shed opposite the house came into view.

"They found some stuff in the exterior garage of the house," MacLean said. "Deputy Miller was just going to show us. Deputy Miller, you can proceed to the garage now? Thank you for showing us the body again."

"You got it," the voice said.

Miller's phone swiveled to a sturdily built wooden shed that had been bleached by the sun. Two doors were open, revealing two white-clothed crime-scene techs inside.

They turned with annoyed looks at the man pointing a cell-phone camera in their direction.

"We have a link to Sluice–Byron County SD in Colorado here," Miller said as he approached the two men.

"What?" one of them asked.

"Hello there!" MacLean waved.

"They can't see you, sir," Lorber said, placing a hand on MacLean's shoulder.

The sheriff slapped the ME's hand away.

"Uh ... hi." The CSI squinted at the phone.

"Sheriff Will MacLean, here. Thanks for your assistance on this. We have a case involving Ethan Womack up here in Colorado. We're pressed on time and need to see what you guys have."

The man seemed to relax a little and nodded. "Oh, okay." The man next to him had a DSLR camera and snapped photos of something on a workbench.

"One second, please, sir," Miller said, his face filling the screen.

The video went dark for a second while Miller spoke in a low voice to the men inside the shack. There were mentions of "sheriff's orders" and "cooperation," and then the video appeared again.

The CSI said, "Okay, sir. I've just been fully briefed. We'll go ahead and show you what we have."

MacLean downturned his mouth and nodded. "Thank you, uh ..."

"Sergeant Gains, sir."

"Sergeant Gains," MacLean said, "this is of the utmost importance. We have lives on the line up here. Please proceed."

"Of course, sir." The man was now centered in the video feed on the screen. He bent over and picked up a black vest. "We're finding a lot of scary stuff in here. This here is level-three-A body armor, standard for Taos SD's SWAT team." The man raised a bulletproof vest and poked his finger through a hole. "See that?"

"Armor-piercing rounds," MacLean said.

"Yes, sir. There are two of these vests, all shot to shit." The man pointed to the side and Miller followed, turning the camera view outside.

The video brightened, then dimmed to show hilly, desolate country covered in sage brush. "You can see there are two shooting berms set up out there. Looks like they see more action than our department range."

Two bumps rose from the otherwise board-flat land.

"Did you see the trophies inside?" the CSI asked.

MacLean frowned. "No. What are you talking about?"

"Fifty Caliber Shooters Association trophies," the CSI said. "Turns out Ethan Womack is a seriously gifted shooter. Works at a local gun shop called T 'n' T Guns. We have two units on their way to speak to them. But from the looks of this shack, he could set up shop right here."

The camera swung back to the interior of the shed, and Gains's latex-covered hand twirled a long rifle round in front of the cellphone lens. A two-toned bullet jutted from the cartridge case. "Fifty-caliber armor piercing." He pointed and the camera focused for the first time on the wall inside the darkened shed.

"Wow." Lorber whistled.

Guns hung from every square inch.

"Two M16A2s," Gains said, "a couple of M4s, Glock 17, Glock 21, two Beretta M9s, just like the one our friend inside used to shoot himself, among an assortment of other gems our military uses. So you guys were the ones who tipped us off to Ethan Womack, huh? I heard he killed somebody up there and stuffed him in a trunk."

MacLean cleared his throat. "Yeah, well, that's what it looks like at the moment."

"You said you have lives on the line up there," Gains said.

"I'm not at liberty to discuss."

"Yeah, all right. But let me tell you what." Gains made a show of pointing at the wall of guns. "I'm seeing some spots that look like there used to be guns hanging there, if you catch my drift." He held up the cartridge again. "And I'm not seeing the fifty-caliber rifle that fires this. Which is probably the same one that landed him second place in the local FCSA tournament last year."

MacLean exhaled and wiped his forehead. "We understand. Thank you, Sergeant Gains."

"I'm also seeing an empty hook in his line of handguns."

MacLean folded his arms and turned toward his deputies. "Thank you, Sergeant Gains."

They watched in silence for a minute, and Patterson saw Wolf eyeing his watch. She pulled out her cellphone and checked the time. 3:13 p.m.

"Hold on," Miller said. "One second, please." He spoke to a man next to him and then his face filled the screen again. "I'm told we sent over Ethan Womack's cellphone information. Did you receive it?"

Wilson held up a packet of paper. "We did, thank you!"

"Okay, good. I'm also told that we've sent over a personnel file on Ethan Womack and his deceased brother."

"Yes," MacLean said. "Thank you. We received everything. Listen, we're going to shut down for a bit now. Thank you for your cooperation. We'll be in touch, all right?"

"Yes, sir."

At MacLean's order, Lorber ended the live-link session and closed the laptop.

"What is this?" MacLean asked. "Wrong place, wrong time for Rachette? Who is this guy?"

Wilson fumbled with the stack of papers in his hand. "Ethan Womack: thirty-nine years old. Born in Taos, New Mexico. Aggravated assault two years ago … looks like he was in a fist fight with a fellow employee. Put him in the hospital with a ruptured spleen."

"Now he works at a gun shop," MacLean said.

"Says here his victim was a fellow employee of T 'n' T Guns in Taos. Same shop he works at now."

"Looks like he was found to be, quote, mentally deficient by the court."

"What?"

Wilson kept reading. "He had severe head trauma when he was a child. The man was sentenced to a mental hospital, where he spent four months and was released. This gives a doctor's name."

"Let me see that." Lorber took the page and read it. "He was put in the loony bin and was released. Sees a doctor now on a weekly basis. No more details than that here."

MacLean raised his eyebrows. "Thank you for that professional analysis."

Lorber handed the sheet back to Wilson.

"What about this deceased brother of his?" MacLean began pacing again. "Give us the rundown on him."

"Okay ... Paul Womack. Forty-three years old. Born in Taos. No priors. Was in the 75th Ranger Regiment, US Army." Wilson looked at Wolf. "Says he was stationed at Fort Lewis. You were stationed in Tacoma."

Patterson, along with everyone else, watched Wolf closely.

A perplexed look crossed Wolf's face, and then he shook his head. "Never heard of him."

"Why does he have Rachette?" MacLean looked at Wolf. "He's army. He was stationed the same place you were. When?"

"Served from 1998 until 2002," Wilson said. "He was ... geez, dishonorably discharged and put in federal prison for shooting and killing two civilians in Afghanistan."

MacLean was on Wolf again. "You sure this doesn't ring a bell?"

Wolf blinked and said nothing, which served to amplify the suspicion of everyone else in the room.

"You don't know him?" Wilson asked.

"No," Wolf said.

Patterson felt her sweat glands fire. What was Wolf doing? He was protecting Rachette, she reminded herself.

MacLean zeroed in on her next. "Did you guys go to Beer Goggles?"

She had trouble thinking through all the implications of telling these men about Rachette's true predicament, what they could and couldn't share about what she and Wolf knew, what they'd learned, and what it would be plausible for an outsider to know.

Speak, moron! She felt her face flushing hotter.

"Yeah, we did," Wolf said. "We talked to Jerry Blackman and a guy named Tyler Eggleston who frequents the place and drank beers with Rachette last night. He said you were there, too, Yates."

Yates nodded, looking uncomfortable as the new center of attention. "Yeah. I was there at the beginning of the night. I told everyone that a few minutes ago, before you and Patterson were here."

"Okay, okay," MacLean said. "So what did you guys find out?"

Wolf shrugged. "Rachette was there, drinking like he always does. They didn't see anyone suspicious. I checked the receipts for Ethan Womack's name, which wasn't there."

"He could've been in there and paid cash," MacLean said. "You didn't have his picture, did you?"

Wolf shook his head.

MacLean pulled the stack of papers from Wilson's hands and held up one of the sheets. "Here he is."

They all stared at Ethan Womack's mugshot photograph.

The man's dark-brown eyes stared into the camera like he'd just asked it a question and was waiting for an answer. His lips were full and shiny, and his jaw hung open, revealing crooked teeth. He had the most prominent brow Patterson had ever seen, other than in drawings of Neanderthal people in history books.

"Whoa," Lorber said.

The placard said Taos Police Department and was dated two years previously.

"There's a DMV printout in there, too," Wilson said. "1986 Ford F-150. Color: black. No photo."

MacLean snorted. "This guy's seen as mentally deficient by a New Mexico court and yet he has a driver's license and works at a gun shop?"

No one answered.

MacLean shook the mugshot photo. "You have to shove this picture in their faces down at the Beer Goggles. Nobody's going to forget seeing this guy. And ask them about this black Ford F-150. You get a list of everyone at the bar?"

"The people with Rachette," Wolf said. "We'd have to go back to get more names."

"So do it. And show everyone this mugshot." MacLean held out the paper until Wolf took it, then shoved the packet of papers into Wilson's hands again.

"What about his cellphone?" Wolf asked.

"Shit." MacLean turned and paced. "His cellphone."

Wilson flipped to another packet of paper marked with a New Mexico Wireless logo. "Got a ping map here that shows he came into Rocky Points four days ago. Monday at 3:10 p.m. he pinged on our cell towers. Is that how you read it?"

"Let me see that." Lorber took the papers.

Patterson edged closer and got on her toes to see. The map showed a series of dots connected with blue; they followed along the fastest highway route from Taos and up through the center of the Rockies to Rocky Points.

The next page showed a Summit Wireless map with Ethan Womack's local movement.

"He went downtown." Lorber shrugged. "Looks like he hovered around Main Street. Right in our vicinity, in fact. Then, poof. He shut off his phone."

"Did he go to the Beer Goggles?" MacLean asked.

"No. But his phone shut off on Tuesday and never came back on. Could've gone anywhere after that and we'll never know."

MacLean looked at Wolf. "Beer Goggles. Go."

Wolf nodded, then turned to Yates and Wilson. "You two go. It'll be better to send new faces. You might be able to get a fresh perspective out of Jerry."

Wilson glanced at MacLean to check and then nodded. "Let's go."

"So what are you gonna do?" MacLean asked.

"Patterson and I have a hunch we might've missed something up at the shooting site."

The sheriff narrowed his eyes, then nodded. "Fine. Let's move."

CHAPTER 20

WOLF PULLED up one of Patterson's office chairs and sat down next to her. He stayed silent, watching her fingers tap in a blur on the keyboard—entering numbers into cells and clicking the mouse in different spots.

He checked his watch. "Six minutes."

"His number is still not registering on the network." Patterson clicked some more keys and tapped the trackpad on her laptop. "He's not turning on the phone until the last minute. Or maybe it'll be a different phone." She shook her head and checked a cable inserted into the back of her computer. "Ethernet's still connected. Calling from a different phone would be the smart thing to do. For a mentally disabled guy, he seems pretty smart."

"Or whoever's with him is."

She grunted in response.

Wolf felt useless sitting next to her so he stood and looked out the window.

The sun glinted off wet trees, rooftops, and asphalt. The storm was a black hole behind the northeastern mountains and a low cloud clung to the eastern side of the valley, shining white.

"Anyway, even if it's a different number, I'll run it and we'll get a location. I just have to type fast."

Wolf said nothing.

Four minutes and thirty seconds.

"If it's the same number, I'll hit the enter key and we'll have a good chance of getting a location. Here, I'll hit it now." She pressed the enter key. "Nothing."

Wolf walked to the other side of the room and studied a picture of her, Scott, and Tommy. The kid had her eyes and Scott's mouth. The freckles were all Patterson. A perfect hybrid of the two. Father and son gazed upon each other, smiles alive on their faces.

Given the tension of the situation, Wolf was surprised to feel a smile fading from his lips as he turned back to the window.

Patterson's phone chimed and vibrated on her desk.

With lightning reflexes she picked it up. "It's a text, and it's a different number." She dropped the phone onto the desk. Another blur of fingers on the keyboard. Then she pushed back. "There. I have a location!"

Wolf stepped around the desk and picked up the phone. The blood and flesh on the screen made him flinch.

"Downtown. Somewhere within two hundred feet of Third and Main. I can't get more specific than that."

Wind Shade Bliss was located on Third and Main, and Wolf's already skyrocketing pulse redlined.

He pocketed the phone and ran out the door.

"Wait for me!"

CHAPTER 21

WOLF WAS unable to find a parking spot in front of the art gallery so he stopped in the middle of Main Street and got out, blocking traffic behind him.

Spilling more than one glass of wine, Wolf and Patterson pushed through a crowd of people who'd gathered out front and entered the gallery. Jazz played over speakers in the corners of the room, and the people packed inside turned to look at them as if a pair of moose had barged inside.

Wolf ignored the stares and spotted Lauren in the corner, talking to Baron.

Finishing a breathless laugh, she saw him come in and her face went crimson.

Craning a finger, he turned away and looked for Ella.

Lauren threaded her way through the crowd. Any embarrassment, and Wolf had seen it loud and clear, left when she saw his concern. "What's happening?"

"Where's Ella?" he asked.

"She's in the back room with the other kids. What's going on?" Lauren watched him look past her toward the back doorway. Her face dropped and she began pushing people aside. "Excuse me. Excuse me."

He followed her close.

When she stopped abruptly he almost ran into her and Patterson crashed into his side.

Lauren exhaled like she'd explosively decompressed and held up a hand. "Right there. She's right there. Now what the hell is going on?"

The back room had been converted into a children's arts and crafts space for the occasion, and a half-dozen children were working on lumps of clay.

"Dave!" Ella jumped up and came over. "Look at what I'm making. It's a mountain."

"What's happening?" Baron stood at the doorway.

Wolf felt Lauren's eyes burning into him as he studied Ella's sculpture. "Oh, wow. Looks great."

"Go back and work on your sculpture, honey." Lauren's voice had a sharp edge and Ella did as she'd been told. "Now, what are you guys doing in here?"

"Is everything all right?" Baron shuffled closer and loomed next to Patterson.

"Please, Baron. We're okay," she said.

Baron rolled an icy glare towards Wolf and left.

Patterson backed away and melted into the main-room crowd behind him.

"Sorry. We have a—"

"A situation?"

Wolf met her gaze for the first time.

Her pupils had contracted to points. She shook, staring at him like he'd just slapped her across the face. This woman had been through soul-ripping trauma twice in her life—both times almost losing her daughter.

The children were staring at him, concern etched on their faces.

"Everything's okay," he said with a smile that he hoped looked genuine.

The back door to the gallery was open, letting in a shaft of afternoon light and a fresh breeze.

Wolf grabbed her hand and brought her outside to the dirt alley muddied by the storm.

When they were out of sight of the children he wrapped his arms around her. "I'm sorry. I'm so sorry. I was just worried."

She leaned into his chest. "What's going on? Talk to me."

He pushed her back to arms-length and softened his expression. "I have to go."

"Go where?" She studied his expression. "Are you in trouble?"

He pulled her into another hug but she pushed back. "Talk to me. Why did you think Ella was in trouble? Are we in danger?"

Wolf thought about that. "No. We traced a call and it came from this vicinity, so I was just making sure you were okay."

"What call? You're tracing someone near here? Is it somebody dangerous? Do we need to be worried?"

"No. Listen, they're not going to stick around. They're running from us."

Lauren rubbed her forehead with a shaky hand.

"I really have to go." The window was closing and he needed to start looking for Ethan Womack. Patterson had gone out the front.

Lauren nodded and said nothing.

"How's it going in there?" Wolf asked.

She rolled her eyes, a hint of a smile tilting her lips. "It's going fine, or at least it was. Go."

He kissed her and watched her go back inside.

CHAPTER 22

PATTERSON IGNORED scathing looks as she exited the art gallery and went to the edge of the crowd that had spilled onto the sidewalk.

"Hey, Heather."

She heard a familiar voice behind her and turned, then immediately regretted it. Chet Chamberfield worked with Scott up at the mountain and was attracted to her, or desperately wanted to be her friend, or something. He talked her senseless every time they saw one another.

"You checking out the art? Lauren Coulter. You know her?" Chet sipped his wine. "I think she's dating your former boss, Dave Wolf? Isn't that right?"

She looked up and down the road. What did she expect to see? Ethan Womack standing with a cellphone in his hand, staring in her direction with a holy-shit-I've-been-caught expression?

"Good stuff. I'd recommend checking out the Cave Creek landscape. It's one of the bigger ones on the right when you walk inside. How's Scott doing?"

"Listen, Chet. This isn't a good time."

"Oh." He took another sip. "Why's that? Something going on?"

"Goodbye, Chet." She looked him in the eye and walked away.

"Yeah ... okay. Geez, what was her problem?"

She headed south and studied the patrons alongside the road in the immediate vicinity. Then she studied the crowd she'd just ditched, carefully avoiding looking at Chet again.

On the drive there, she and Wolf had searched the traffic for a 1986 black Ford F-150 and seen none. Scanning again, she got the same result.

Ethan Womack had changed cellphones before he'd texted the second message, which meant he was, despite the "mental deficiency" listed in his file, an intelligent person. The guy had trophies for long-distance fifty-caliber shooting. And as MacLean had pointed out, he had a driver's license and a job. That sort of man wouldn't be standing out in the open. Nor sitting in his truck on Main Street, watching her.

Still, she got the sense that she was being watched, though that was the norm for her ever since the Van Gogh killer. But he could've been working with someone else. They'd already established that to pull off the crime would've been difficult for one man.

She honed her focus like a laser beam and scanned the crowd in front of the art gallery. No one drew suspicion.

She checked her watch and calculated that six minutes had elapsed since she'd received the text. If there was more than one of them, they were probably long gone by now.

That text message.

She allowed herself to dwell on the recent memory. There'd been blood and a severed finger. She'd only given it a glance before trying to trace the number, but that's all it had taken to etch that picture on her mind for the rest of her life.

Poor Rachette. He would be sweating right now, his hand in unimaginable pain, waves of nausea probably flowing through him. She sweated for him just thinking about it.

Turning back in the other direction, she walked past the

crowd and took some deep breaths, scanning both sides of the streets.

Wolf appeared at the next corner, and she was confused at first, then realized he must have exited the building from the back door and come around.

"Anything?" he asked.

"No 1986 Ford F-150. No one who looks like Ethan Womack." She searched her pockets for her cellphone and realized that Wolf still had it. "Can I see my phone again? I want to look at that message again."

He gave it to her and got in close to look.

A second later, the photo glowed on the screen. Rachette's severed digit lay on a wood surface, and beneath the severed end pooled fresh blood.

"My God," she said.

The message underneath said: *If you both fail to make the meeting point in time, he dies. If you tell anyone, he dies. I'll be watching.*

Following the picture were a set of coordinates and two words: *Midnight tonight.*

"I'll be watching?" Patterson asked. "So it is one guy."

Wolf said nothing.

"Midnight tonight." Sweat broke out on her forehead. The edges of her vision started dancing and she looked up to stop vertigo from taking over.

"Read those coordinates to me." Cradling his phone, Wolf waited for her.

She read them off and dizziness took hold, but she got the coordinates out of her mouth without her voice shaking.

She felt like she was on a ship out in the middle of rough seas, teetering on the plank with a sword to her back.

When she opened her eyes, Wolf had his cellphone held toward her, showing the map of the coordinates.

The picture slowly resolved into a narrow, east–west valley, dozens of miles south and west of them, on the other side of

Williams Pass. A blue dot pulsated near the base of a white-capped mountain.

Wolf pinched and zoomed out, then waited for the spotty mountain cell service to resolve the picture again. "I've been there. That's remote."

Patterson said nothing. All she could think about was Tommy. Her little boy was probably sleeping right now, cuddling his new stuffed tiger.

"Dark Mountain," Wolf said. "Thirteen thousand plus feet. The spot he has on here is at the foot of it. Probably at least eleven-five up there," he said, meaning eleven thousand, five hundred feet. She'd been up the road before, but never hiked the way in.

"So, we hike in." Patterson's voice sounded hollow in her own head.

"There's a road that offshoots from Highway 734." He pointed. "Goes up a few miles, then the rest is a hike. Probably four or five miles of walking." He checked his watch.

Patterson swallowed and took long, deep breaths.

"It's going to rain again tonight, isn't it?" She closed her eyes, feeling like she was hyperventilating.

Wolf held out his hand. "Could I please see your car keys?"

She opened her eyes and turned to him. "What? Why?"

"I need to see something."

She fished them out of her pocket and handed them over.

He put them in his pocket.

"What are you doing?" she asked.

"I'm taking your keys."

"Why?"

"Because I don't want you to drive anywhere."

She shook her head. "What do you mean?"

"I'm doing this alone and I don't want you following me up there."

They stared at one another.

She felt a tear form in the corner of her eye. Her chest heaved and the only noise she made came from her labored breath.

"There's no good ending to this thing," Wolf said. "I'm not going to knowingly march you into an ambush."

Patterson shook her head with little conviction. She thought of Tommy again and closed her eyes. "I can't," she said.

"Ethan Womack wants me. His older brother killed himself because of me. And he's taken Rachette to make sure I show up, so he can take revenge. On me."

She wiped her eyes. "But he's saying we both have to be there. Why is that? Why's he involving us?"

"He's hurt. He worshipped his brother, and now his brother's dead. He's trying to inflict as much pain as possible on me by involving you and Rachette."

"He's going to kill Tom when he realizes I'm not there."

"He may or he may not. But I'm not going to play that game." He put a hand on her shoulder. "There's no way in hell you're going up there with me. And you know there's no way Rachette would let you go if he were here right now."

The tears flowed down her cheeks. "If something happens to you two, how will I live with myself?"

Wolf shrugged. "I'm not going to let anything happen. And I'm not giving you an option. It's not up to you. This is my call, my decision."

"You're not my boss anymore."

He turned and left her standing alone. Despite the screaming voice inside, demanding she go after him and help, she stayed where she was.

CHAPTER 23

WOLF STARTED the engine and pulled forward, unclogging the traffic that had built up behind his SUV.

He ignored Patterson, who stood on the corner like a statue, and flipped a U-turn, then accelerated up Main to the county building and parked in the rear lot.

His phone vibrated and displayed MacLean's name.

"Yeah?"

"They got nothing at the Beer Goggles. How about you?"

"No. Nothing. That earlier rain was heavy. Any footprints or other signs are long gone by now."

"I've chartered a plane to New Mexico. The only clues to follow are going to originate down there. And with a deputy's life on the line, I'm not going to outsource the work and watch it on Facebook while playing with my dick."

"I agree. Good move," Wolf said.

"So, get your ass in here. Flight leaves from Ashland airport in an hour, and we take a chopper in ten minutes."

On cue, the noise of an approaching helicopter seeped through his vehicle and appeared in the sky above the county building.

He leaned back in his car seat. "I'm not going."

There was a brief silence. "What the hell do you mean you're not going?"

"I have to stay here."

"The clues are down there, Wolf. If you want to—"

"I'm not going. I'll be here, ready to act when you guys find something important. That's the end of our conversation."

MacLean exhaled. "Okay, whatever you say."

The line went dead.

Wolf stared at his phone and tapped the map application. His cell hooked up to the county-building wireless network and the map materialized quickly.

He scrolled south of the meeting point again and zoomed in.

With glazed eyes, he stared at the screen, and when his phone went dark and shut off, he let it sleep, because he no longer needed the display.

Like magnets turned so that their opposite poles lined up, the seemingly unfathomable events of the day were snapping together and forming a line. And the line led to a place that boiled his blood.

Moving fast, he got out and went to the rear hatch. He opened it and pulled out his emergency backpack, then fished inside for his Garmin handheld GPS.

He shut the hatch and climbed back into the driver's seat, plugged in the GPS, started the car, and made sure the charge light came on.

As the GPS downloaded an update, the helicopter noise ramped up again, and outside a Bell 429 helicopter ascended from the roof and disappeared into the southern sky.

A minute later the GPS was ready, so he entered the coordinates and studied the area closely. The trail he'd have to hike was 4.7 miles long. The meltwaters of Dark Mountain fed a thin stream that ran the length of the valley and the trail would have to cross it once. Wolf zoomed in on where the hiking trail crossed the river and saw a footbridge. The structure looked sturdy enough from a hundred-foot-height zoom, but he knew the water would be running high.

He zoomed out and did some calculations.

His dash clock glowed 4:38 p.m.

That left him seven hours and twenty-two minutes to get to the top of a five-mile hike through rugged terrain—a hike that started thirty-nine miles away.

Most of the drive was highway, then a dirt road meandered into dense forest and up the valley until it ended at the trailhead. The last two miles of road were labeled as jeep trail, which meant it might be hairy. Especially during melt season. And surely after the rain they'd just received. Then there was the weather forecast for tonight, which called for more of the same.

If the drive took two and a half hours, say three for good measure, that put him at the trailhead at 7:39, which would be about an hour before sunset.

Hike the 4.7 miles beyond that at a one mile-per-hour trudge and he'd arrive at 12:39—leaving him thirty-nine minutes late and Rachette dead. At two miles per hour, he'd be there at 10 p.m.

He was confident he'd be there before 10 p.m.

He had plenty of experience with long, grueling hikes. Marches with fifty-pound packs on their backs—ruck marches—had been numerous the first seven days of RIP.

That's how he'd gotten to know Paul Womack: by hiking in front of him. The man had jabbered constantly, telling anecdotes and dirty jokes. Anyone who marched in Paul Womack's vicinity was subjected to it, but nobody complained. He had a gift for making his fellow soldiers laugh.

Wolf backed out of the parking spot, thinking about Paul Womack's open head glistening in the New Mexico sunlight.

He cracked the windows and let a fresh breeze flow through the cab.

Looking in the rearview mirror, he stared at his own eyes and saw broken capillaries, a wrinkled forehead, and baggy eyelids. He was half the Special Forces soldier he'd once been. He hoped that was enough to prevail over the evil that awaited him.

CHAPTER 24

RACHETTE HEARD a noise and opened his eyes, then realized his own moaning had woken him up.

As before, he itched like hell, but now he was soaked in sweat. Pain coming from his hand fueled nausea.

Blinking, he saw a different view than last time. Rafters and the underside of an A-framed roof filled his vision now. Gray daylight filtered through the gaps in the shack's wood.

The straw dug into his back.

The blankets held in the heat. Too much heat. He was so hot.

He thrashed underneath the blankets, somehow pushing them aside to let the cool air caress his naked body.

His left hand throbbed and it now dawned on him that his hands were lashed in front. His legs were no longer pulled up behind him and he lay on his back. The hair on his arms stuck to crusted blood on his belly.

"You need water."

Rachette blinked and searched for the source of the noise. A shadow approached, its movements accompanied by the sound of a thousand tinkling bells. It came close and then bent down next to him.

"Here."

A man spoke to him, Rachette realized for the first time.

The man's prominent brow came into focus and he recognized it, though he failed to remember where from.

"You need water." He held out a bottle with the cap off.

Rachette sat up and put his lips on the opening, and the man tipped.

He coughed and spat the water onto his chest, which felt so good on his burning skin. My God, he was so hot.

"Again."

He drank greedily from the bottle until the water was gone, then collapsed on the straw.

The ice-cold liquid made his body tingle from the inside out. A breeze flowed in from the door, which was propped open with a rock, and it wicked the sweat from his body. All at once, the memories came flooding back and he realized where he was.

Unibrow, that was his name, turned and walked to a pallet of water bottles on the floor. There was that sound again when he moved, like he wore bells, or ... chains.

Rachette saw them now.

Unibrow picked up a bottle and turned around. Rachette saw that the man's wrists were handcuffed together. A much longer chain was attached to the cuffs and ran to a metal bar under the workbench. Like a dog on a leash, he had a range of around ten feet. As the man approached with the water, Rachette thanked God he was within that range.

"What's your name?" Rachette asked.

No answer.

The man unscrewed the bottle and poured the water down Rachette's throat.

With a full belly, he collapsed to the hay. Then he turned over retched, and water shot out of him like a firehose.

The man stumbled back, then bent down next to him again. "Drink. I think you got a fever."

With detached interest, Rachette studied his new hand. A

blood-soaked makeshift bandage made from what looked like T-shirt fabric bound the red stump where his pinkie had been.

He turned over and heaved all the water out.

"Here." The man tilted the water bottle up to his lips.

"Forget it."

The man stood with a blank look.

Rachette eyed his handcuffs. "Were you handcuffed last time I was awake?"

No answer. No head movement.

He'd been hogtied and facing away from this guy before. Earlier, a hangover had clouded his mind, and then there was the whole distraction of Lucky Charms barging in and chopping off his freaking pinkie.

A noise begun deep in his gut and he rolled to his side, heaving again. This time nothing came out.

After what felt like an hour, he rolled onto his back and caught his breath.

The guy stood unmoved.

"What's your name?"

A blink. "Eeth ..."

"Eeth?"

"Ethan." Ethan turned away and set down the bottle on the workbench.

Rachette noticed that the toolbox no longer sat near the doorway. "Where's the bearded guy?"

"Gone for now."

Rachette's shivering intensified, so he sat forward and pulled the blankets over him. They were damp and smelled like piss, and that sparked the memory of having to take a leak before that asshole cut off his finger.

"What's his name?"

"I don't know."

"Who put this bandage on me?" Rachette closed his eyes and waited for the blankets to do their job.

"I did."

He shivered and rubbed his legs together for warmth, then cracked his eyes and craned his neck to see if Ethan was staring at him again. But the man's back was still turned, and Rachette saw the angry scar cutting across his shaved head.

"What happened to your head?" He closed his eyes and lay back again, wondering if he'd just crossed a boundary, then decided he didn't care.

No answer.

Cracking his eyes again, he saw Ethan rub a hand over the scar.

Ethan's jeans looked like they'd been washed a few months ago, if at all. But the blood smeared on one pant leg looked fresh.

"You know what happened to my friend last night?"

Ethan turned around, and although darkness swallowed most of the shack, Rachette could see tears running down his face. "They killed him."

Rachette had already suspected as much, but the news still made his chest constrict. "Who's *they*, Ethan? Do you know? What's going on?"

He had trouble seeing Ethan's face through the dark now. A breeze picked up outside, sounding like a howling wraith.

A flash lit the doorway. Seconds later, thunder shook the shack and rolled into the distance.

Ethan looked up like he'd heard the voice of God, and then he walked to the propped-open door. The chain snapped him to a halt and he seemed completely caught by surprise. He grunted, pulling on the restraints as hard as he could.

Rachette watched the chain's connection to the underside of the bench with intense interest.

The man's rage flowed and a primal scream came from his mouth. But he failed to budge the chain or the bench. Then he lay down on his back and tried to kick the rock free from the door, but still he failed to reach. And when lightning flashed, this time closer, Ethan ducked underneath the workbench and put his hands over his head.

"We'll be all right," Rachette said, startled by the man's animalistic fear.

There was a knock against the roof, and then twenty, and then a thousand as hailstones and fat rain drops pelted the shack.

Two consecutive lightning bolts struck, each followed by thunder.

"Or not," he said under his breath.

Rain mist flowed inside the door and through the many cracks in the walls, but the roof seemed to be holding the brunt of it out.

Ethan pulled his head inside his jacket.

Another flash. More thunder.

Hailstones pelted the entrance, skittering across the dirt inside.

He watched another bolt of lightning lick the ground on the other side of the valley.

When the thunder hit, Ethan rolled to his side and a muffled cry came from his coat.

Rachette ripped aside his blanket, almost passing out from the pain in his hand. Sitting forward on his naked ass, he spread his knees, since his ankles were bound tightly, and got up.

He teetered and landed back on his butt, and the pain throbbed anew in his pinkie.

"Ahhh, shit." His voice was inaudible over the raging storm.

Again, he pulled his feet underneath him and tipped forward, this time standing up. His head felt light, like a helium balloon rising to the ceiling. He stood still until the wave of dizziness finally passed.

Gritting his teeth to stop the chattering, he hopped over the blankets and onto the dirt. Each time he landed, hailstones assaulted the bottom of his bare feet and pain shot up his legs, which protested from hours of inaction and the fever coursing through his body.

As he neared the door, his feet slipped on mud and shot out from under him. Landing on his side, rain and hail pelted him like a shotgun blast. He rolled, kicked the rock away from the door with his heels, then swung it shut with his feet.

Almost shut.

It slowed on the wind and blew back open.

"Fuck you!" Again, he rolled, got into position, and kicked the door. It slammed home against the jamb and caught.

The darkness was absolute. Rachette sprawled in the mud, shivering harder than ever.

He used his hands and feet to inch himself back towards his makeshift bed, grunting through the pain in his finger every time it hit the ground. He fell when he reached the hay, landing on his face and chest. Then, with shivers wracking his body, he rolled onto his back and began searching for the blankets.

"Ah!" He reached through the darkness but found nothing but more dried grass. Rolling to his right, he sat forward and tried again, but there was nothing.

There was no sound now but the chattering of his teeth in his skull.

Thrashing some more, panicked squeals started coming out of his mouth.

You're going to die, said a voice in his head, and he believed it.

"Help," he called out, just as a pair of strong, warm hands grabbed his shoulders and forced him into the hay. Then a scratchy blanket was pulled over his skin, then another. And then weight pressed down on him.

Ethan's hands moved over the course wool, rubbing the heat back into Rachette's shivering form.

Rachette had a half-thought about the gayness of the moment but, as he felt the warmth returning to his body, decided he would have added some Liberace music if it meant surviving another day.

"Thank you," Ethan said. "Thank you."

"Hey, yeah." Rachette winced at Ethan's vigor. "No problem."

CHAPTER 25

THIS FEVER IS KILLING YOU.

More images swirled in Rachette's mind, accompanied by flashes and booms, and Lucky Charms pouring water on his head, spiking the water bottle off his scalp.

"Wake up!"

He opened his eyes. A white-bearded man filled his vision.

Shit.

He instinctively held up his hands, willing himself to burrow into the straw, away from this man with the tin snips.

"Ha ha ha!" Lucky Charms's laugh thundered. "See? Got the kid shitting himself. Check his butt cheeks for mud."

Another man laughed with startling aggression.

The shack bustled with activity. The door was propped open, letting in subdued light and air that smelled like rain. Clouds clung to the side of the mountain where Rachette had seen lightning strike earlier. Had that been a dream? Hadn't he kicked that door closed?

"Okay, okay," the other man said. "Back it up. Let him breathe, and let's get this unloaded before another storm rolls in."

Steller's jays hopped on the ground outside and made incessant noise.

"The fuck are they doing here?" Lucky Charms stepped to the doorway, raised a gun, and shot.

Rachette flinched at the deafening boom and saw one of the birds explode in feathers.

Lucky Charms laughed again.

"Christ, asshole! Put that away!" A third man came up fast and pushed Lucky Charms out of the doorway. He was the same age and body type—mid-fifties or sixties, tall and overweight on top of an athletic body. Judging by how fast Lucky Charms had flown out of the doorway, and the tumbling sound outside, the guy was strong as a bull.

"Here. Pick this shell up," one of them said. "It's something like this that's going to ruin everything. Then I'm gonna shoot you and tell them you did all this."

The conversation traveled outside, then dropped to a murmur as crunching footsteps receded.

A squeak echoed, and then came the sound of a door opening, or maybe a tailgate dropping.

Ethan stood in the corner, looking out the open door with the same fearful expression Rachette had seen during the thunderstorm.

He remembered the door. And the blankets. And Ethan rubbing heat back into him.

"Hey," he said.

Ethan flicked a glance at him and then looked back outside with rapt attention.

"What are they doing?"

Ethan zipped his jacket all the way up and said nothing.

"Hey."

No response. Ethan pulled his coat collar up over his mouth and stared.

Rachette decided that jacket for him was like a security blanket to a child. That, and it was an expensive-looking piece of clothing compared to the rest. The sides of his leather boots were worn, and the laces were held together by their last threads. The jeans were like tissue paper. But the jacket was brand-spanking-new, with silver buttons on the breast pockets.

Grunting echoed outside, and then the sound of something heavy sliding on metal, like an object being pulled out of the back of a truck. Behind the strains of men, liquid sloshed inside a large container.

Ethan's eyes widened.

"What's that?"

No response.

Outside the doorway, feathers tumbled on the breeze. The Steller's jay's leg twitched, and the bird received a jolt of life and tried to get up, then flopped on its side and lay still again.

"One ... two ... three!"

More grunts, and then a thump.

"One ... two ... three!"

Rachette heard a scraping sound. As it got louder, a blue container came into sight through the cracks and he smelled gasoline.

Something told him the fuel was not for gassing up their cars.

The banter started up again and a flurry of feet approached the doorway.

Lucky Charms appeared with his pistol. He paused, aimed at the bird, and finished it off. Tucking the smoking gun in his pants, he walked inside with a satisfied grin.

Locking eyes with Rachette he said, "How's the wee pinkie?"

"The shell, asshole!"

Lucky Charms's laugh shook the building as he watched his compatriot pluck the brass off the work bench.

Rachette said nothing as the procession of men entered—Lucky Charms, two men with identical bodies but different shades and lengths of hair, and then a man with shorter hair, much younger and fitter-looking than his cohorts.

His lip twisted into a snarl, because the last man he recognized well.

"You," he said.

CHAPTER 26

"DAVID WOLF, the man with the brightest aura in Rocky Points." Fabian Michaels looked up from a book on his glass merchandise counter and smiled. "What brings you in? Looking for a crystal for your new lady?"

Driftwood hanging from rope clanked as Wolf stepped into the entryway of the spiritual shop known as Fire and Ice on Main Street. Shutting the door, he saw no customers inside.

"Uh, no. Thanks."

"Hey, you know, I'm going to stop by her art exhibit tonight. That girl can paint, brother. She is one gifted person. I'd like to buy some of her art, but I need my online sales to pick up a little. Besides, I have a couple of new toys on the way." Fabian winked. "Nice doozies you'll have to come check out."

Wolf glanced behind him back out the window. Two people walked by, oblivious to the tiny storefront selling aura-enhancing knickknacks.

"Dreamcatcher?" Fabian pulled his wavy blond hair back and whipped it into a ponytail with a practiced move. "Wind chimes? Got some seriously boss new wind chimes made of beetle-kill pine. Look at those. Blue-tinged wood, see that? And the timbre of the clapper hitting beetle-kill tubes is something for the ear to behold."

"I'd like to buy your M4."

Fabian blinked. "Thought you of all people would have one of those."

"I ... no. I'd had enough of them in my army days so I never bought one."

"And now you need one today?"

Wolf nodded.

Fabian swallowed. "Why are you in here asking me?"

"I know you have one in back."

Fabian's relaxed gaze landed on Wolf and stayed there. "All my firearms are properly registered."

"I know."

"And I store them here legally. I don't sell anything." He looked past Wolf.

"I know."

Fabian let the silence draw out for a beat, then asked, "You need my help?"

"I just need your gun."

Fabian narrowed his eyes. "I don't have an FFL attached to this address." Bracelets tinkled up his arms as he held up his hands.

"Listen, this isn't a sting operation. You helped me out a few years ago. I need you to help me out again, without asking questions."

Wolf referred to a crew of local men he'd assembled to help combat a drug cartel that had borne down on Rocky Points. Fabian Michaels had been there, standing tall with the aforementioned M4 assault rifle across his chest, and Wolf had never forgotten it.

Wolf had a pair of hunting rifles and a Walther PPK at his house, which were ineffectual against the threat he faced. And, besides, the drive home was a trip he had no time to make.

Fabian Michaels was a spiritual shop owner and diehard NRA member, two things that clashed in everyone's mind but Fabian's. Fewer bigger fanatics of firearms existed in Rocky Points, and that said something for a town in the Colorado mountains.

"Not a sting?"

"Not a sting."

Fabian shrugged and gestured to the door. "Lock it."

Wolf locked the entrance and followed Fabian behind the merchandise counter through a beaded curtain.

The back room was ten by ten feet, with work tables lining two walls. Jewelry and other craft projects were piled and spaced evenly on top of them, labeled with multicolored Post-it notes. The room seemed to be the source of the lavender scent emanating through the shop.

Fabian produced a set of keys and released three heavy locks on a black door. He opened it and slid inside, and then clicked a light switch. A fluorescent bulb flickered on and then hummed, illuminating another space that smelled like gun oil. The amount of weaponry adorning the walls gave the Sheriff's Department armory room a run for its money.

"Have two Colt M4 series carbines, as you can see." Fabian took one from the wall, pointed it down, and pulled the charging handle back. He checked the chamber, pushed it closed with a metallic "snick," and handed it over to Wolf.

Wolf took the weapon and repeated the process. He brought it to his shoulder and aimed at a spot on the wall. A vision of an eight-year-old boy materialized in the crosshairs of the scope. With closed eyes, he lowered the weapon.

"Sighted it in yesterday," Fabian said.

Wolf saw the other M4's bulkier scope. "Night vision on this one?"

"Yeah. You need it?"

Wolf nodded and handed back the gun.

"This one has a BAE systems thermal-imaging scope with

switch-over night vision. Best of both worlds without having to use head-mounted NVGs, so you don't ever have to lower the rifle." Fabian took it down and checked the chamber. He handed it over and showed Wolf the power and adjustments, then went and shut off the light.

The room went pitch black until Fabian pulled out his cell-phone and bathed the space in a soft glow. "Try it out."

Wolf put his eye to the scope and saw a bright white silhouette of Fabian's hand waving in view. "That's the thermal setting, obviously. Here, you can dial it up for more red." Fabian twisted a knob and his hand turned to the color of glowing lava. "You see that?"

"Yeah," Wolf said.

"Hit this switch for night vision."

Wolf did so and the display turned to standard night-vision green.

"Pretty cool, eh?"

Wolf lowered the M4. "Yes."

He wondered what kind of scope Ethan Womack would have on his .50 caliber sniper rifle. Probably something similar since he'd set a midnight meeting.

Fabian flicked on the light and shrugged. "Need anything else?"

"How much?"

"Do you actually want to buy this stuff? Or do you need to borrow it?" Fabian scratched his head and put on a pained face. "I'd rather you borrowed it."

Wolf nodded. "Okay, how much?"

"To what?"

"To rent it."

"Yeah, right. Just bring it back to me, how about that?" Fabian smiled easily and gazed into Wolf's eyes. "I can see you're troubled with that, though. You sure you don't need my help?"

Wolf ignored the question. "You have something I can put this in?"

Fabian eyed him for a few more seconds, then bent down and retrieved a black Pelican case and opened it up on the workbench. He detached the scope and seated it in a cutout, then placed the M4 inside. "Hundred eighty rounds enough?" he asked, holding up three high-capacity magazines.

"That should be good," Wolf said, hoping he was right.

Shutting the case, Fabian said, "Hope you know what you're walking into. You sure you can't use my help?"

"Yes, I'm sure. But thank you."

"You deliver this thing back to me," Fabian said. "Then, you know what? Payment is that you have to buy one of those beetle-kill wind chimes. Those things are clogging up the corner of my shop. They sound like the Three Stooges bonking their heads together."

Wolf smiled. "It's a deal."

They walked back out into the main shop. Wolf took the weighted plastic case and Fabian locked up his armory behind them.

Wolf waited for Fabian to join him at the entrance.

"Thank you."

Fabian looked past him and pushed open the door. "Hey, ladies."

A pair of women with their noses pressed to the window backed away.

"Are you open?" one of them asked.

"Sure am."

Wolf squeezed outside.

"Hey! Wolf!"

Wolf turned around.

Fabian finished ushering the two women into his shop and raised a finger. "Wait there for one second." He disappeared inside and reappeared a few moments later with a wad of clothing in his hands.

Stepping close, Fabian gestured to the south. "You hear the weather forecast for tonight?"

Wolf nodded. "More thunderstorms."

"Yeah." He pushed the clothing towards Wolf. "Take all this. Got a rain coat, fleece gloves, winter hat, and a sweatshirt right there."

"I have some supplies," Wolf said, catching the body-odor whiff coming off the clothes.

"Good. Now you have more. Just in case, right?"

Wolf eyed the dark skies beyond Williams Pass and checked his watch—5:13. Fabian was a spiritualist and a former marine, and he was being practical.

"Thanks," he said, and he meant it.

Fabian squeezed his shoulder. "See you later." He disappeared back into his shop. "Now, ladies, I want you to look at these wind chimes. Are you familiar with beetle kill—"

The door slammed shut.

CHAPTER 27

HEATHER PATTERSON HAD WALKED the seven blocks back to her office through the blurry lens of her tears. She'd retrieved her extra set of car keys from her desk drawer, carefully keeping out of Bryce's sights. Then she'd driven to the Sluice–Byron County building.

She'd seen the helicopter lifting into the sky on the drive over, and she'd also caught sight of Wolf leaving in his SUV.

Since that moment, now sitting in her car in the rear parking lot of the county building, shame gripped her heart and wouldn't let go.

She'd never felt such a tearing of her soul. Rachette was in trouble, his pinkie severed by a crazy man who'd already killed Pat Xander, and now she'd let Wolf go up and face him alone.

She had the coordinates for the midnight meeting spot on her phone. She could simply defy Wolf and make her way up the trail behind him without him knowing. But Ethan Womack had guns —fifty-caliber sniper rifles—and probably planned on using them. Which meant going up there was likely a one-way ticket.

"Shit!" She slammed her hand down and rested her forehead on the steering wheel. The sound of her frantic breathing filled the silent cab.

"What's the plan here?" she asked herself out loud. "You gonna follow him?"

She leaned back and flicked her eyes to the picture of Tommy taped to the inside corner of her windshield. Normally her two-year-old's smile brightened her mood every time she looked at it, no matter what shit assignment she was on, but right now, it failed to do the job.

Three years ago, she would've been riding shotgun with Wolf, and if he'd had a problem with it she would've followed him. Plain and simple. Now, the primal love for her son overwrote everything in her DNA. David Wolf had put his life on the line to save hers before, and now she'd let him go into the darkness alone.

There had to be a way she could help.

If she had to bet on who'd win in a fight, David Wolf or Ethan Womack, she'd bet on Wolf every time. But she knew little to nothing about Ethan Womack. He was a tournament shooter and had set the time and place for a meet, which gave the man hours to prepare. Not only that, but he was mentally impaired due to head trauma. What did that mean? He had a record. Aggravated assault meant to harm somebody with intent to kill, or without regard for life. Had his head injury turned a dangerous man into an even more lethal one? Had his brother's suicide put him over the edge?

She leaned her forehead on the steering wheel again. *Shit.*

"You can do both," she said out loud, not knowing yet what she meant.

She lifted her head and watched a deputy walk through the building's rear automatic doors.

What do you mean? she thought. Then out loud she said, "You might be able to learn something that might help him. You can help and stay out of harm's way."

But how?

Either way—out loud, or in her head—her words sounded like a coward's.

A thought tickled her brain, and a voice told her to shut up with the self-pity and listen.

She stared into nothing, thinking about Ethan Womack. She thought about Pat Xander's car being pushed off the side of the road, Rachette's phone, the spent cartridges, and the pool of Pat's blood. Ethan's fingerprints were on all of it.

She thought about the last text message. It had said, "I'll be watching."

Looking around, she saw nobody watching her. It had been an empty threat. There was no way Ethan Womack could be watching her because he'd have to be in two places at once.

With a light feeling in her stomach, she wondered if her car had been compromised. Was there a video camera in the rearview mirror feeding out a video right now? She twisted the mirror, looking at the back side of it, then shook her head and took a sobering breath. She had the most sophisticated alarm system money could buy. If anyone passed gas near her car, much less planted a device inside it, the thing went berserk.

"There are others involved," she said. Staring out the window, she tried on that idea for size.

The anonymous caller had led the Sheriff's Department to the crime scene, which had led to Ethan Womack's fingerprints easily identifying him as the culprit.

She blinked.

Maybe Ethan Womack was being framed. The thought made her pulse jump.

Wolf had gotten the video, which added a motive to the equation—that Ethan was pissed that his brother had killed himself and blamed Wolf.

The crime scene had shown who did it, and the video had given them the reason.

It was all tied up in a bow – but a little too neatly.

Who else would want to come after Wolf, *and* had a connection to Ethan Womack?

Somebody who was mad at Wolf from his past. Someone connected with the army. Maybe a former Ranger.

She knew little about Wolf's past because he liked to keep it that way. Rachette had once told that Wolf had shot an eight-year-old boy in India. Or was it Sri Lanka? Wherever it was, thinking about that gave her the same sick feeling now as it had hearing it back then, and that was enough reason to never seek confirmation from Wolf.

She shook her head, steering her thoughts back on track. Why else lead the cops to the crime scene, slathered with your own prints, unless you want the cops to know your identity?

Ethan was mentally impaired. Was he easily manipulated? A pawn in someone else's game?

But he was a fifty-caliber tournament shooter and armed to the teeth. He had an aggravated-assault charge on his record.

She stared out the windshield some more, trying to put the pieces together, but the darkening storm clouds to the south were taunting her. They were telling her she'd let her boss go into the darkness alone.

Wolf was going to be ambushed. Picked off from a thousand yards.

Ambushed by him? Or by them?

There was her subconscious again, telling her more people were involved. If she was right, figuring out who could be her ticket to becoming useful. Maybe she could even ambush the ambushers.

She picked up her phone and dialed.

A few rings later Charlotte Munford-Rachette answered. "Hello?"

"Where are you?"

"At the station. Where are you?"

"I'm downstairs. I need you to come let me inside."

CHAPTER 28

6:04 P.M.

Wolf's head hit the Explorer's ceiling as he barreled through another pothole.

He'd made the drive up and over Williams Pass in record time, passing every vehicle he came upon without hesitation. The descent past the Cold Lake turnoff and into the Ashland Valley was where he could really open up the engine, and where he'd clocked himself going over a hundred and twenty miles per hour with the windshield lights twirling and siren screaming.

That stretch of relatively flat, straight road had been short-lived, however, because the location he had to find was up a county road that shot west off Highway 734.

County Road 997 was a 17.3 mile stretch of road that burrowed its way into steep mountains, gaining a lot of altitude in its short distance. What started as flat dirt climbed to rocky switchbacks, and now he was in dense forest and had seen smoother ground in bombing ranges.

More than a few miles an hour would risk catastrophic vehicle damage. Over and again, he had to creep to a complete stop to pass over some of the rocks without tearing a hole in something vital on the bottom of the SUV.

According to his Garmin GPS, he only had two miles to go, but he swore he could've walked faster, and after another few minutes at crawling speed he was prepared to pull over and do just that. But the road mercifully smoothed for the last mile and he glided further up the valley at just under ten miles per hour.

Finally, he came to the end of the line—a small clearing where the road stopped and a narrow trail up into the trees began. A brown sign, pitted by a shotgun blast, said Dark Mountain Lake—4.7 miles.

He parked and got out into air that felt thin, even to a Colorado native who'd lived in the Rockies all his life. A chill burrowed into his jacket. The lead-colored sky darkened by the second and a low rumble of thunder came from up a steep-walled valley that lay in front of him.

Wasting no time, he zipped up his jacket and tightened his boot laces for the hike. He put on his backpack, which contained his emergency dry clothing, the Garmin GPS, and Fabian's fetid gear for good measure.

He shouldered the M4, put a hand on his Glock, pocketed his multitool, and locked his SUV, hoping he would see it again.

With a hard exhale, he marched past the sign into the dripping forest.

Right. Left. Right. Left.

"Henning! Henning!" Paul Womack slapped the unconscious squad leader on the cheek. "Wake up! Hey!"

Wolf fired another burst toward the rock outcropping. The wind blew heat from his barrel back in his face.

A Taliban fighter stood from his cover and caught one of Wolf's rounds in the forehead. A pink mist puffed behind the enemy's head as he dropped, and then the action ground to a halt.

Wolf aimed, waiting for more movement. None came, but he kept his rifle raised.

Two medics rushed over and knelt next to Henning. "What happened?"

"Artillery round landed right next to him," Womack said.

"He's cyanotic."

"Suction."

Through the ringing in his ears and radio chatter Wolf could hear Henning gurgling.

"Suction!"

The second medic, SPC Mac Johnson, put a suction bulb that looked like a turkey baster down Henning's throat and started pulling out clotted blood.

Wolf flicked his eyes between the action on the ground next to him and the threat ahead.

Womack had his own rifle raised now, scanning the brown, rock-strewn landscape that had served as their enemies' ambush point.

Mac removed the helmet and assessed the damage to Henning's head wound. "Shit."

Wolf looked down and saw that shrapnel had become lodged deep in Henning's temple.

"Airway cleared," Mac said. "All right." He pulled out a J-shaped tube and put it down Henning's throat.

A ground-mobility vehicle pulled up and stopped a dozen yards away.

"Wolf, Womack," the first medic ordered, "get him onto the GMV."

Wolf nodded. "Yes, sir."

They were sitting ducks and everyone knew that more artillery shells could be on their way, so they moved fast.

Womack grabbed Henning by the shoulders and lifted while Wolf took his legs.

The sergeant was thick and muscular, and lifting his dead weight took more than a bit of straining.

Just then, Wolf spotted another enemy rise from the rock outcropping and point the muzzle of an AK-47 at them.

"Incoming!" Wolf froze, then backtracked toward the GMV.

Red blossoms opened up on the Taliban fighter's chest, dropping him dead. Mac had seen the enemy at the same instant and fired a three-round burst.

In the commotion, Womack stumbled and released his grip on Henning's shoulders.

As if in slow motion, Wolf watched Henning's head drop to the ground, sounding like a sack of sand as it made direct contact with the spot where the shrapnel was embedded.

Wolf's knees nearly buckled from the firing of his nerves. "Oh, shit."

Womack stood with his arms out, staring down at Henning with wide eyes.

"Go! Go! Go!" someone yelled from the GMV behind them.

Womack blinked, looking left and right as if trying to find someone else to take his place.

"Come on!"

At the sound of Wolf's voice, Womack snapped out of his trance and picked up Henning again. They moved quickly to the GMV and two Rangers helped them put the sergeant in the back.

As the GMV drove away, Wolf and Womack were left exposed in the open. Sensing that Womack was still reliving earlier moments, Wolf gripped his shoulder and pulled him toward an ancient rock wall.

They sat down heavily behind the cover and Wolf eyed his friend. "You okay?"

"I dropped him." Womack's skin was whiter than the snow capping the mountains in the distance.

"He fell, Paul," Wolf said. "We were taking fire."

Womack closed his eyes and tilted his head back. "Shit, shit, shit ..."

Wolf felt sick to his stomach at the sight of his friend's soul tearing apart. He'd forged a bond with Womack as they'd walked through the fires of hell together, but this was too much to bear.

"I pulled him away from you," Wolf said. "It was my fault. I thought I'd shot all the enemies. I should've known there was another. We wouldn't have been caught off guard."

Womack turned to Wolf and looked like he was going to say something, like *That's bullshit. I dropped him. Thanks for trying, though.* Or something snappier. Paul Womack had a way with words.

But instead his friend's eyes grew distant and he said, "Fight's over."

The fighting might've been over, but then again there could've been more combatants in waiting less than a click away, ready to fire more artillery, and air support still hadn't arrived to make sure they were all vaporized.

But Womack stood up and walked away from Wolf.

Nearby thunder snapped Wolf from his memories. What little sky he could see through the forest canopy was dark, and the sound of howling trees rolled down the valley until the surrounding pines were creaking back and forth.

Rain spattered the ground, and then Wolf. They were fat beads mixed with pea-sized hailstones, but he was sheltered well inside the forest and had only felt a few drops. So far.

Keeping his pace, he pulled out the GPS and found a blank screen due to weak signal. He knew GPS signals propagated through the worst of elements without degradation, but passing through thick forest was another issue. If he wanted to find his spot, he'd need to be in the open.

He hoped his waterproof backpack performed as advertised.

His watch said 7:13. Still plenty of time.

The air crackled and a flash lit everything, and before he could flinch thunder cracked.

Somewhere inside the forest to his left, a tree crashed to the ground. An animal shot across the trail ahead of him in a blur, and he caught a glimpse of a bear before it vanished into the woods.

Wolf checked his rear and upped his pace into the teeth of the storm.

CHAPTER 29

PATTERSON REMEMBERED how much she hated squad-room coffee and dumped another packet of raw sugar into the cup and stirred.

There was another flicker of lightning outside and ridiculously close thunder.

Damn it. She looked at the hot cup of coffee in her hand and thought about Wolf and Rachette again. Disgusted, she dumped the liquid into the sink.

"I know the feeling." Charlotte stood looking at her. "I can't picture eating or drinking anything. I just keep thinking about where Tommy is." Charlotte began to cry again but put up a hand to stop Patterson from comforting her.

"Shit." Charlotte turned around and sat in front of her computer. "When is he gonna call us back?"

They both stared at the desk phone for a moment.

Patterson went back to pacing the room, then, with renewed restlessness, walked to the kitchenette and dug under the sink, finding a box of chamomile tea. She held up the box toward Charlotte, then dropped it back under the sink and closed the cabinet.

Charlotte stared through the room and rubbed slow circles over her belly with her hand.

The sight made Patterson close her eyes and tilt her head to the ceiling. She wasn't a religious person, but she considered herself spiritual and in touch with her inner self, which she felt gave her intimate knowledge of the workings of the rest of the universe.

She was never one to pray or attend church. But now she pleaded to a higher power, something outside herself altogether, to help them. To give them all a break.

And she asked for relief from all the guilt. She'd let Wolf and Rachette down and, if that wasn't enough, she'd kept the truth a secret from Charlotte.

Charlotte had closed her eyes now, continuing her belly rub with her other hand.

But there was no way Patterson was going to tell a pregnant woman that her husband was not just missing, but hogtied, naked, and freezing on a bed of hay like an animal. And, oh yeah, remember Wolf getting his pinkie blown off a couple of years ago? Yeah, your husband's finger's been severed, too. So he's probably convulsing and delirious with fever right now.

"Hey." Deputy Yates marched into the squad room with a line of deputies behind him.

"Screw it," Charlotte said. "I'm calling him back again."

Charlotte dialed and planted her elbows on the desk. She pressed the phone to her ear.

"What's going on?" Yates asked Patterson.

"We're calling a deputy in New Mexico for the tenth time."

"I meant, what's going on? Where the hell is Wolf?"

Patterson felt heat rise in her face. "I don't know."

Yates looked at her. "Shit. We need him right now. He's not answering any of my calls. This isn't like him, and I'm starting to get worried. Have you talked to him?"

"I did earlier." She shrugged. "He said he was looking into it. He didn't want me with him. What was I going to do?"

Yates shook his head and watched Charlotte dial her phone again. "Okay, why's she calling a New Mexico deputy for the tenth time?"

"Eleventh now."

"Why?"

"Trying to figure out what's going on down there. We had a deputy who was working with us for a while, then he went quiet. Supposedly they're in Ethan Womack's place of employment."

"The gun shop?"

She nodded.

"Hello? Hello!" Charlotte sat straight. "Hey, yeah ... okay ..."

"She's through," Yates said.

They watched Charlotte nod and grunt into the phone for a few seconds and then Yates said, "Okay. Listen, with MacLean and Wilson gone, and now Wolf AWOL, I'm in charge."

Patterson nodded. "Okay."

"So I want to have a sit-room meeting in fifteen, all right? You two can brief us on what you're finding out, and then we need to get a handle on what we're going to do. Wandering around a few hundred square miles looking for a beat-up Ford F-150 is like ... I don't know ... hard. And waiting for MacLean, Wilson, and Lorber to let us know what they found isn't gonna cut it. We gotta get proactive."

She held back telling him that that's exactly what she and Charlotte were doing. Yates only wanted to help and he had nothing to do. He wanted direction. With their deputy in danger, they all did.

"You got it," she said.

Yates turned around. "Nelson! Let's go."

Deputy Nelson broke off from the other group and followed Yates. They walked to the darkened situation room and opened it up, flicking the lights on and disappearing inside.

Charlotte plugged her free ear with a finger. "Okay ... okay ..."

Patterson went to the edge of her desk and sat.

"Okay." Charlotte looked up at her.

The two of them had started the past hour like everyone else: waiting for Sheriff MacLean, Dr. Lorber, and Undersheriff Wilson to give them an update on the situation down in New Mexico. But that had meant sitting and twiddling their thumbs while the three men flew in a helicopter to Ashland and caught a turbo-prop flight to Taos.

Of course, after that, they'd have been shuttled by vehicle to wherever they were going, who knew how many miles from the airport, then briefed on the situation.

That meant at least a four-to-six-hour wait before getting anything meaningful from their away team.

So, they'd taken matters in their own hands and picked up the phone, starting with the sheriff himself in Taos. The man had been reluctant to speak to them at first, but Charlotte poured on the tears and pleaded. She showed her whole hand, telling the man she was pregnant and desperate to know what had happened to her husband.

When he'd tried to placate her, she freaked and demanded to speak to someone who could help, said she wasn't going to take no for an answer. Of course, none of it had been a ploy or an act and the sheriff had no choice but to give in, handing her off to work with one of his deputies. That deputy had handed her off to the next.

And so it had gone on for two more phone calls until she got hold of a deputy named Gritzel.

Now they might as well have been in the Taos Sheriff's Department vehicles, because they had a confidant on the inside.

Charlotte twisted her face as she listened to Gritzel's voice in her ear. Then she clicked her computer mouse. "Okay, yes ... all right, I'm opening it now."

She hung up. "He's calling on Skype."

The icon on her computer screen bounced and chimed.

"I love this dude," Patterson said, leaning closer, because not only was Gritzel a responsive, helpful individual, he also embraced technology. During their previous conversation, it had been his idea to swap Skype addresses so they could have this little powwow in the first place.

Charlotte clicked the video-call button. A deputy filled the screen, facing their direction, looking like he sat at a computer. Two more uniformed men stood behind him, looking over his shoulders.

"Deputy Gritzel," Charlotte said. "Thanks for including us."

Gritzel nodded. "You got it." He was young with freckles and a mouth full of haphazard teeth only a mother could love.

"These are Deputies Hendershot and Ulfers," he said. "Guys, this is Deputy Munford and ..."

"This is Heather Patterson. Detective Heather Patterson," Charlotte lied.

"Yes, this is Detective Heather Patterson."

She waved and the two deputies behind Gritzel looked nonplussed to be staring at the two women, or rather, to have the two women staring at them.

"Whatcha got, Deputy Gritzel?" Patterson asked, wondering why the two men were there in the first place.

Gritzel's fingers clicked on the keyboard.

"We made it to Ethan Womack's place of employment, T 'n' T Guns, here on the north end of Taos. My sergeant is finishing up questioning the employees."

Charlotte cleared her throat. "What are Ethan Womack's fellow employees saying?"

Deputy Gritzel shrugged. "They're acting shocked about the whole thing. They say he was their best gunsmith. Never caused any trouble at all. He was a little different, quiet-like, had some sort of head trauma when he was a kid, but they say he's overall a great employee. Apparently, some sort of savant with guns. Worked really fast."

"And what about the aggravated assault?" Charlotte asked.

"According to the owner himself, the guy deserved every bit of the beating he received. Called him retarded and made fun of his mother in a sexual way, who had died a month prior, mind you."

"Jesus," Patterson said.

"Yeah."

"Do they know about his brother's suicide?" Charlotte asked.

"No. They seemed shocked about it." Deputy Gritzel looked over his shoulder.

"Yeah, shocked." The man behind him concurred.

"Did Ethan ever have anyone else in there with him?" Charlotte asked. "Any friends?"

"No. They say he was a loner. Like, true loner. No friends. Just his brother, who'd recently started showing up because he'd got out of Leavenworth."

"Are all the other employees accounted for?" Patterson asked.

Gritzel gestured to the colleague behind him.

"Yeah," the deputy said. "It's two brothers who own this place and then two employees, one of which is Ethan Womack. Four people total, and the other three are in there."

"What about other people who came in with Ethan in the last few days?" Charlotte asked. "Nobody hanging out with him? Nobody suspicious coming in and buying guns, maybe?"

Gritzel shrugged. "I don't know."

Charlotte sighed heavily.

Patterson put a hand on her shoulder. "Deputy Gritzel ... what about his house? Anything new there?"

"Besides Paul Womack's body, the shooting trophies, the missing fifty-caliber ... what else? I'm hearing Paul Womack's been dead for a good seventy-two hours, but that's not final until the coroner gives his report, which your sheriff will be present for in a few hours."

"How about those shooting competitions?" Patterson asked. "What do the gun-shop owners say about that?"

"The guys working in this place act like it's a harmless thing, like a boy scout going to an archery contest. Nothing violent-minded about it." Gritzel's hand grew large as he pointed at the computer screen.

Patterson scratched her forehead. "Was there internet browsing history on his home computer?"

"No home computer."

"No home computer?" She sounded more surprised than she'd meant to. She thought about the highly-edited suicide video and how it had to have been done on a computer. But where?

"What about his work computer?" she asked.

Gritzel tapped his nose with his finger. "That's what we're doing now."

He reached down, picked up the camera, and swiveled it to show them.

"And?" Patterson asked.

"And I'm in his browsing history ... looks like he googled Deputy David Wolf and did some clicking around to articles about Rocky Points, and your Sheriff's Department. Jesus, you guys had the Van Gogh killer last year." The deputies behind him looked interested now. "You two work the case?"

"Send the links over, please," Charlotte said.

"Okay. Emailing you now."

"Thank you, Deputy Gritzel. You're a good man."

"Forward me that list when you get it," Patterson said to Charlotte.

Charlotte received the email a few seconds later and sent it on.

"What about video-editing software?" Patterson asked.

"What about it?" Gritzel asked.

Charlotte looked at her, clearly confused.

"Is there any on his work computer?"

Gritzel clicked around and leaned into the screen. "I'm not seeing any. Why?"

"Nothing. Never mind." She sat down at the desk next to Charlotte's and shook the mouse. It came to life slower than a teenager on Saturday morning so she got up and paced, listening to the conversation.

"Notice the top of the browsing history," Deputy Gritzel said. "He searched for cheap hotels in Rocky Points, Colorado."

"Hey, that's my desk." Yates appeared behind them again.

"Yeah, thanks. I'm using your computer." Patterson raised her voice to talk to Gritzel. "Did he make a reservation?"

Gritzel leaned into the screen again. "Looks like the last tab he closed was somewhere called the Edelweiss Hotel ... and, yes, there's a reservation email in his inbox. I'm forwarding it on."

"Edelweiss?" Yates hitched up his duty belt. "Let's go."

"Wait for me." Charlotte pointed at Yates.

He froze at her tone. "Okay, then let's go."

"He's not going to be there," Patterson said.

"And how do you know that?" Yates asked.

Heat rose in her face. "I don't know. I'm just saying ... a hotel? He kidnaps Rachette and takes him to a hotel? I'd think it would be somewhere more remote. Like a shed, or a shack, or ... something."

"Yeah, well, if you get a thought of where that might be then let us know," Yates said. "Otherwise, we'll follow this bright flashing clue over here. Okay?"

"Listen," Charlotte said to her screen, "thanks. We'll be in touch." She typed out a message. "Here's my cellphone number. Please keep me informed if you guys come up with anything else."

The call ended and Charlotte got up so fast that her chair spun three circles.

"Aren't you coming?" She looked over her shoulder at Patterson.

"Yeah, you coming?" Yates eyed his desktop monitor.

Patterson checked her phone and saw the email from Charlotte had come through. She didn't need Yates's gerbil-powered computer to see the links, and besides, this was not her squad room anymore, and Yates's question wasn't really a question.

"Yeah."

CHAPTER 30

7:45 P.M.

Wolf was outside the cover of forest now, walking along the swollen river. Rain and hail pelted him, made worse by the buffeting headwind. Lightning flashed everywhere, often hitting the mountains nearby, but the thunder was drowned out by the sound of the raging torrent of water sliding downhill.

In the deluge, he'd lost track of the trail, made invisible by the jumping hailstones and raindrops.

The hooded jacket kept the rain off his torso and head, but his sopped denim jeans pulled over his legs with each step.

In the current downpour, he dared not look at the GPS to get his position. Like his backpack, the device was advertised as waterproof, but he wasn't going to push his luck with a field test.

With at least two and a half miles to go there was no sense worrying about it.

He marched on with his hands thrust in his pockets.

Right. Left. Right. Left ...

"Promoted?" Womack looked at Wolf. "You? We'll be taking orders from you now?"

Wolf stared at his friend, then out into the pale-brown Afghanistan landscape outside the forward operating base. He waited for a chuckle, any indication that Womack was kidding, but none came.

"So, you're now our squad leader," Womack said in a let-me-get-this-straight tone.

Wolf narrowed his eyes. "Henning's in a coma in Germany. There was an opening. I didn't ask for the promotion. They gave it to me."

Wolf and Womack were both corporals, but Wolf had been chosen. Clearly Womack was bent out of shape about it. "You're acting like I'm rubbing it in your face or something."

"That's exactly what you're doing, isn't it?" Womack's voice rose. "That's why we're talking right now, right?"

"We're talking right now because we're friends, Paul. HCC just told me I'm in charge of nine men's lives now and I wanted to talk it over with my friend."

Womack packed a Copenhagen in his lip and pocketed the can—another subtle jab. Copenhagen cans were passed back and forth between the two men, not put away without offering to the other.

Wolf chuckled to himself. "Ever since the Sergeant Henning incident, I can't help but notice a marked difference in our relationship."

"Relationship?" Womack spat between his boots. "What are we, chicks?"

Wolf smiled. "Okay."

"Okay, what?"

"What the fuck's your problem?"

Womack stood shaking his head.

"What?" Wolf stood with him.

"Did you tell the commander about what I did to Henning?"

"What did you do to Henning?"

"Don't give me that shit, Wolf." He pointed a shaking finger an inch from Wolf's nose. "Don't give me that bullshit!"

Wolf swatted his hand away. "You want to know what I told the commander? I told the commander we were taking fire and I pulled Henning from your grip. I told him his head hit the ground and drove a piece of shrapnel further into his brain and it was my fault that he's sitting in a coma and his wife and kids can't wake him up. I told him that to promote me was ill-advised, and that you were the better man for the job. There. Is that what you want to hear? Because it's the truth."

For an instant, Womack softened his expression and looked into Wolf's eyes, and then, like he'd done for two days, the man shut down and turned to walk away.

"Nope." Wolf slapped a hand on his shoulder and stopped him. "You're not walking away until you—"

Womack pushed him with both hands and Wolf landed on his ass.

He methodically got up and into Womack's face. "Try that again."

Womack did, and Wolf deflected both arms, pulling and twisting at the same time, bringing Womack down on his back with Wolf on top of him.

"Hey!"

"Hey!"

Their scuffle had been noticed by a group of Rangers coming out of the exercise tent.

As the sound of boots approached, Wolf glared hard into Womack's eyes. "What the hell's wrong?" he asked.

They were pulled apart by strong arms of other men from other squads, then sent on their merry ways in separate directions.

Walking backwards, Wolf waited to catch an over-the-shoulder glimpse from Womack. But none came.

The latest tendrils of lightning spreading across the sky made Wolf skid to a stop and consider a question that twisted his gut: *where was the bridge?*

There was another flash and he saw it again: a jagged line of rocks and steep cliffs straight ahead.

The cliffs on the map had been well beyond the crossing, he remembered clearly now. The reason a walking bridge spanned the river in the first place was because of this impassible terrain, no more than a hundred yards into the rain ahead.

He pointed his headlamp at the raging white water. Foliage on both banks was submerged and being pulled downstream.

Shit.

He pulled off his pack and took out the GPS. Powering it on, he crouched and blocked the rain. After a minute of powering on and satellite acquisition, it showed his position at three tenths of a mile past the bridge.

There was no way he would've walked past it.

His confidence wavered as he remembered the violence of the rain that had been falling only minutes ago. Three tenths of a mile ago he'd been more swimming than walking.

Using satellite-photo view, he zoomed in on the bridge again. He was no engineer and looked at it from space, but he'd have bet money that the bridge was now drowning in at least five feet of water.

He shut off the GPS and returned it to the backpack. Then he shouldered the bag and looked back downriver.

He decided that daydreaming or not, there was no way he'd have passed up the bridge.

Whatever had happened, he was faced with two choices: to spend time he didn't have hiking back downriver to find the over-looked bridge or to stay here and get across by other means.

He flicked his headlight to the stream again.

A chunk of a dead pine tree floated past him into the darkness. Another piece of wood slid by, and then what looked like a whole sapling. He estimated the river's width at twenty feet, and even if he'd had a jet boat he'd have given only fifty–fifty odds of making it across.

With a growing sense of urgency, he stared back toward the rocks. Upstream was a dead end.

Another bolt of lightning reached across the sky, lighting the valley like a flash bulb. The river was a white, writhing snake that disappeared into the trees far down the way he'd come.

He checked his watch: 7:59.

He pointed his headlamp down at the slick, rocky ground and ran back downstream.

CHAPTER 31

THE EDELWEISS HOTEL, located on Wildflower Road just off Main Street, was normally a quiet and quaint white-painted Swiss-style chalet. Tonight, SBCSD vehicles swarmed the place and the façade flickered red and blue.

Patterson watched deputies talking with one another out of her rain-streaked windshield. She knew from experience that they'd be relaying rumor mixed with legitimate information to one another, like a childhood game of Telephone.

From behind her steering wheel she'd seen the events as they'd unfolded earlier. Yates, forcing Charlotte to stay back at a safe distance, had taken two other deputies inside. They'd not found Ethan Womack. She suspected he'd either never showed up for his reservation, or had for a night or two and hadn't returned since.

Ethan Womack had moved on to worse accommodations. More straw and dirt, less flowers and yodeling soundtrack.

As a steady rain pattered the car, she looked down at the glowing cellphone in her lap.

She rolled through the internet links Gritzel had gotten from Ethan Womack's browsing history.

Tapping the next link in line, a *Denver Post* article flashed up talking about the Cold Lake murders. She read quickly, pausing at the mention of her and Rachette's names. This article was the first in the line of links that mentioned Patterson and Rachette. This had to be what had given Ethan Womack the idea to involve them.

Three knocks hit her window next to her head. "Jesus."

Pressing the start button on her Acura, she lowered the window and Yates's glistening face came into full view.

"He's not in there."

"I gathered. Any clues?"

"None. Busted down the door. You think MacLean's gonna be pissed at the bill?"

"I think under the circumstances he'll let it slide."

Yates nodded. "He was booked here for four days. According to the manager, left after two. She hasn't seen him since. Left his toiletries in the bathroom." Yates nodded at the phone in her lap. "You talking to Wolf?"

"No. He hasn't gotten in touch with me. How about you?"

"No. Jesus. What's he doing? I've called him a dozen times. MacLean's on my ass to get hold of him, too."

"Why? Did MacLean find anything out down there?"

"No. He just wants to talk to Wolf." Yates took off his hat and slapped it against his leg. "All right. We're gonna head back and have a sit-room. Figure out where everyone's searched for this truck of his, and where we need to go next."

Patterson nodded. "All right."

"You coming?"

"Yeah. I'll be there."

Yates looked at her cellphone again, slapped her roof, and walked into the rain toward the huddle of flashing department vehicles.

After rolling up the window she stared out the windshield, wondering if she should take the initiative, too, and call Ethan Womack's head-doctor, whom the away crew were interviewing down in New Mexico. Maybe looking into the man's mind could yield a clue. But MacLean and Lorber were reportedly on top of that and she'd have to wait.

She raised her phone and continued skimming the current article.

When she was done, she closed it out and tapped the next—another article on the deception and corruption involving the Sluice–Byron County Sheriff's election two years ago.

The article was a spin-off of Lucretia Smith's original exposé, detailing the information that Wolf, Rachette, and Patterson herself had compiled—how a town councilwoman, Judy Flemming, had worked in tandem with the sheriff-elect hopeful, Adam Jackson, to try to make the current department look bad and increase Jackson's odds of becoming the next sheriff.

Just like Lucretia Smith's article before it, the knock-off mentioned Deputy Greg Barker by name and how he'd been fired for his involvement, and detailed other deputies being injured in an unrelated incident—one being Chief Detective David Wolf, the other his deputy detective, Juan Hernandez, who'd since been let go by the department because of said injury.

She skimmed fast and went to the next. Each article was a cannibalized version of the prior, with the same information reported in mostly the same words.

"No map links."

She realized then that she'd been doing a lot of talking to herself lately.

Her phone rang and displayed Sheriff MacLean's name.

"Hello?"

"Where's Wolf? You talked to him?"

"No, sir."

"No?"

"I haven't seen him or talked to him since this afternoon," she said.

There was a long silence.

"You there?"

"Yeah. All right."

"Have you and Lorber talked to Ethan Womack's doctor yet?" she asked.

"Yes, and he's offering nothing we don't already know. Ethan Womack suffered a head injury when he was younger, which makes him a socially awkward individual. We're trying to press him more but he's not talking. Doctor–patient confidentiality." MacLean exhaled long into her ear. "Have Wolf call me if you talk to him."

"Yes, sir."

There was a click and the call was dead.

Okay, fine. Scratch the doctor.

Damn it. The clock was ticking.

That made her think about Scott. He was at home, alone with Tommy, being understanding and not calling, assuming she was busy and had work to do ... but he was probably worried by now. She dialed his number.

"Hey," he said.

"I'm totally late, I know."

"What's going on?" Tommy cried in the background.

"With me? Nothing. What's happening over there?"

"Oh ... he's mad that I'm not giving him another cookie."

"He's probably just tired, huh?" she said.

"Yeah." The crying quieted. "Okay, I'm in the other room now. Ah, bliss. What's happening?"

"Nothing. I was just calling to let you know I'm going to be late."

"The Metrosexual running you ragged tonight?"

She smiled. "Yeah."

They sat in silence for a beat.

"I love you," she said, hating the finality in her tone.

"I love you, too. Come home."

"Will do. Don't wait up."

The call ended.

Where was she?

"Map links," she said, pulling up the Ethan Womack's work-computer browsing-history email again. She was right. There were no map links.

The man had somehow gotten the jump on Rachette on the way to his house, which was up a rather desolate road. He would've had to study a map to see where Rachette lived.

And then there were the coordinates up near Dark Mountain. How had he chosen the desolate spot for a meeting place?

He could've come to Rocky Points and gone to the library to use a computer, she decided. He could've asked a waitress at the Sunnyside for a hiking spot for loners. A million other things could've explained how he'd learned his way around.

She closed the phone internet browser and went back to the last message received. She tapped the coordinates marking the meeting point, and the map application opened.

A blue dot appeared in the middle of the screen surrounded by digital gridlines.

She wondered how far Wolf had hiked. How hard was he getting hit by rain?

The map load took forever. "Let's go!"

Rocky Points was known for skiing and craft beers, not cutting-edge cell network speed, so she breathed through the new wave of anxiety and waited.

Deputy vehicles began streaming out of the parking lot. She saw Charlotte still standing outside under the porte cochère, talking to Yates.

The phone flickered as the map finally emerged. She ticked the aerial-view button, which made the load process start all over again.

"Damn it."

Mercifully, the map loaded faster, showing a snow-covered

peak on the left side of the screen, earth-toned terrain and endless pine trees on the right.

Pinching her fingers on the screen to zoom outward, she waited for the map to populate again. Most of the road details disappeared, so she zoomed back in and swiped to study the area.

The meeting spot lay at the top of a narrow valley lined with steep-looking mountains. The thumbtack was in a bowl formed by the surrounding peaks. Next to the marker was a small, shining lake.

She'd never been to the area. The peak directly left of the dot was called Dark Mountain—elevation 13,210 feet, according to the label.

It only took a tiny twitch of her finger to look over the northern edge of the bowl, a trek that would've taken a hiker most of a day and all their energy.

Cold Lake slid into view—dark blue surrounded by a sea of green trees.

Well-to-do people had carved clearings in the forest and erected summer homes off the southern tip of the lake. They were well-spaced and at the current zoom level she saw them all at a glance.

Her eyes traveled from the edge of the lake southward to the top of the mountain overlooking the meeting point. To walk the distance from one of the houses to Dark Mountain would've been formidable—through thick trees to the tree line, and then steep, rocky terrain above.

Furthermore, the homes were all multi-million-dollar struc-tures, sturdy, large and built with modern materials. The few outbuildings she saw were big and topped with stone tiles.

Closing the mapping app, she checked the first picture of Rachette she'd received. She saw dirt underneath the hay pile Rachette had been laid on. There was a sliver of wall behind him made from bleached and warped wood. Darkness filled gaps between the planks.

In other words, an old beat-up shack. Not the outbuilding of a multi-million-dollar home.

Opening the maps app again, she scrolled south, past the blue dot and over the southern wall of the bowl. Again, the map disappeared and digital gridlines took its place.

"Damn it."

Slapping the phone on her leg, she stretched her neck.

Charlotte walked across the parking lot towards her.

Patterson took off her seatbelt and was about to climb out to meet her halfway when the phone screen flickered, displaying the aerial images.

The blue marker pulsed at the top of the screen now. In the middle, was a line of snow-covered peaks, and in the valley to the south, just below the southern edge of the crescent peak dubbed Dark Mountain, stood a single structure casting a shadow.

Her heart hammered in her chest as she pinched her fingers and studied a basic square building that had been twisted into a parallelogram by years of standing in the elements. A two-track road stitched the ground east and west, passing feet from it.

Charlotte had stopped outside and was talking to Yates again. Yates held up his phone and Charlotte reluctantly went back and took it. Maybe MacLean was on the line wanting to talk to her.

Patterson zoomed back out on the map and followed the two-track road to the east. Swiping her finger, she traced a meandering stream down the valley until it leaked into the larger valley below. There, the two-track became a regular dirt road and connected with Highway 734. The junction of the two roads was only a few miles south of where Wolf would've turned off earlier tonight to hike to the coordinates.

The ambush scenario became clear. Ethan Womack had driven up this road with Rachette and held him in this shed. The meeting spot was one valley to the north. Between the two valleys was a ridgeline—the perfect perch for a shooter with a fifty-caliber sniper rifle.

Quickly, she swiped back to the structure, then followed the two-track the other way.

Again with the gridlines.

Her heart pumped wildly now and sweat spread under her armpits.

Outside, Charlotte stood by the hotel, nodding and saying few words into the phone pressed to her ear.

The aerial-view images materialized again, and Patterson followed the two-track west between two mountains. It curved south, and then, surprisingly, it swung to the east.

The road widened and was marked as Turkey Hill Ranch Road.

Swiping further, she waited again for the picture to materialize. And then it did, revealing a complex of buildings in a clearing. They were painted red and white, with cattle strewn about in the surrounding green fields that cut into the forest. Machinery littered the space near one of the buildings, and three pickups were parked in front of another.

Overlaying the map was a hyperlinked label: Turkey Hill Ranch.

She tapped it, and when a website came up she scoured the page for the names of the owners. She found none, but saw mentions of a company called Cormack Holdings and an association called Johnstone Beef Growers.

A soft knock ripped her from her reading.

She lowered the window, revealing Charlotte's drawn face.

"Hey."

"Hey." Charlotte's upper lip trembled and she gazed into nothing with stoic stillness.

Patterson put the phone on the passenger seat with the screen down and climbed out. Wrapping Charlotte in a hug she said, "We'll find him."

Charlotte sobbed and leaned on Patterson's shoulder without wrapping her arms.

The emotional outburst lasted a few seconds and then Charlotte backed away, wiping her nose. "So what's happening? I saw you reading something on your phone. You find anything in those articles?"

"Uh, no. Well, I see that Ethan Womack probably found out about us through those articles. They mention me and Tom a few times. But ..." Her subconscious interrupted her with something, but failed to elaborate.

"But what?"

Patterson shook her head. "I don't know."

Yates pulled his vehicle up to the front of Patterson's Acura and rolled down the window. "Situation room in ten minutes!"

Patterson nodded.

"You coming?" Charlotte asked.

She furrowed her brow, hit hard by the desperation in her friend's voice. "Of course, Char. I'll be there."

Charlotte turned and climbed into the vehicle. Then they drove away with hissing tires.

Patterson got back inside and studied the website page some more. After another minute of fruitless reading, she cursed the tiny, sluggish device in her hand and called Bryce Duplessis.

"Yo," he said in greeting.

"It's me."

"I know."

"I need a favor. Are you in the office?"

"No. I'm at home enjoying a glass of wine."

Patterson hesitated.

"Of course I'm in the office. What do you need?"

CHAPTER 32

"YEAH, well ... if you had come up with a better plan, we wouldn't be following her now."

Rachette's health slid downhill, and fast. He could tell by the way sleep called him. All he wanted to do was close his eyes, but this guy had no volume knob on his voice.

"What? I can't hear you! Damn reception ... what? Yeah, I can hear you. Then just run her off the road and shoot her in the head with his gun."

That remark made Rachette blink awake. He stared at the wool blankets, wondering who this guy was talking about. A woman. Charlotte?

"Charlotte." His voice sounded like a vacuum cleaner.

He was so thirsty.

"He's coming ... he's up on the ridge in place ... we're ready, so just keep following her ... then we'll have to deal with it. Correction: you'll have to deal with it. And you're gonna have to go all in. We can't have her walking around after tonight, understand? ... Huh? ... Yeah. Well, like Dad used to say, 'Put your shit back in your ass!'"

Rachette smiled and passed out again.

CHAPTER 33

"NOPE," Bryce said. "Dead end there."

Patterson sat staring at the now quiet Edelweiss Hotel through streaks of rain. "Shit."

"Cormack Holdings' registered agent is a firm in Denver called Gander and Mesner."

"You know anyone there?"

"I'd have to look into it tomorrow. Why? What's the big deal?"

Patterson closed her eyes and sagged into her car seat.

"So we're going to need another day of looking in on Chandler Mustaine, by the way."

She cracked her eyelids. "What?"

"Yeah. Twenty-seven photos and you got zero usable shots of his face."

"No, I didn't ... yes, I did."

"You got him with a hat and self-tinting glasses on, which look like mirrored Ray-Bans in the photos I'm looking at."

"Are you kidding me?"

"Nope. It's kind of comical. But, anyway, no big deal. Just head back next weekend. Miss big-tits will be back in town, or the other one. Either way, there'll be another chance soon. I'm not worried about it."

She was going to tell him that Chandler Mustaine had seen her in the trees as she'd fled the scene, which was going to make another time very difficult, but then decided she didn't give a shit. "Okay."

Hanging up, she swallowed and looked at herself in the mirror. She reached over, pulled open her glove compartment, and took out her Glock 17 nine-millimeter tucked in a paddle holster—just like the department issue she used to have.

She had one magazine inserted and two spares lying underneath the paperwork in her glove.

After staring at the oiled weapon, she looked over her shoulder toward Main Street. Then she looked down at herself, dressed in slacks and a blouse, with shoes built more for show than for usefulness. The coat draped on the back seat would repel rain for a while, then sop it up like a sponge. But the rain was letting up, wasn't it?

"Fuck it," she said. "Let's go."

She started the car and flicked the wipers, then twisted the lights and drove.

"Who are you talking to?" she asked, pulling onto Main, south toward Williams Pass, and the two partners who needed her.

CHAPTER 34

WOLF FIRED AGAIN into the tree and went around to the other side to assess the damage he'd done. Ten of the 5.56 millimeter bullets had left fist-sized holes in the opposite side of the sopping-wet ponderosa pine.

He put both hands on the trunk and pushed. The tree felt as immoveable as a healthy ponderosa growing in Rocky Mountain soil normally did.

The bridge was gone. The water had severed it from its moorings and shoved it up onto the opposite shoreline, which explained why he'd not seen it earlier. The water flowed just as fast, if not more intensely, than before. If there was a better way to cross the river, he wasn't seeing it.

He fired another few rounds.

The rain had stopped now, but water continually dripped off the branches above Wolf, let loose by the vibrations of bullets ripping through its thick trunk.

He walked out into a clearing and checked the sky. A patch of stars twinkled through a break in the clouds. The weather was rolling out, which was one obstacle gone, but the river ran higher than ever, swelled by the runoff collecting in the bowl up the valley and pouring out like a shotgun blast.

One more time, he looked up at the tall pine and clicked the gun to full auto. He ducked underneath the canopy and aimed carefully, his theory being that if the exit holes came out toward the water the tree would follow that direction once he'd put enough lead through it.

He squeezed, firing off six, seven, ten rounds, trying to concentrate his fire in the center of the trunk. It sounded like a cracking whip, if a whip'd had full-auto mode, and the noise rolled up and down the valley as he paused between bursts.

He gave it a push again, and thought he felt it give a little.

After another long squeeze of the trigger and the gun kicking in his arms, the empty click told him he'd gone through sixty rounds and the tree still stood. Without hesitation, he slammed another magazine home and squeezed off more rounds until, finally, he saw the tree jolt.

He stopped and stared at it, wondering whether it had only been the gun's recoil playing tricks on his mind. Then he felt the fresh cascade of water coming off the branches above him and knew he'd finally cut through.

He placed the M4 on the ground and put his full weight behind, pushing against the tree. Then it creaked and shuddered, and started falling away from him. The last thing he wanted was the trunk to split and kick back into him with the force of a Mack truck, so he picked up the gun and ran away, hearing popping and cracking and then a whoosh as it landed in the river.

With wide eyes, he ran to the side and raked the headlamp beam over the tree to the other bank. The water frothed through the branches and underneath the downed behemoth, but it held firm against the battering.

He shouldered the M4, avoiding the scorching barrel, and walked to the cracked base of the fallen tree. The air was saturated with the scent of pine sap and gunpowder, which, along with his victory, energized him to move.

He climbed up onto his makeshift bridge, and it only took a

few steps into the maze of branches to realize that crossing was going to be harder than he'd expected. But he moved steadily, pointing his headlamp, grabbing branches for balance when he could, and inched his way over the water.

When he reached the center of the raging torrent, he felt the tree move underneath him, and then it began to roll. Sidestepping, he slipped on the soaked wood and landed squarely on his crotch.

His testicles took the brunt of the fall and nauseating pain overpowered everything.

The tree kept moving.

Gritting his teeth, he got to his hands and knees and scrambled forward as best he could. The strap of the M4 caught on a branch and pulled him back, and he almost toppled into the water, but his foot landed on wood and he pulled hard, freeing himself just in time.

Another step—another two feet.

The rotating underfoot stopped as he neared the other side. Then the tree jolted and the rushing water changed in pitch, and he saw that the end of the tree behind him was buried in whitewater. A second later it began creeping downstream, and then it broke loose.

Needles poked his face as he scrambled forward, and he watched in horror as the front end backed into the water.

Without thinking, he dove sideways toward the bank, but came up short of solid ground and plunged into the icy liquid.

The shock to his system was made worse by the rip current that sucked him under and sent him tumbling. There was no up or down, only rolling.

Almost instantly the air in his lungs was gone, and they convulsed, begging for air.

He felt rock underneath him and he kicked off it, managing to get his head above water and suck in a tiny breath before he went back under.

An instant later, he felt a shattering pain against his back as he ran into something. He twisted around and grabbed bark-covered branches. The tree had wedged to a stop and caught him like a net. Water piled behind it, submerging his head, and he struggled to stay above the frothing torrent.

With numb fingers, he gripped hard and pulled himself up. As he lay draped on the trunk, he sucked in a breath, and then something hit him on the head and he fell off. The blow stunned him and it took a second to realize that the ponderosa pine was rolling like a paddle wheel and the rotating branches were now pushing him under.

He clawed and pulled his way out from under the murderous wooden arm and managed to pull his torso up out of the water and onto the trunk again.

The tree seemed to jam itself home into a stable position, and that was all the coaxing Wolf needed to climb up.

With water pouring off his face and flowing down his body—over his back, down his pants, into his boots—he got up and walked over the slick wood.

He stumbled and slipped, raking his body through the branches as he moved toward shore. Then something cracked and the tree lurched, and like a boat backing away from a dock, he felt the pine swing downstream. He dove off again and held his breath, but his time he crashed face-first into a bush.

Panting, he rolled onto his back and watched the dripping branches pull away from him and disappear.

As shock wore off, he sat up and took stock of his situation.

He looked over his shoulder and saw the suppressor muzzle of the M4 still on his back, and his daypack was securely fastened underneath that. He ran a hand over his waist and felt the Glock still in his paddle holster.

All in all, he figured he'd come out all right, and he was on the other side of the river.

Then he realized he was shivering.

CHAPTER 35

HE STUMBLED out of the bush and unslung the M4 and the backpack. As he unzipped the bag, he was hit with the stench of Fabian's clothing, and then relief that it was dry.

He sloughed off his rain jacket, the long and short-sleeved shirts beneath it, his sopping jeans, underwear, and socks, and started putting on the dry clothing.

His teeth chattered uncontrollably and he stumbled while poking a leg into the dry jeans—both signs that he was hypothermic.

A fire was out of the question. He had a lighter, but then what? Everything was wet.

He zipped the jeans, put on the spare long-sleeved shirt and sweatshirt, and donned some new socks. Shoving on his winter cap, he felt something slide down the leg of his pants. He kicked and a small black box clattered to the ground.

Even with the life evaporating from him, he paused at the sight. He bent over and picked it up, then fumbled with numb fingers and opened the box. The diamond ring he'd once offered to Lauren shimmered inside the velvet case.

He thought of Lauren's smiling face, and then Ella's.

He shut the box and dropped it in his backpack, and with

renewed determination pushed his feet into the sopping boots. After a few seconds of fumbling with the laces, he gave up and tucked them inside instead.

With the distraction of death tapping him on the shoulder, he was surprised by a lucent idea that had come to him. And instead of leaving the wet clothing, he packed it in the bag and shouldered it again.

He grabbed the rain jacket, strapped on the M4, and marched fast.

"Let's move. Team One, go."

Titus, Chambers, and Womack got up from their cover positions and jogged toward the cluster of huts they were calling Objective B, or Bamyani to the locals.

Intel described Bamyani as a town with a population of a hundred that had been known to house Taliban combatants. Wolf saw it as another group of huts perched on a hill in the middle of three thousand years ago.

Wolf, Chan, and the rest of the squad watched on as Womack dragged behind Titus and Chambers. On any other given mission, Corporal Paul Womack would've led a foot-blistering pace, but the man they'd once known was gone.

"What's his problem?" PFC Chan asked next to Wolf.

"Henning," Wolf said.

Wolf decided then and there that he had no choice but to report Womack to command. News that Sergeant Henning had died of his head injuries had reached them two days prior, and now Womack had gone from borderline insubordinate to walking zombie.

"Move, Womack," Wolf said into his throat mic.

Womack upped his pace, catching Chambers as they reached the exterior of the first building.

Once Womack caught up with the others, he passed them and

took position next to the doorway, which, like most of the structures in Afghanistan's countryside, had no door.

A second later, without the go-ahead order from Wolf, he disappeared inside with gun raised.

"What the hell's he doing?" Chan asked.

"Get in there after him," Wolf said into his mic.

Before Chambers and Titus reached the doorway, yells and a burst of gunfire came from within the hut.

"Cover!" Wolf said, running out from behind the wall to the building. "Status! Status!"

"Enemy down, enemy down," Titus's voice came through the earpiece.

The rest of the squad followed and took up positions outside the hut, and Wolf walked in to assess the damage. A young man, no older than sixteen, was splayed on the ground with a stripe of gunshot wounds across his chest. An AK-47 lay on the dirt floor next to him.

"What happened?" Wolf turned to Womack.

Womack's blue eyes flashed. "I shot him first. That's what happened."

"You didn't wait for my order."

"Thank God, I didn't. Or we'd all be dead."

They stared at one another.

A demon lurked behind Womack's eyes, red-rimmed and bloodshot from five nights straight of drinking beer.

"Sir, sir!" Chambers pointed out the door.

Gunfire erupted outside.

They ducked for cover and Wolf edged to the doorway.

"Clear!"

A man sprawled on the ground outside, an AK-47 lying next to him, a similar line of gunshot wounds seeping through his ragged clothing.

"Anyone hit?" Wolf asked.

"No, sir."

"Shit. Let's move!" He turned to Womack. "Stay close to me."

"Sir, yes, sir!"

Wolf ignored the insubordination in his voice and left out the door.

There was one main road through the town, which was the equivalent distance of one block of shops on Main Street in Rocky Points, but it felt like a mile in the current circumstances.

A full hour later, they'd searched and cleared every building. Besides the two combatants killed earlier, they uncovered no more threats, only elderly men and dozens of women and children who were shocked and scared after watching a group of technologically clad warriors methodically sweep through their town.

Like many times before, the team rounded up the non-combatants into groups and put them in huts so they could keep a close eye on them.

"Secondary sweep," Wolf said, and Titus and Chan walked to him.

Another Ranger herded the final stragglers into one of the buildings.

"How many do we have?" Wolf scanned the buildings behind them with his NVGs.

"We have thirty-nine women, twenty-seven children, eleven men."

"Okay." His men looked calm-eyed and ready for action, save for Womack, who darted his M4 back and forth between the buildings.

"Womack, you stay with the non-combatants." Wolf remembered the bag of candy and the swarm of giggling children.

"Sir, yes, sir!"

The other Rangers watched with wary eyes as Womack snapped a crisp salute, turned on his heels, and ducked inside. The silence of the countryside township deepened.

Wolf nodded to Chan. "You take the other hut."

With too many non-combatants for one building they'd split them into two groups.

"Yes, sir." Chan ducked into the building next door.

As the sun brightened the eastern horizon, Wolf and the rest of the squad fanned out and began methodically clearing the town again.

Experience told them that they'd overlooked plenty of hiding spots and the danger wasn't over.

"Watch your asses," Chambers said over the radio.

Tense chuckles swept over them. Once, the previous month, a different squad had carried out a mission a few miles away. A Taliban fighter had been hiding on a rooftop for hours when he'd decided to open fire, hitting a Ranger in the ass with two AK-47 rounds.

"Good call," Chan said, stepping up on a crate to peer onto the surrounding rooftops. "Clear here."

There was a three-round burst of gunfire and yelling from behind them.

They ran. And as they came back out to the main road, the shrill sound of dozens of simultaneous screams put Wolf's heart in his throat. There was desperation and horror in those noises and they were coming from women and children. And in that instant, he knew that Paul Womack had done something seriously wrong.

Wolf had stopped shivering, which was either good or a sign of imminent death. He decided that since he was sweating, moving quickly, and upright, the threat of hypothermia had passed.

Still, he felt weakened, like a blood-sugar crash could be coming on, so he stopped and unstrapped the backpack. Inside were two protein bars, which he unwrapped and ate greedily. After a few bites, he realized that his water bottle, which had been clipped to his backpack, was missing.

Sneaking up to the edge of the still-raging stream-turned-river, he cupped his hands in the icy water and sucked down a dozen gulps.

9:03 p.m.

At this rate, he'd be plenty early.

Again, he pulled the Garmin GPS out of its zip case and hit the power button, then waited for the map.

He studied the screen and set the zoom wider, then checked the valley to the south.

With numb hands he grabbed the M4 and brought it to his shoulder.

He put his eye to the scope and saw a clear night-vision-green image of the surrounding terrain. The nitrogen-purged interior of the rifle scope was free of fog on the inside chamber and free of streaking on the outside lens glass.

The weather was cooperating too. The rain had stopped and the clouds were moving to the east, revealing larger patches of stars and a half-moon that slid in and out of view.

He saw no movement up the trail or behind him. When he switched it to thermal-camera view the image turned black and white, and then he dialed up the knob to show heat as red.

Like his hands and feet, the surrounding landscape ahead and behind was cold. Nothing. He focused on the top of the ridge of Dark Mountain, sweeping from left to right. Still no red, so he lowered the gun and hit the scope power switch.

According to the numbers on the screen, he was 0.73 miles from his destination now. He studied the map again, then the valley, matching the picture of a rock outcropping on the screen with the real thing.

Behind it, the towering bowl loomed.

He shut off the GPS, zipped it in his backpack, and got moving again.

CHAPTER 36

THE HIGHWAY PAVEMENT at the bottom of the valley was dry in spots now, and Heather Patterson risked pushing the speed of her Acura MDX to just under eighty miles per hour. Her eyelids were glued open and she had the high beams on, scanning the landscape left and right for wildlife. Fragrant sage oils and the scent of rain seeped through the vents.

She made good time, but had to check her speed and switch back to low beams often as oncoming traffic passed by. The last thing she wanted was to be pulled over.

Even so, every vehicle she'd come upon she'd passed, and she blew by another minivan now.

Pulling back into the right lane, she checked her rearview, focusing on a set of headlights far behind. For most of the drive she'd been watching the vehicle closely as it copied her moves, driving way too boldly for the average layperson. They could have been a teenager, she supposed—a college kid headed down to Ashland, trying to make good time and latching onto her psycho driving by making the same passes, assuming she'd get a speeding ticket before they did.

She relaxed when the headlights remained behind the receding reflection of the minivan. Then she eased into her seat some more when another mile went past and it looked as if she'd lost the vehicle altogether.

Adrenaline steadily dripped into her veins and there was nothing she could do about it.

She flicked on the high beams once more, illuminating the sage shrub-covered landscape and a green sign with a big arrow pointing right: Cold Lake National Forest Access/Dark Mountain Trailhead—17.3 miles.

Passing the turnoff Wolf had taken, she felt another stab of guilt hit her, then reminded herself that she was potentially tiptoeing inside the lion's den right now. At seventy-five miles per hour.

Her dash clock read 9:03 p.m.

Movement caught her eye and she jammed the brakes. An elk, standing massive with a rack of antlers, materialized in the oncoming lane. It reared and whipped its head to look at her, eyes gleaming in the headlights. Then it walked into her lane.

She swerved right and the car vibrated as she ran over the rumble strip. Then it shuddered as she mashed the brake harder.

The elk took another step.

She was either going to flip off the side of the raised highway and slide on muddy terrain through a barbed-wire fence or collide with the huge animal.

There was too little time to register the thought as the animal grew in the windshield.

Instinct took over and she cranked the wheel left, and at that very instant the elk lunged forward.

The jumping animal flashed by and then there was nothing but the long road ahead of her.

She let off the brake and let go of her breath.

"Shit."

Her body hummed and her hand shook as she tucked a strand of hair behind her ear.

Damn it, she had to stay focused. Her chances of helping her friends were already slim. Add smashing into a thousand-pound animal at seventy-five miles per hour and they'd be zero.

Another green sign reflected in her headlights out the windshield.

Normalizing her breath, she coasted and then slowed. As she eased onto the shoulder, mud spattered on the underside of her car until she came to a stop.

The sign read: Turkey Hill National Forest Access—10 Miles, with an arrow pointing right.

She leaned into the windshield and looked up the dirt road gouged into the sage and then into the monolithic mountains making up the western wall of the valley. Rachette was up there, but if she took this route, she'd pull up to the shack like it was a drive-thru restaurant. One manned by Ethan Womack wielding a fifty-caliber sniper rifle that fired armor-piercing rounds he was good at shooting, if the trophies told anything.

Ethan Womack would not be expecting a visitor to come up his tailpipe. But to Patterson this felt too direct. Turkey Hill Ranch was calling her, with the circuitous route that climbed out of the cattle property and up to the same shack from the opposite direction.

Headlights crested the horizon behind her and she let off the brake. Pressing the gas, she passed the turnoff and pulled back onto the highway, her tires sloughing off the mud as she upped her speed to sixty-five.

Ambush the ambusher.

Or was it ambushers? she asked herself again.

The turnoff for Turkey Hill Ranch was less well advertised 1.7 miles later. In fact, there was no sign at all, only a widening of the shoulder and a dirt road shooting perpendicular to the west off the highway.

She jammed the brakes and barely made the turn. As she skidded to a stop on mud, her headlights illuminated a cattle guard with a red and white sign: Private Drive—No Trespassing.

She drove across, her car vibrating on the grate, and then she slowed to a stop at a metal swinging gate blocking the road.

Another no-trespassing sign reminded her she was unwelcome.

Headlights from the highway lanced off the gate and she decided to douse her own.

Now sitting in the dark, she listened to the soft whisper of the vents blowing on her face and waited for her eyes to adjust.

The road beyond the closed entrance went straight for a stretch, then curled left up a gentle rise into pine trees. In those trees, just over some low hills, sat the Turkey Hill Ranch. Past that ranch, the road bent around, climbed in elevation, and eventually curved back east to the shack—her back entrance to the action.

In other words, she had to pass through this gate.

A car hissed past on the highway and she watched the taillights disappear. To the south, the outskirts of Ashland twinkled on the valley floor.

In Patterson's experience, subconscious thoughts found their recognizable form in the quietest of moments, and especially after exciting or traumatic events—like, say, hard exercise, or almost nailing an elk at seventy-five miles per hour.

Like an animal out of the dark, a thought sprung into her mind now.

After shifting into park, she picked up her phone, pressed the unlock button, and was glad to see some decent reception bars. She opened her email and navigated to the list of links representing Ethan Womack's web-browsing history.

She opened the first article and skimmed. Then closed it and went to the next. Then the next. It took her less than a minute because she was looking for something specific in the articles— one single word—and, yet, she'd failed to find it.

When she was done, she closed her phone and put it back in the center console.

In all the stories and corruption allegation exposés—any that involved Wolf, Rachette, and herself—none had mentioned the word finger. Or the other, closely related word she would've settled for: pinkie.

They all mentioned that David Wolf had suffered a gunshot injury to the hand, because that had been the official statement released from Sheriff MacLean a week after the events. But there was no mention that Wolf had gotten his left little finger clean blown off by a nine-millimeter bullet fired at point-blank range.

So why was somebody cutting off Tom Rachette's left pinkie and sending a picture of it to them?

Clearly the injury was a taunt, referring to Wolf's past. Trying to re-open the wound, so to speak.

Sure, everyone in town knew what had happened to Wolf, but how would Ethan Womack have known?

She shut off her car and got out.

The air was still and quiet, thick with post-rain fragrance. Feet crunching, she stepped over a puddle and walked to the end of the gate.

A rusty chain hung off a steel post and she saw that the gate wasn't locked. Relief should've been flooding through her at this moment, but that feeling was muted by apprehension. She pushed, and the gate's hinges sang as it swung all the way open.

A pickup truck went past on the highway, then disappeared.

She jogged to her car and hopped in. She turned it on but kept the lights extinguished and drove beyond the gate. Then she got out and swung it shut again.

She turned to run back to her car but stopped, realizing that as the last truck had passed she'd seen the silhouette of a mailbox alongside the highway, a few paces on the other side of the cattle guard.

She looked up the ranch road. The coast was clear. Then up the highway. No one was coming. She vaulted the gate and sprinted.

A few seconds later, and after stepping gingerly over the yawning slats of the wet metal grate—thank God she never wore high heels—she pulled open a rusty mailbox and found a stack of mail.

She patted her pocket and cursed herself for leaving her phone in the car. A cloud obscured the moon, making it hard to see the names and addresses on the mail. Still, if she stared hard enough she could see.

Current Resident.

Turkey Hill Ranch.

Cormack Holdings.

A car came over the rise from the south and bathed her in blinding light. Her back was to the passing vehicle and she kept it that way. Now exposed and feeling like she'd been caught red-handed in a federal offense, she shrugged away the anxiety and took advantage of the light, flipping faster through the pile of envelopes.

Turkey Hill Ranch ... Cormack Holdings ...

She stopped at the next one and her face dropped.

Cormack Barker.

"Holy sh—"

Squeaking brakes pulled her gaze to the highway. She saw the same pickup truck that had passed in the opposite direction a few seconds previously. A man's face was pressed to the driver's-side window, and when they locked eyes, Patterson's skin crawled.

The man was smiling.

She put the mail back inside and slammed the door.

Stumbling on the cattle guard, she almost broke her leg as her tiny foot slipped into one of the gaps.

A throaty roar came from the pickup truck as it turned around on the highway.

She sprinted back up the road, her eyes watering from the rushing wind, and seconds later hurdled the gate with adrenaline-fueled ease.

Just as she got back into her car, headlights swung onto the road behind her.

She mashed the gas and the Acura's wheels spat dirt.

As she sucked back into her seat, she saw in the vibrating rearview that the truck had come up sideways to the gate. Then a cab light flicked on and a door opened.

The curve came up fast and she hit the brakes and cranked the wheel just in time.

She leaned into the window as she followed the road left. The man down at the gate wasn't following her, though with his cab light on she could see him putting a phone to his ear.

She considered his bearded smile, and the headlights she'd thought had been following her all along, and had a feeling he was more than just a concerned neighbor.

Then she entered the trees and the truck disappeared.

CHAPTER 37

WOLF LAY on his belly and crawled up to some rocks. Once there, he got to his knees and studied the terrain ahead. A lake shone silver in the moonlight, surrounded on three sides by the steep slopes of Dark Mountain, jutting skyward like a giant's castle walls.

Like a firefly sitting in the bottom of a salad bowl, a tent squatted next to the water, lit within by a yellow light.

He cringed as a stream of icy water bolted down his neck between his shoulders. Sopping-wet clothing draped over his head and back, and any body heat he'd stoked within himself on the jog up the valley was sucked away by the second. But he'd figured that if he had a thermal-camera night-vision scope, then his enemies could have the same, so he was trying to mask any heat signature he gave off.

It was 9:41 p.m. and he'd arrived. Two hours and nineteen minutes to go and somebody already had something set up for him.

The trail was a thin tendril shining in the moonlight, entering the bowl and leading straight to the glowing tent.

He flipped on the thermal camera and began scanning.

There were no heat signatures near the tent or in it, and after a few minutes he'd still found nothing in the valley.

His early arrival had been anticipated, so how about his thermal-camera scope? A thermal blanket could block a heat signature easily enough, rendering anyone lying in wait invisible.

He pulled back on the zoom and scanned again, still seeing nothing on the slopes, then swept left and up to the top of the southern ridge.

Like a blob of amorphous red gas, he saw a heat signature up top.

Setting the zoom to max, the red blob grew in the scope, and though the figure took no better form than a bead of light, he could see that it moved.

A perfect perch for a sniper.

Or a rancher.

"There you are," he said under his breath.

Years ago, back when Wolf had been a third-year deputy and Tom Rachette and Heather Patterson had still been battling zits in high school, he'd been called to a horrific traffic accident on the other side of Williams Pass, just near the turnoff to Cold Lake.

A woman named Ellen Mink had been driving with her teenaged son, Chad, in the passenger seat, and they'd gone off the road, flipping the vehicle multiple times. Not wearing a seatbelt, Ellen had been thrown from the car an unfathomable distance from the mangled vehicle and died. Chad had been belted and survived, though injured badly enough to put him into a two-day coma.

When Chad had regained consciousness, he'd told a story of a truck carrying a cattle trailer running him and his mother off the road near the Cold Lake junction. Other memories of the crash were hazy or had left the boy's mind altogether, but he'd remembered the four-leafed clover painted on the side of the trailer and the words Emerald Isle Ranch as it'd veered into their lane and struck their car.

Naturally, upon hearing the news, Wolf had started the process of talking with the Emerald Isle Ranch owner, a man named Cormack Barker. Except Sluice and Byron county had not yet merged and the ranch was across county lines, so Wolf had gone to the sheriff to the south for help: Will MacLean.

Wolf, his then boss Sheriff Burton, and a young newly elected Sheriff MacLean had gone in together to the Emerald Isle Ranch.

The ranch was big with hundreds of cattle, and Cormack Barker had two brothers who helped him run the place—two brothers who'd kept their distance and their mouths shut that day.

Cormack had either acted or was genuinely surprised, because his cattle truck, he pointed out, was without markings—no logo at all, and no indications of having recently run a car into the sage up the highway. Sure, his ranch logo was a four-leafed clover, and his ranch name was indeed Emerald Isle Ranch, but his cattle trailer was a beat-up maroon piece of junk without any artwork painted on it.

On inspecting the trailer, they all saw rusted edges and no evidence of trading paint with Ellen Mink's car. And, clearly, no one had painted over or removed logos from the trailer.

When asked to produce registration paperwork, Cormack had it handy, though to Wolf's eye it looked suspect. Perhaps doctored. There was more damage to the paper than expected, given that it had probably sat in a file cabinet for most of its life. It reminded him of the time he'd changed two Ds to Bs on his fifth-grade report card before showing it to his parents.

And upon further inspection of the property, there was no sign of another trailer, which seemed odd considering how many cattle were on the ranch.

Cormack Barker was a donor to Sheriff MacLean's campaign and there was to be no further investigation, as clearly stated by the Byron County sheriff. Burton promised to comply and, in the end, the whole thing fizzled out.

Wolf had continued, however, though he never found a solid link to where that phantom trailer had gone, nor did he find someone else who'd claimed to have ever seen it. Other than the boy, that is.

As he talked to the business associates of Cormack Barker—the veterinarian in Ashland, the slaughterhouse owner on the eastern plains—the picture became real clear. Cormack Barker had bought the silence of everyone associated with the Emerald Isle Ranch.

At the slaughterhouse in Greeley, he'd seen ten trailers on the owner's property. Two of them had had fresh paint jobs. Without a warrant, however, standing on a ladder and scraping off the new paint to check underneath was out of the question.

Finally, after a year, he'd had to stomach justice not being served for Chad's mother.

During those long months of Wolf's unofficial investigation, Cormack Barker had renamed Emerald Isle to Turkey Hill Ranch.

That had rubbed Wolf wrong. Just like the cattle trailer, Cormack had effectively painted a new ranch name over the old, tarnished one.

Then Greg Barker, Cormack Barker's only son, had eventually gotten hired by MacLean. And when the two counties merged, Wolf had been working side by side with a Barker. That had rubbed Wolf wrong too. Especially since the son was every bit of a lying, conniving bastard as his father had been all those years ago.

Wolf remembered Greg's words in front of the art gallery.

I hear there's an opening in the department for detective.

Wolf had been stewing over that comment ever since he'd seen the location of the meeting spot on the map. Rachette had been hogtied at that very moment, and Barker had been standing there, talking to him, Lauren, and her seven-year-old daughter, telling them he'd done it.

The coordinates they'd been sent referred to a single valley on the northern edge of their vast tracts of land. The Barkers were being brazen about it, or stupid. The line was thin with that family.

Finding the connection with Ethan Womack proved difficult, however. Nothing in his memory jarred loose any explanations. As far as he could tell, the only thing the Barkers and Womacks had in common was the direction of their blame—towards Wolf.

So how might they have connected? Ethan Womack could've recruited the Barkers' help after Paul's suicide. Perhaps his anger sent him on a quest for like-minded fellows—other men bent on revenge against David Wolf.

After studying the red signature some more, he moved on and scanned to the right, following the top of the ridgeline all the way to the other side.

It seemed that one of them waited alone. Ethan Womack had a skill set suited for the job of sniper, but it could've been any of them.

There was only one way to find out.

Wolf ducked back down and behind a rock wall that stood on the side of the trail and blocked him from view from the enemy above.

His watch read 9:45 p.m.

The same wall of rock that hid him from view now became a ridge of granite that ran from the valley floor to the top of the ridge above. He estimated the trek up would take an hour, and he'd be undetected the entire way.

Then, at the top, he'd be able to ambush the ambusher.

He peeled the wet clothing off his head and shoulders and stuffed it in his backpack, then climbed.

CHAPTER 38

PATTERSON EYED the rearview mirror for the thousandth time and leaned closer to the windshield to see.

"Shit, shit."

The moon hid behind another cloud, and with her headlights off she dared not creep above five miles per hour. The forest on either side of the road was tight and dark, yielding no view into the trees, and the gravel road was made of dark rock that seemed to appear only milliseconds before she drove over it.

A map glowed on her phone in the passenger seat. The pulsing blue dot showed her location on aerial view, though gridlines filled most of the screen. When she next had a chance, she'd get a top-of-the-line GPS and take a sledgehammer to her phone.

She had to be close to the clearing she'd seen before. Then there'd be a series of buildings on either side of the road—the Turkey Hill Ranch.

The Barker ranch.

Thinking of Greg Barker made her hands tighten on the wheel.

How was this asshole involved in all of this?

Perhaps the answer could provide sense where previously there'd been none.

Rachette had been taken, and those responsible had demanded not only Wolf's attention but Patterson's too. Why? Because no other single family in the entire county had more pent-up anger toward the three of them, that's why.

She, Wolf, and Rachette had compiled evidence regarding Greg Barker and his involvement in the political corruption and relayed it anonymously, under the pseudonym of Black Diamond, to Lucretia Smith, the one reporter they could find ruthless enough to publish the story.

One thing she'd learned in her years living in Rocky Points: secrets weren't secrets for long. The Barkers must've learned the truth of Black Diamond's identity.

Or maybe she was off. Completely off. Maybe the proximity of the Barker ranch was a coincidence.

Because a random guy from New Mexico was also involved. Or, at least, he seemed random. Then again, he was anything but random, wasn't he? He was the brother of a man who'd been in the army with Wolf. The brother of a man who'd just committed suicide on video. And Ethan Womack, already damaged by his childhood head trauma, now blamed Wolf for the whole thing, if his angry edited version of the video was anything to go by.

The moon sloughed off its cloud cover at the same time the forest opened, and Patterson jolted at the sight of a dark figure on the side of the road.

A cow stood motionless, staring at her as if mocking her frantic thoughts. Dozens of the animals littered the rolling landscape.

As she edged over a hill, a complex of buildings came into view, ablaze with light.

Then she spotted something more sinister and came to a halt.

A tractor and a pickup truck were parked lengthwise across the road. A man holding a rifle across his chest stood underneath a lamp post next to the vehicles. The man had a thick torso. He wore a flannel hunting coat and jeans. His face was smeared in shadow.

What the hell was this?

As she checked the rearview mirror, headlights flicked on behind her, searing her eyeballs.

Twisting in her seat, she noted the height and spacing of the beams, and the throaty growl of its idle, and decided the truck from the highway had followed her after all.

She leaned forward to escape the glare and saw the man under the lamp post talking on the phone.

Her phone lit up and rang. The screen showed the same number from the previous text message.

"Hello?"

"Roll down your window and throw your gun out."

The guy under the light ahead pocketed his phone and she heard the truck engine in her ear speaker. "Are you behind me?" she asked, trying to delay so she could think.

"Throw the gun out now or else I'll give the word to shoot your partner in the head." The man's voice was gravelly with a slight accent she took to be Irish. She recalled hearing that Barker's father and his brothers were first-generation immigrants.

Fear gripped her, clamping her chest like a vise as she lowered the window. She glanced at the photo of Tommy. His smile seemed to sadden, like he was saying goodbye.

She flicked her gaze between the man ahead and the rearview.

"I couldn't hear what you just said. The reception's bad on my phone."

"I'll give you five seconds. Five, four, three ..."

Staring at Tommy, she separated the Glock from the paddle holster, then threw the holster out the window as far as she could. It skipped off the road and into an irrigation ditch off the shoulder.

A spotlight swiveled from the truck behind her and landed on the spot; there was her empty paddle holster among the weeds.

"Nice try. Now throw your gun out," the voice said. "Five, four, three ..."

She closed her eyes and tossed the gun. It clattered on the road outside.

"Good girl."

"Fuck you."

"Drive forward until your car is in the light. Then stop and shut off your engine."

"Five seconds. Four, three ..."

"All right, all right." She let off the brake and coasted forward.

The truck behind moved with her, then stopped where she'd dropped her gun.

As the headlights receded in her mirror, she saw a husky Barker man climb out and pick up her gun, then get back in his truck.

While they tightened the noose she was a whimpering prisoner with a hood over her head.

But what could she do? They had Rachette, and they were going to kill him.

She looked at Tommy's picture again. So what if they did? That was their plan, right? They were going to kill her, and they were going to kill Rachette, no matter what. And in a couple of hours they'd meet Wolf two valleys over and kill him. They'd been watching her. The text had been telling the truth.

She clenched the wheel with soaking wet palms. Except for her lungs, which were pumping at a mile a minute, her body felt locked in rock.

These guys were cattle ranchers, and they were roping her from the front and back and taking her down. This was a slaughter.

Staring death in the face, she morphed her frantic breathing into rapid breaths, psyching herself up for action, though she still didn't know what form it would take. She rolled her shoulders, trying to release herself from the paralyzing cast of fear.

The guy underneath the light stepped toward her now.

She flicked another glance at Tommy, then checked the rearview. The headlights behind her grew. And then the truck parked and the guy climbed out again.

The man with the rifle stepped in front of her vehicle, shielding his eyes with one hand against the truck's headlights behind her.

Patterson saw an opening and struck before it closed. She flicked on her high beams and stomped on the gas pedal.

The tires skidded for a millisecond, then lagged for another as the silicon brain inside did its thing and applied power to all the right places. Then the car screamed and shot forward, sucking her back in the seat.

The man on the road halted and one of his boots slipped. He tried to right himself and point the rifle at her at the very moment she drove over him.

A rifle shot sound merged with the thump of his body against the front and bottom of the car.

The Acura rose and dropped and then she jammed the brakes, cranked the wheel right and hit the accelerator again, driving off the road and up onto a freshly mown, lush green lawn. If they put up a roadblock, she'd go around it, and if a dickhead with a rifle stood in front of her, he'd be squashed.

The car bounced up a small rise and her headlights painted the side of a red-and-white building.

The grass was soft and wet, and the car slid sideways as she turned the wheel left. She flipped a full one hundred and eighty degrees before she even knew what had happened.

The headlights from the truck and the Acura shone over a twisted body lying on the road.

"Shit," she said.

Through her open passenger window, she heard the man moaning in the dirt, like he was in shut-down mode.

"Cormack!" The other man ran to him.

Somewhere in the night, a cow lowed in response to Cormack Barker's agony.

"You bitch!" The other guy raised a pistol in her direction.

A bullet smacked her windshield and the view vanished behind a web of cracks.

Under a hail of bullets, she shifted into reverse and backed up past the pickup and tractor. Once past the blockade, she cranked the wheel and got back on the road.

She shifted back into drive and leaned side to side, trying to see through the windshield.

"Damn it!" Without thinking, she punched the glass.

It bowed out against her two-knuckle shot but held firmly in place.

"Ahh!" She bared her teeth and grabbed her fist, then stuck her head out the side window and pushed the gas.

She slitted her eyes to block the wind and tears streamed back on her temples.

The road ahead climbed up and turned into the pine trees. As she rounded the corner she ducked into the cab and looked over her shoulder just in time to see two headlights bouncing off the lawn and back onto the road.

CHAPTER 39

LEGS CRAMPING, lungs burning, Wolf re-assessed his fitness halfway up the slope. Following a web of game trails, his zigzag route was steep and treacherous, passing through veins of scree and up and over rocks.

One wrong move would send a rock tumbling hundreds of feet, disturbing the otherwise still air and revealing his sneak approach. Then there was the issue of keeping himself on the mountain. The more he pushed, the more sluggish and uncoordinated his muscles became. Still, he dug deep to maintain a steady pace.

As he came across the third pile of animal droppings, he paused and wondered if he'd been looking at a mountain goat or bighorn sheep instead of a Barker or Ethan Womack. Where did those animals sleep?

Shaking off the thought, he continued, staying close to the rocks that hid him from the heat signature on the ridge.

The hidden route meant that the tent at the bottom of the valley was also out of sight, and the longer the climb took, the more anxious he became to get to the top and take another look through the scope.

Finally, he edged his way closer to the top, and as the rocks thinned out he could see down the ridgeline. There was no cover beyond the final outcropping in front of him, and there'd be none on the rounded ridge above.

He ducked down behind a boulder and put the scope to his eye.

The signature was still there, much closer now, and when he clicked over to full zoom the shape of his ambusher sharpened.

His stomach twisted.

For a long few seconds, he stared through the glass, wanting the image to miraculously change, but his would-be sniper turned sideways, and the outline of a cow was unmistakable.

With heart pounding, he sat and aimed down at the valley floor, switching back and forth between the different settings on the scope. Still no movement or other heat signatures.

Perhaps somebody was down there, lying invisible under a thermal blanket after all.

His watch read 10:29.

Maybe he'd caught them in the act of setting up for him and nobody was there yet, which would've been beyond amateur.

Keeping the M4 raised and his finger on the trigger, he rose and walked to the top of the ridge.

A southern wind gusted on the peak, wicking the heat from his body, then settled into a steady breeze.

The landscape on the other side was more gradual and forgiving than the terrain he'd just climbed out of. A smooth hill descended and then flattened out where the shack beckoned.

Behind the structure was another ridge, much lower than where he was now, and beyond that were waves of moonlit mountains and Ashland's pool of twinkling lights on the valley floor.

Keeping low, he raised the rifle and gazed through the scope again. Zooming in, he focused on the small building and saw three different heat signatures glowing through the wood façade. Two appeared to be standing and one was horizontal.

Rachette had been lying down on a bed of straw in the first

picture. And now that they'd severed his pinkie, it stood to reason he'd be lying down. Which meant he was still alive. That was good. He took a breath of relief. Very good.

He did the math: Cormack Barker, Greg Barker, Cormack's two brothers, and Ethan Womack. Add Rachette, and he was looking for six heat signatures and saw only three.

Not good.

Dialing back the zoom, he saw another blob of red near the shack, then another, then a dozen more. Cattle were roaming free, which explained the cow up here on the ridge.

He swept the scope back up the ridgeline towards the animal. It stood motionless, chewing away.

There was no vegetation on the ridge whatsoever, so what was it gnawing on all the way up here? And for nearly an hour while Wolf had climbed the mountain?

Wolf tensed and got to his feet, sensing that something was very wrong.

"Freeze, please," a voice said behind him.

CHAPTER 40

PATTERSON ROUNDED the corner and the headlights disappeared behind the pine trees.

She pictured the man holding his gun in one hand, the steering wheel in the other, foot slammed all the way to the floor, the engine roaring as he looked out a perfectly functioning windshield. She visualized the murderous rage flowing through his body after witnessing her drive over his brother.

The next turn to the right was sharper than she'd anticipated. Leaning her head out the window while cranking the wheel towards a road disappearing around the front of her car was tricky, but she feathered the brakes and negotiated the turn until the road straightened again.

Stealing a glance to the left, she saw tree tops silhouetted against the moon. The slope down to the base of the trees looked steep and rocky.

What was her brilliant plan here? The man was going to catch up in seconds, point a gun, and pick her off as she leaned out the window. She had no weapons, and no chance of outrunning him.

He was out for blood. He'd already shot up her car.

She clenched her teeth and ignored the icy fingers of fear

running up and down her back. Yeah, well … she was out for blood too.

She needed a plan, and she needed it now. This instant.

Pulling the car to the right side of the road, she ducked inside the window, gripped the wheel with both hands, and jammed the brakes, cranking the wheel toward the drop-off.

The tires scraped, and she clenched her eyes and gritted her teeth, hoping she'd stay on flat land until she stopped.

After a long skid, the vehicle came to a stop and rocked back and forth.

She put it in park and pulled the door handle, forgetting she'd have to unlock it first.

"Shit."

She pressed the button and stepped out.

Light grew brighter on the trees as the truck's engine rose in volume.

She got back in and shifted into drive. Then, without hesitating, she dove out of the open door.

On her knees, she watched as her car lurched forward and dipped over the side of the road. She wondered if the underside would catch, but it continued without resistance, and then, just like that, her forty-eight-thousand-dollar baby was gone.

Two separate noises competed for her attention: first, the sound of her car smashing into the trees below. Second, the truck's engine lowering in pitch, about to round the corner and paint her with high beams.

She sprung to the uphill side of the road and skidded onto her ass as she realized she'd chosen the wrong spot for her maneuver. Looming above her was a steep incline.

The truck skidded around the corner.

She dove into the drainage depression on the side of the road, splashing into a puddle.

"Dah!" The cold was excruciating, but she dared not move

because the truck was now out of sight. If she couldn't see him, he couldn't see her.

For now. Until he got closer.

She lay still and prayed. The water seeped into her meager office clothing, cradling her breasts like icy hands, and she thought about Chandler Mustaine reeling his mistress in through his front door.

"Come on, come on ... see it. See it."

The engine's roar approached fast, grew almost deafening, and then the headlights passed and a cold breeze swirled over her.

Then he jammed the brakes and skidded to a halt.

The cold was unbearable now, and she flexed every muscle in her body to counteract it. But she dared not move.

The night lit up as the truck's reverse lights came on. The tires crackled and the engine growled.

She stared at the ripples in the pond, every fiber of her being wanting to turn around and look, but she kept still, watching the light grow around her. She felt the weight of the truck vibrating the ground, heard the brakes squeak, then the lights shut off and the truck stopped right next to her.

With the headlights behind her now, and the red taillights to her front, she was theoretically in the dark, so she dared to peek over the edge of the depression.

The truck had a high clearance, and underneath it she could see layers of shadowed mountains and the lights of Ashland in the distance.

Legs climbed down out of the driver's-side door and stood for a moment. They turned around, as if about to crawl back inside. Or maybe he was about to duck down and say, "Gotcha!". But the truck's spotlight beam swept down over the edge toward her car.

This was not her plan all along. She needed to wake up!

There. A rock larger than her fist, with one side smooth and the other a jagged point, sat at the edge of the puddle. With gritted teeth, she picked it up and crawled underneath the truck.

She probably made noise, but the gurgling engine inches above her head smothered all sound.

And then it shut off.

She froze as the night went dead quiet, save for the engine's ticking.

The man bent down and picked up a rock, and she saw his oily black pistol in his other hand. He stood straight and launched it through the air.

A metallic clank pierced the silence.

She was perched in a pushup position, every muscle flexed. The pain of exertion, along with the cold, became almost unbearable, but she blocked it out, slowed her breathing, and continued to wait while the guy threw another rock.

Clank.

He turned around and climbed up into the cab. The suspension squeaked as his weight shifted inside. She heard a moan, and then another.

"You're all right," the man said. "Be quiet, pansy."

The driver talked to an unconscious man with multiple fractures and probable internal bleeding that would kill him in the next hour. Pansy.

The moaning continued and light sprayed from the driver's-side door.

If he started the truck, she'd have to roll into the center to avoid the oversized wheels, though with one check in the rearview mirror she'd be exposed as he drove away. Mentally, she rehearsed rolling as hard as she could over the edge once she was clear of the wheels.

But there was no way this guy was going to just leave. He had to be sure of this annoying woman's demise, didn't he?

Patterson's muscles trembled, water dripped, her jaw shivered, but still she dared not move. What if there was a pebble placed perfectly next to her toe, just waiting to scrape off another rock and make just enough noise for the guy to bend down and see her? And shoot her point-blank.

The truck rocked and legs appeared again. When the man stepped down she collapsed to her knees, unable to bear the pain anymore.

Holding her breath, she wondered why he appeared to be hesitating. Maybe he had heard something.

She decided that if he bent down again, she would attack with every fiber of her being.

Tommy's smiling face flashed across her mind and she steeled herself for action.

Another moan came and the man stepped aside and slammed the door. There was a click and a puddle of light bathed the ground next to her.

She tensed, and then she noticed the water streaming off her, inching its way toward the man's shoes.

Then a shrill digital ring pierced the silence, and a lightning bolt passed through her body as she thought of her phone. But it was inside the car down in the trees.

"Hey," the man said. "Yeah, I've got her ... I'll bring her up in a few minutes ... when I get there."

The man stepped over the edge.

Immediately he slipped on his ass and skidded down out of sight.

"Goddammit!"

He slapped his flashlight hand on the edge of the road and pulled himself upright, putting his face at eye-level with hers.

Then he saw her.

She scurried out from under the truck, found her feet, and dove off the edge of the road over his head.

The gun went off, and then again. Heat stung the side of her face but the bullets had missed her.

Flipping over him, she grabbed the coat fabric on his shoulder with her left hand, pulled herself in, and bludgeoned the top of his head with the rock as hard as she could. It thudded onto his skull.

Retaining her hold, she landed. Her momentum and the blow to his head brought him off his feet and down the hill with her. She let go and tried to control herself, but ended up rolling down the decline, tangling limbs with him.

Her body flipped backwards again, then again, and she stopped with a violence that pushed a bark from her lungs.

For agonizing seconds, pain filled her torso while swirling red light filled her vision.

The daze lifted and she realized she'd smacked against the back of her car.

The man's fall had been just as horrific, but he was moving.

She tried to suck in air and couldn't. The edges of her vision went dark. The sound of a million tinkling bells filled her ears and her entire body tingled. Like a dying fish, she convulsed, her chest heaving up and down.

All the while, the man was getting to his feet. He was almost there. His face was covered in blood, streaming onto bared teeth.

Then cool air poured into her lungs. She took a breath, and then another. The feeling trickled back into her hands. And then her feet.

"You ... bitch ..." He clamped a huge hand on her neck and then reinforced it with the other.

At least he'd lost the gun, she thought, as he choked the life out of her.

She lifted her left arm and draped it across both of his, then twisted to her right. But he was heavy and strong, and with her back against the car she had little leverage.

But he was dumb, too, and he drew his face close to hers and smiled. So she dug both thumbs into his eyes and pushed, then plucked them both from his skull.

He screamed, his agony matching his brother's, and stumbled backwards.

She spear-handed him in the throat, feeling her fingertips break through the larynx under his sandpaper skin, and his scream turned to gurgling.

He became rabid, punching out as fast and as hard as he could. She ducked to the side and his knuckles connected with the Acura like a hydraulic hammer.

She rolled out of danger, got to her feet, and roundhoused him in the side of the head. And then she stomp-kicked him until he went still.

CHAPTER 41

"I SAID FREEZE!"

Wolf wanted to roll, to shoot, but the voice was still without form, the exact location hidden in the rocks behind him.

"Drop the rifle on the ground. Do it or I'll just shoot you here and you'll never see your buddy again."

Wolf dropped the M4.

Footsteps crunched toward him from behind.

"Drop your Glock, too."

He yanked out his paddle holster and threw it aside.

The footsteps got closer.

"Take off the backpack."

He turned around and shrugged it off his shoulders. "Hi, Greg."

"Toss it."

Wolf threw the bag, at the same time debating whether to rush him.

Barker kept his rifle aimed at Wolf and sidestepped the flying backpack, letting it skitter to the ground behind him.

With his rifle leveled at Wolf's chest, he toed the M4. "See? I knew it. I told my dad and uncles you'd figure it out and come early. I knew you'd have a thermal cam scope and would see my heifer up on the mountain and think it was us. And I knew you'd pick this very spot to climb up. I'm a top-notch detective, Wolf. Always have been."

"Back in the day you were hired by MacLean as a political favor. You never earned your spot. And you're a shit detective, Greg. And everyone knows it and that's why you're unemployed."

"But now I have a gun trained on your ass." Rage amplified his voice. "And nobody else knows about that. I bet you didn't realize I knew about Black Diamond, did you?"

Wolf ignored the question and wondered where the other two people were.

"Like I said, Wolf, I'm a brilliant fucking detective. It took me all of three weeks to figure out who Lucretia Smith's source was."

He smiled, his teeth gleaming in the moonlight.

"Man, I've been thinking about this for a long time. I've watched you, you know. Thought about picking you off with a single shot to the head more than once. Had you in my crosshairs a few times. No, I bet you didn't know that, 'cause you're a shit detective.

"Wanna know what else I've seen? Your girlfriend's naked body." Barker nodded, clearly enjoying the anger darkening Wolf's expression. "Seen her more than a dozen times, I'd say. I've seen you give it to her, too. Pretty good, pretty good. Not nearly as hard as I'll give it to her. Don't worry, she and Ella will be safe and sound when you're dead and gone. I'll make sure of that."

"Not if I blow your head off first," Wolf said through clenched teeth.

Barker ignored him. "Didn't want to bring the midget, huh? I don't blame you. She's annoying as shit."

Wolf shrugged. "She stayed home."

Barker smiled, the expression coming too quickly for Wolf's comfort, and then laughed. It sent a shiver up Wolf's spine.

"She showed up at the ranch a few minutes ago." Barker held up his phone. "My dad and uncle are on their way up with her now, so she'll be joining us shortly. We were watching. Saw you leave her in Rocky Points. And, in case you're wondering, I had a plan for that just in case. But you know Patterson—never could just keep her nose out of things. So she came straight to us."

Wolf studied Barker's face. "Bullshit."

He rolled his eyes. "She showed up at the ranch gates. My dad and uncle have her now. You can believe it or not. It doesn't matter to me."

Wolf knew he was telling the truth.

"You know, I'm feeling good about this. Finally, after two years, here we are, and I'm satisfied. They say revenge is best served cold, but I personally like it piping hot. Well done. Charred black." He flicked his muzzle down the hill toward the shack. "Let's head down and I'll show you what I mean."

Wolf hesitated. Maybe Patterson was here, but she wasn't as hardheaded as Wolf. With any luck, Patterson had figured out the Barkers' involvement and told everyone, and the cavalry was coming. If so, then why had she come alone to the ranch? Where were the flashing lights? He decided he needed to draw out the process as much as possible, just in case.

Barker raised his rifle, aimed carefully, and shot.

Wolf felt the concussion of the bullet ripping the air next to his head.

A high-pitched squeal came from the cow on the ridgeline.

He turned in time to see a dark shape fall into the steep side of the bowl, then tumble over rocks and off a cliff.

Barker waited for the sound of the rolling livestock to stop and laughed. "Jesus, I had that thing tethered to a chain. Snapped it right off." His face darkened. "Unless you want to follow her down, it's time to move. I'll give you five seconds."

CHAPTER 42

"AND HOW DID you and Ethan Womack hook up?" Wolf asked.

The reply was nothing more than the sound of Barker's crunching footsteps. Every attempt to get the man to speak had been met by silence on the walk down. Barker was holding his hand close.

They were down the hill now and near enough to the shack that light pouring from the entrance lit their way. The structure was old, built by a previous generation of men and neglected since.

A beat-up Ford F-150 that Wolf recognized as Ethan Womack's was parked pointing west, as if it had driven up the county road from Highway 734. Greg's newer-model Chevy pickup pointed east, so that the two trucks were nose to nose.

A blue tank stood against the wall of the shack next to the entrance. Judging by the smell in the still air, it contained gasoline, which was good for a family of psychos who liked their revenge served well done.

"Inside," Barker said as they reached the exterior of the building.

How did Ethan Womack fit into this? As Wolf walked closer to the structure, he figured he'd learn that in a matter of seconds.

Come on, cavalry.

The silhouette of a large man holding a pistol loomed in the shack entrance. Then as Wolf got closer, the face came out of shadow and he recognized the toothy grin of Peter Barker, otherwise known by his self-proclaimed nickname of "Peat," in reference to the partially decayed organic matter used for fuel and pulled from bogs in his homeland of Ireland.

"Little Davy Wolf. How nice to see you." Peat's smile disappeared and he looked past him. "What the hell was that shot I heard?"

"I had to get this guy moving," Barker said.

"I called you to make sure you were okay."

"I never got the call." Barker reached down and twisted a knob on a radio on his belt. "Oh, yeah, forgot to turn it back on. Didn't want this asshole hearing me."

Peat shook his head. "Your dad's not responding to my calls or the radio."

"I'll try him."

Peat waved Wolf inside with a silver semi-auto pistol while Barker put the radio to his mouth. "Dad, come in."

"Peat," Wolf said, nodding.

"Come see your little buddy. I think he's conscious." Peat grabbed a water bottle from a workbench and, keeping his gun trained on Wolf, poured it onto a formless pile of blankets resting on the hay.

When the bundle didn't move, Peat pulled back the fabric, revealing Rachette's pale, naked form. He poured some more, and this time the water splashed on his face.

Rachette remained perfectly still.

Wolf stepped into the hay next to his detective and knelt. He put a hand on his forehead and felt intense heat. Better than the alternative, he thought.

Rachette's hands were tied in front with rope. Crusted blood painted his torso and the finger wound oozed pus through a makeshift bandage. A fecal–urine stench rose to meet Wolf's nose.

Peat backed away and waved a hand. "Whew. Well, he's not looking too good. Probably something to do with the infection in his pinkie—sorry, where the pinkie used to be." Peat laughed and it sounded like someone shoveling rocks.

Wolf took Rachette's wrist and felt a weak and slow pulse. He pulled the blankets back up and glared at Peat.

"Awwww, poor guy's hurt, huh? Well, he'll be fuckin' dead like you and that little bitch in no time. Where they at?" he asked Barker.

Barker held up his radio. "They're not answering."

Peat tossed the bottle at Wolf and Wolf blocked it without breaking eye-contact.

Peat seemed entertained and began to laugh, but his mirth turned into a coughing fit.

"Jesus, old man," Barker said, "you have to quit smoking."

Peat raised a middle finger.

In the corner, next to the workbench, stood a thin man watching in silence. He was dressed in ratty jeans and a black winter coat zipped to his chin. On his head was a winter cap pulled low over his ears.

Wolf recognized him as Ethan Womack. He had the same blue eyes as his brother, although Ethan's held less fire.

"Ethan," Wolf said.

"Yeah," Peat said. "Our new friend Ethan. Come on. Say hi, Ethan."

Ethan stood unmoving, his shoulders slumped. His wrists were cuffed together and attached to a chain fastened to the work-bench. His prominent brow was fixed in a relaxed position and he stared, unblinking, at Peat.

"Chatty guy," Peat said, hitching a thumb and shaking his head. "Guy was armed to the teeth when we found him. Wearing a flak jacket and had a fifty-cal sniper rifle in his truck. That and this Kimber 1911." Peat displayed the silver pistol in his hand. "You're lucky we stopped him before he got to you, Davy."

Wolf narrowed his eyes and looked at Barker, who was now standing inside with the rifle on his shoulder. "What is this?"

"This guy was following you for days." Barker hitched a thumb to Ethan. "I saved you. You're welcome."

"I don't get it."

"You don't have to get it," Peat said. "But you move and I shoot you in the head. Get that? Now sit next to your friend and shut up."

Rachette's head lolled as Wolf sat down next to him.

"Call him on his phone," Peat said to Barker.

"I don't have reception."

Peat pulled out a cell and dialed. "Worthless, you know that? Jesus, one bar. Reception's a joke."

"Yeah, well, we are at twelve thousand five hundred feet, so." Barker shook his head and looked at Wolf as if to say, can you believe this guy?

"I'm not getting them," Peat said. "Either of them."

The cavalry, Wolf thought, this time letting the hope fill him.

"Like you said, reception's shit. They'll come when they come."

"No, it's ringing." Peat eyed his nephew. "They're not answering."

"It's ringing on your end. Who knows? ... they're probably busy tying her up, or scraping her dead body off the ground or something." Barker winked at Wolf.

Wolf caught movement in the corner of the shack and they all looked.

Ethan Womack had come out to the front of the workbench, and Peat and Barker turned toward him.

"Hey, there. What's going on?" Peat asked, lowering his phone and putting it in his pocket.

"I have to ..." Ethan's eyes shifted back and forth. "... have to pee." He looked like a child trying to lie about eating the last cookie.

Barker and Peat exchanged a glance.

"What do you think?" Barker asked.

"I think the screwing around is over, that's what I think. Let's get this show on the road." Peat raised his pistol and pulled the trigger.

There was a click.

Ethan crossed his hands in front of his face and took a step back.

Peat nonchalantly racked the pistol slide. Aimed it again.

"No, wait!" Barker yelled.

Peat shot Ethan in the chest.

Wolf closed his eyes as Ethan flew back like he'd been kicked by a horse. Through the ringing in his ears he heard Ethan crumple on the ground. When he opened his eyes, Peat's pistol was aimed at him.

"Wait a minute." Barker raised Peat's aim. "Stop! You've already screwed this up. How many times do we have to go over this? If we want to make it look like Ethan and Wolf got in a shootout, then why would Wolf have shot Ethan with Ethan's gun?"

Peat creased his forehead and lowered the weapon. "I don't know. So they switched guns somehow. Got in a fist fight and ended up with each other's guns. Boom. Shot each other. They're gonna be fried to a crisp."

"You're dumber than a cow."

"Okay, so give me Wolf's gun."

"How about you pull the chains off this corpse and I'll take care of the rest of this, okay, old man?"

"Suit yourself." Peat crouched down next to Ethan. "He's still breathing."

Barker looked annoyed at the news. "I'll take care of it. Get the fucking chains off."

Barker pulled Wolf's pistol from his paddle holster and stepped forward. His eyes were calm pools of hate, and there was zero hesitation in his movements as he raised the weapon.

"And what about the cow you shot up there?" Wolf asked the first question that popped into his mind, then kept talking. "How are you going to deal with that cow carcass with your bullet lodged in it? They're going to find that."

Barker nodded. "That's a good point. Thank you, Chief. I'll have to deal with that."

"When? During or after this place is sky-high in flames? A big fire like this one's gonna draw attention. You'd better deal with that cow first."

Barker laughed. "Or I could just shoot you, then go deal with it, and then set you guys on fire."

Wolf swallowed.

There was a squeak outside, and then the sound of an engine with crackling tires.

Barker lowered the gun. "There they are. You know what? I'd rather you and Patterson experience this together."

Peat walked to the door with an armload of silver chains. "Let's get her in here and get this done. Is he serious about the cow?"

Barker nodded absently, looking like he'd just been pulled out of a dream.

"Then we're going to have to haul it out. We're supposed to be down at the ranch, ignorant of all this, not up here shooting cows at the same time it went down. You're worried about whose gun killed who, and you're leaving bullets in cow carcasses? Like you said, those forensic guys can figure—"

"All right!" Barker pointed his pistol at his uncle. "Just go get her."

Peat smiled with something that looked like pride and disappeared through the doorway.

"What the fuck?" Peat said.

CHAPTER 43

"Huhhhh ... huhhhh ..."

The guy's moaning had gone past the point of making Patterson uneasy. Now her sanity wavered.

"Shut up!"

Like a snoring man woken briefly, he stopped and started again. "Huhhhh ..."

She'd left one man dead on the side of the road three miles back, and as if the horror of that wasn't enough, now her failed attempt at murder sat in an unnatural position next to her. Every bump in the road drove him closer to death.

Twice she'd retched, and the more noise this guy made, the stronger her urge to vomit.

"Huhhhh ..."

That was it. She stopped and heaved out the door until there was nothing left. She sucked in deep breaths while the cool air dried the sweat on her forehead. By the time she'd pulled herself back inside and shut the door, she was a new woman.

Now she let the anger flow through her again. Let this man suffer. They'd both gotten what was coming to them. And if Greg Barker and Ethan Womack were up here with Rachette, they'd get what they deserved, too.

The dash clock read 11:39 p.m. Did that mean Wolf was twenty-one minutes from an ambush one valley over? Would Rachette be in the shed?

She was above the tree line now and the road finally swung to the north. Remembering the aerial view of the road, she knew she was close. A mile, maybe less.

One positive in this otherwise abysmal situation struck her: before his head had been mushed, the man had taken a phone call and said, "I have her. I'll be up there in a few minutes." Or something to that effect.

When she'd tried to figure out who'd called him, his phone had been locked with a PIN. But the fact remained, whoever he'd spoken to was expecting him in this truck with her as a prisoner, which meant she had the element of surprise.

She drove over a rise and saw light in the distance. Two pickup trucks were parked nose to nose, one of which she recognized as Ethan Womack's old Ford F-150. The other looked like Greg Barker's newer ridiculously lifted and tricked-out pickup. The light she saw poured out of a shack next to the vehicles.

Getting her bearings, she gazed north to a barren ridge. Wolf would be on the other side. Which meant someone had to be over there waiting for him. Maybe they'd even moved Rachette there.

"Huhhhh ..."

She pictured a fifty-caliber sniper rifle being pointed at her right now and decided: so be it. It would put her out of her misery.

Leaning into the windshield, she let off the gas and coasted the big pickup down the final stretch, keeping a sharp eye on the doorway and the newly acquired pistol in her right hand.

She got closer, and then closer still, until she could've thrown the pistol and hit the door.

She clicked on the high beams, so anyone trying to look through the windshield would be blasted with light, and got out.

Rounding the back of the truck, she saw a white-bearded man exit the shed with his head down.

She stood still at the tailgate and watched him through the windows.

He tossed something on the ground and it clanked. Then he squinted into the headlights and put a hand to his face. He walked to the passenger door and ripped it open.

Patterson moved fast around the back of the truck and raised the gun.

"What the fuck?" Cormack Barker spilled out onto the white-bearded man. "Cormack!" He struggled to lower him to the ground. "Cormack ... where's Shamus? What happened to—"

"Freeze right there," Patterson said, pointing the gun.

The man swiveled around fast.

She took a step back and leveled on his center mass. "Shamus is dead. I killed him. And I'll kill you next if you move."

A movement near the doorway to the shack caught her eye. Greg Barker leaned out, pointing a gun at her.

CHAPTER 44

WOLF HEARD desperation in Peat's voice through the thin wall of decayed wood. Then he heard Patterson.

The sound reached Barker's ears at the same time, and he snapped out of his reverie and inched his way to the door with the Glock poised to fire.

With each step Barker took, Wolf was pulled with him, his muscles tensed to spring. And then Barker forgot the world inside the shack and ducked out the doorway.

Wolf ran at full speed, tackling him just as the pistol went off.

CHAPTER 45

PATTERSON'S HAND exploded in pain as her pistol spun to the ground.

She bent down to pick it up and hesitated. Shock overcame her at the sight of her left thumb. It was bent back and bleeding profusely—the muscle fibers underneath the skin of her palm exposed.

A boot filled her vision and connected with her face, and then she was eating dirt.

Blinking, she came to and searched frantically for the pistol on the ground. She found it, pointing at her face. "Get up!"

She got up and swayed, then tumbled to the ground as the man pulled her. A sharp, metallic blow hit her in the back of the head and warmth flowed down her neck.

She lay still, listening to grunting and shuffling accompanied by the occasional slap of fist on flesh.

A few moments later, she realized that Wolf and Barker were fighting, wrestling on the ground near the open doorway to the shack.

Barker was on top, raining savage blows onto Wolf's face. He was a much bigger man and she knew the odds were against her former boss. But then again, she'd seen Wolf do the impossible before.

On cue, Wolf caught Barker's fist and must've dug into a pressure point because Barker howled in pain and rolled sideways.

Wolf landed a few punches.

Kill him! she thought with gritted teeth.

The two separated and stood.

Barker wiped blood off his lip, put up his fists and bounced on his toes.

"Yee-haw!" The man with the white beard fired a shot in the air. "Okay, this is what I'm talking about!" He looked down at Patterson and stomped kicked her.

She'd suffered broken ribs before and knew the pain it brought. She had no doubt that bone had just been cracked near her armpit.

"Let's go, bitch!" Greg said to Wolf, slapping his own chest.

Wolf dove at him and they circled toward Patterson, then behind her and towards the back of the shed.

Turning would cause more pain than she could bear so she rested her head on the ground and listened. She heard more blows, more feet shuffling, more taunts from White Beard, and the sound of Greg Barker gaining confidence with each fist connecting with flesh.

Barker grunted one last time as he landed another hit, and then there was nothing but the sound of his heavy breathing.

The man with the beard was back near the truck, examining Cormack. "He's hurt bad. We have to take him to the hospital."

"Yeah? And how's that gonna go down?" Barker said between quick breaths. "We need a private doctor."

Patterson heard footsteps, and then Greg grabbed her by the hand and dragged her. A whimper escaped her lips. It felt like the sharp edges of broken ribs were cutting tissue inside of her.

"What did you do to him? What did you do to my dad?"

She resisted telling him she'd just run over his ass with a few thousand pounds of Acura. The guy didn't need more goading into a dark place. He was already there and Patterson didn't like the looks of it.

Barker dragged her through the doorway and up onto a lump of blankets resting on hay. "It's time to have a bonfire."

The blankets stirred, and she realized Rachette was underneath them.

A few seconds later, Barker and his uncle came in carrying Wolf. They dropped him next to her and backed up.

"All right. Let's finish this right now," Barker said. "First thing's first. I'm gonna blow Wolf's head off, and I want you to watch it."

Barker studied her. She was lying on her side, facing in the opposite direction to Wolf.

"Turn around so you can watch."

"Go fuck yourself." The act of talking punched her ribs with pain again.

Barker bent down and grabbed her by the hair, flipped her over, and dropped her so she faced Wolf.

He stared up with vacant eyes. Both his lips were split and oozing blood while his jaw wriggled side to side.

"Where's Ethan?" White Beard's voice was frantic.

Barker twisted. "What?"

With Barker on his heels, White Beard walked to the doorway. When he stopped, the two men collided.

"Move it! Get out there an—"

A boom rocked the interior of the shack, like someone had cupped their hands and slapped Patterson's ears.

The two men's heads exploded and she closed her eyes as warm flesh hit her like shrapnel.

She held her breath, feeling tiny droplets bathe every inch of her exposed skin. And then the grisly shower subsided.

CHAPTER 46

THE SOUND RIPPED Wolf out of semiconsciousness. Like standing on the highway in a windstorm, he felt tiny particles hit his chin.

Warm, pink mist swirled and rained down. Shutting his eyes, he knew that one of his detectives had just died.

As he waited his turn, Jack's image filled his mind and he concentrated on it. His son's steeled expression told him not to worry, that he could take care of himself, that he'd be all right without his father.

Lauren's pretty, freckled face appeared next. She stood in a meadow with Ella in her arms. The little girl's green eyes were squinted like her mother's as she laughed at one of Wolf's jokes.

Behind them a murky form stood in front of blazing white light. Then it sharpened into a familiar, shapely silhouette—Sarah, his ex-wife and the only other woman he'd ever loved.

The hallucinations disappeared, and when Wolf opened his eyes a man stood over him, cradling a tournament-modified fifty-caliber sniper rifle.

"Are you okay?" Ethan asked.

Wolf blinked through a persistent red blur, wondering if he heard things correctly.

"What are you going to do?"

Wolf turned his head toward Patterson's voice. "You're alive." Relief hit him like an avalanche at seeing her sitting up next to him.

She ignored him and looked up at Ethan Womack. "Ethan, what are you doing?"

Ethan looked genuinely confused. "I'm seeing if you're okay."

"Oh," she said. "Okay, thanks. Can you please lower the rifle?"

"It was my fault," Wolf said.

Ethan's eyes flashed and then narrowed.

"I dropped Sergeant Henning. I pulled him from your brother's grip. I shouldn't have put him in the hut with those women and children. It was my fault."

Ethan stared at him with unblinking eyes. "You have to call an ambulance."

"Can you please put that down?" Patterson asked Ethan again.

"You have to call an ambulance." Ethan walked to the workbench and put down the gun. "Your friend is very sick."

Patterson turned to Wolf and held out her hand. "You have your phone?"

Fighting through the pain shooting through his shoulder, Wolf dug out his cell and handed it over. "Here."

"You have reception, thank God." She dialed. "It's going through. Tammy, this is Heather. We found Tom. Listen carefully. We need a medevac helicopter near Turkey Hill Ranch Road. Is this phone showing up on the map? ... all right ..."

Wolf sat up and gazed at Ethan Womack.

Ethan stared back with a vacant expression. "You're David Wolf."

He nodded.

"I had something."

"You had something?"

"For you."

"Okay." Wolf narrowed his eyes. "Had what?"

"A video."

"Okay."

Apparently done talking, Ethan sat down on the dirt and watched Patterson.

Straining to keep upright, pain throbbed through every inch of Wolf's upper body, so he leaned back and closed his eyes.

CHAPTER 47

"DAVID!"

Lauren dodged a gurney being wheeled down the hospital hallway and ran to Wolf.

"My God." She stopped and studied his face with the eyes of a nurse. "What happened to you? I came as soon as I heard. What happened?"

"Where's Ella?"

"She's downstairs. I didn't know ... they said you were fine but I didn't want to scare her. She's with a friend of mine from the second floor NICU." She cradled his face with her cool hands and ran a thumb over his mouth.

He ran his tongue over his split lower lip, then the upper. "Got in a bit of a scuffle."

"My God," she said again.

"You should see the other guy."

"I heard something about Tom Rachette being kidnapped, and he's in critical condition. And Heather was hurt, too? What happened?"

Wolf pulled her into a hug, certain the pain in his shoulder meant he'd ripped cartilage or torn a tendon. "Tom's been upgraded to stable. He was severely dehydrated and needed some antibiotics to help the infection in his hand, but his vitals are on the rise. Heather's fine. Dislocated thumb and some cuts."

"I heard his finger was severed. Is that true?"

Wolf raised his own left hand, displaying the stump where his pinkie finger used to be, and told her about the past twenty-four hours in as simple terms as possible.

When he was done, she asked, "Greg Barker? When he talked to us on the sidewalk yesterday morning ... he'd already killed Pat Xander and kidnapped Tom?"

He nodded and pulled her head to his chest. "Try not to think about it."

Though that was easier said than done. Closing his own eyes, he watched a slideshow of bad images. First the dead body in the trunk, then Paul Womack's suicide video, and then Greg and Peter Barker's entangled headless corpses.

He felt desperate to rest but suspected he'd need drugs to find sleep anytime soon.

"How did the art show go?"

They separated and she shook her head.

"What?"

"Oh ..."

"What? What happened?"

Avoiding his gaze, she said, "Let's just say I kneed Baron in the nuts when he tried to kiss me afterwards."

Anger flared inside Wolf, but when Lauren looked up with her shimmering emerald eyes, he smiled, sensing that was all she needed. "Okay. We'll just say that you kneed him in the nuts then."

She smiled and playfully head-butted his chest, and they walked arm in arm down the hall and through some automatic doors.

In the next hallway, laughter spilled out of Rachette's hospital room.

Lauren knocked as they entered.

The window blinds were drawn open, letting in a shaft of morning light from the sun rising between two peaks. Patterson stood at the foot of the hospital bed and Charlotte was bedside. Both wore smiles and wiped fresh tears.

"Hey, there they are," Rachette said with a dreamy lilt.

"Wow, you're looking better," Wolf lied.

His detective's pale skin glistened with sweat. His swollen eyelids were cracked open, revealing bloodshot eyes.

"Just woke up," Rachette said. "I was telling the girls I could smell them."

Charlotte smiled and kissed him on the cheek. More tears spilled as she stroked her husband's stubble.

Patterson backed away and turned to Wolf and Lauren. Eyeing Wolf's face, she said, "I see you're still looking like shit."

Wolf smiled, then put a hand to his lips and groaned. "Everyone needs to stop making me smile."

Lauren cuddled him and made some comforting noises.

"Where're Scott and Tommy?" he asked.

Patterson pointed at the wall. "Down in my room, sleeping in."

"Sounds like a good idea. Been a long night."

"It was." Every movement, every word looked like it pained Patterson.

"I heard you hurt your ribs," Lauren said. "How are they?"

"Not bad. Two hairline fractures." Patterson looked Wolf in the eye for a long moment, then held up her bandaged hand. "We've had some sort of curse put on our left hands, apparently."

Wolf nodded, then locked his gaze on her's. "Thank you. I don't know how the hell you did it, but thank you."

"You're welcome." There seemed to be a hint of shame in her voice.

He knew nothing of the details yet. The rest of the night had been too much of a blur, with helicopters landing and taking off, and flashing vehicles driving up the valley, and his head ringing from Barker's savage blows.

But he knew she'd killed two Barkers to save the two men standing in this room.

"You did what you had to do," Wolf said.

"I personally can't wait to hear the story." Sheriff MacLean appeared in the doorway.

"Hey, Sheriff," Rachette said, sounding like he was about to lose consciousness again.

MacLean walked inside. "Hey, Tom. Geez, he's out of it, huh?"

Rachette closed his eyes and went to sleep, but his bandaged hand remained pointed straight in the air.

Her nursing instincts taking over, Lauren walked to Rachette and guided his hand back to his chest.

"Can I talk to you?"

Wolf nodded and followed MacLean out into the hallway.

MacLean led the way to a bank of windows at the end of the hall and studied Wolf's face. "You look like shit."

"So I hear."

A family of deer stood outside, chewing on grass shoots sprouting between dew-covered sage.

"What happened?" MacLean asked.

Wolf thought about his answer and told his story, starting with the video and ending with Ethan Womack literally blowing Greg and Peter Barker's heads off.

MacLean stared at him. "You knew the Barkers were behind it."

Wolf said nothing.

"Why didn't you tell me?" MacLean's question contained no judgment.

"I had no choice. They had Rachette and I had to take care of it myself."

"Sounds like you got your ass handed to you and Patterson took care of it herself."

Wolf smiled and closed his eyes. "Yeah."

MacLean gazed out the window and petted his mustache. As if he'd been stung by a bee, he slapped his pants pocket and pulled out his phone. "Damn it. Another message from White. DA's office is freaking out about this one. Ethan Womack is off limits until we meet on this. We have his doctor coming up from Taos right now. He'll be in the station this afternoon. Last night, he was an uncooperative asshole. Now that we have his patient in custody, seems he's had a change of heart."

One floor below, Ethan Womack was being treated for three broken ribs where a slug had hit a bulletproof shield somehow installed in his coat. The details of that revelation were still as murky as the past twenty-four hours.

"We need to do a trace on Paul Womack's phone," Wolf said.

"We already did that." MacLean put a palm on the window. "Everyone has a cell nowadays, and when we noticed Paul's corpse was sans phone I ordered a triangulation."

"Where is it?"

MacLean pushed off from the window and turned to Wolf. "Last place it pinged was five miles north of Ashland."

"That's near Turkey Hill Ranch," Wolf said.

MacLean nodded and gazed out the window.

Without asking, Wolf could tell that the sheriff was thinking about Ellen and Chad Mink. "I want to see that phone first." He rubbed a tender spot on his head.

"Yeah, well, you need to rest. Like I said, you look like shit. Dang it." He slapped his leg again and drew his phone. "Yeah ... yeah ... son of a bitch. I have to call White. Just ... get some rest. And when you do get back into the station, please bring a full report." He poked the phone screen and put it to his ear. "And one word for you."

"What?"

"Ice. Looks like a golf ball got sewn into your upper lip."

CHAPTER 48

THE NEXT MORNING, Wolf sat in his cool leather office chair and moved his computer mouse, thankful that the computer screen flickered to life and there was no lengthy booting-up process in his future.

The past twenty-four hours had been spent reclined, though anything but relaxing. Instead of mindlessly watching *The Rifleman* reruns and drinking Newcastles on the couch at home, which he would have enjoyed, he'd been sitting in thinly cushioned hospital chairs waiting for Rachette to regain consciousness.

When that had seemed unlikely for another day, Wolf had reluctantly gone home with Lauren and spent his time writing up a full report for MacLean on Lauren's laptop. The exercise had raised many more questions than answers about Ethan Womack.

For instance, how had Ethan become ensnared by the Barkers in the first place? Had he approached them or they him? The fingerprints on the bullet casings found at Pat Xander's murder scene could be explained simply enough—the gun used had been Ethan Womack's Kimber 1911 pistol. The ammunition was his.

Had Ethan placed his fingerprints all over Pat's car against his will or on purpose?

Scrolling through a list of bureaucratic emails only served to numb Wolf's mind even more.

Standing up from his desk, he gazed out the window and watched the chairlift cables glinting on Rocky Points Resort, stitching the mountain like the scars on Ethan Womack's skull.

A therapist named Tennimen had shown up the previous evening to help with the delicate process of interrogating Ethan Womack. Questioning a mentally impaired person required a level of care that was above and beyond normal procedures, and District Attorney Sawyer White had erred on the side of caution with his recommendations for Ethan Womack's case. Rightfully so, Wolf supposed. But that meant answers could be a long time coming.

He pulled out his cellphone and scrolled to Deputy Charlotte Munford's number, then hovered his thumb over the call button. Deciding against bothering her, he pocketed his phone and sat back in his chair.

Two knocks hit his door and it swung open before he could open his mouth.

"Wolf." MacLean thrust his head inside. "Back already?"

MacLean came in and shut the door behind him.

"Come in."

MacLean walked over carrying a large plastic evidence bag in his hands. Inside was a folded garment Wolf recognized as the jacket Ethan had been wearing when he was shot by Peter "Peat" Barker.

"You seen this shit?" MacLean dropped it on his desk. "This is a Tenzeneta model jacket, made by Carlos Cabrillo Clothing. It's the latest in bulletproof casual wear."

Wolf raised his eyebrows.

"Yeah. Only a few companies in the world doing this type of thing, and T 'n' T Guns in Taos carries a few of these babies. This one right here will run you a cool two thousand five hundred dollars. I talked to Ethan Womack's employer, who said he gave Ethan a thirty percent employee discount last December. Apparently, it took him a year to save up for it. Wore it everywhere, even in eighty-degree weather." MacLean looked like he was picturing himself wearing it. "Can stop a .45 ACP round from point-blank range. Which I can't believe, feeling this thing." He pinched it through the plastic. "The armor inside is bendy. Pick it up. It's not much heavier than a normal winter coat."

Wolf did, and concurred with MacLean's assessment with a nod, then dropped it on the desk.

The sheriff picked up the bag, tucked it under his arm, and put on a serious expression. He dug into his pocket and produced a USB memory stick, then placed it in front of Wolf.

"What's this?"

"We found Paul Womack's phone at Turkey Hill. And we found the original, pre-edited suicide video on it."

Wolf picked it up and twirled it in his fingers. "I asked you to let me see it first."

MacLean's face blushed. "Lorber and I saw it when we transferred the video onto this USB, which I'm graciously giving you now."

Wolf nodded, unsure why he was so self-conscious about others watching it beforehand. His chest and throat tightened, and something akin to dread descended on him.

"And you're sure the Barkers edited it?"

MacLean nodded. "Cormack had a computer with video-editing software on it. Lorber says there's no doubt, and if our resident computer nerd says so, then ..."

Wolf's vision blurred as he twirled the USB some more. He heard the screams of the Afghani women and children echoing in his head.

"He doesn't off himself in it," MacLean said, all seriousness in his voice now. "That noise at the end of the video you got was put there by the Barkers." Knocking on Wolf's desk, he turned and walked toward the door. "I'll give you some privacy. Then come see me, all right?"

He looked up from the USB and nodded. "Yeah."

The door clicked shut and MacLean's cologne whirlwind settled.

Slowly, Wolf bent down and inserted the USB in the computer tower, then pulled up the file directory onscreen. Two files were listed.

The first was named The Barker-Edited Version.

The second, Paul Womack's Original Video.

He clicked play on the first.

"You—witness. Wolf. It's ... your fault. Wolf. It's ... your fault."

"You—witness. Wolf. It's ... your fault. Wolf. It's ... your fault."

Black screen. Pop.

He closed the video player and clicked the next file.

Leaning back in his chair, he took a deep breath. Then he tilted forward towards the monitor and watched as Paul Womack's face flashed onscreen.

Paul stared at his phone from inches away, so close that Wolf could see the freckles on his nose. And then the image swirled and Paul propped the phone on the table, adjusting it to point at a vacant chair.

Carrying a Beretta M9 pistol, Paul Womack walked to the chair and sat down.

"Hello, Wolf." He smiled warmly, the way Wolf remembered the first day of RIP. "There's no way to preface this, so I'm just going to begin. I've always wanted to explain to you who I was, but I was afraid of how you'd look at me. I was afraid you'd walk away from being the best friend I've ever had. I hope that now, after you've met my brother, you'll understand what I meant that day in Bamyani."

The room closed in on Wolf as he thought back.

"Do you remember?" Paul said, pausing enough for Wolf to

retrieve the memory. "Right after you got me out of the hut. After I murdered that innocent woman and her little girl. Robbed them of their lives. Remember what I told you?"

Paul's mouth curled into a smile that failed to reach his eyes. "Of course you remember. And now you see how God repaid me, right? You were there to witness it. It's so awe-inspiring to me that God spoke to me in such clear, uncertain terms. I hope that by thinking back on that day with Henning, you know that God exists. And he's an ironic son of a bitch, ain't he?"

He stared into nothing for another few moments.

"I also hope you realize that nothing was your fault." He glared into the cellphone camera for a moment then sat back. "So what do I want from you? Why am I sending you this? Well, first, I wanted to explain myself. Check. And, sorry, but I must call on my fellow Ranger one last time. Sometimes endings are messy, and this one's going to be particularly bad. So, please, send somebody else here to clean me up and don't let my brother see me with my head falling out of my skull. I've asked him to deliver my cellphone to you. I told him it contained an important video and to not watch it under any circumstances. He's to make sure you watch it before returning home. He'll comply. I told him it was his mission." Paul rolled his eyes. "It's a thing we do. He's gifted with a gun because he always wanted to be like us. He loves to act the part. He's a real good kid." Tears reflected on Paul's cheeks. "A good man. He'll be better off without me."

Paul stared at the gun on the table for a long time, then his eyes slid up to the cellphone camera lens.

"It's a big favor, I know, and you sure as hell don't owe me anything, but still ... I know I can count on you. You were always there for me, Wolfie. Goodbye, brother."

His chair squeaked as he stood up and walked to the cellphone. Again, his face filled the view and tears dropped on the screen. Then it went black.

Wolf stared at the computer for a time, letting a tear slide down his cheek as he thought of the sadness Paul Womack had endured over his life.

CHAPTER 49

WOLF OPENED MacLean's office door and leaned inside. "Sir?"

"Wolf, come in." MacLean gestured across his desk. "I want you to meet Dr. Tennimen."

A man with a head of tight brown curls stood and shook Wolf's hand. "Nice to meet you."

"Likewise." The doctor's hand was soft and he smelled like spicy cologne. He pulled a wool sweater over the waist of his corduroy pants and sat back down.

District Attorney White sat next to him, giving Wolf a hawk-eye stare. "You look like crap."

"Thank you, sir."

"Sorry, no chair." MacLean said.

Wolf was unsure why, but they all seemed to be staring at him. "What's happening?"

DA White took to picking a piece of lint off his pants.

After clearing his throat, MacLean said, "Dr. Tennimen, why don't you introduce yourself and let us know what's going on."

"Right. Thank you. I'm Doctor Tennimen and I'm a psychologist at Taos University, specializing in cognitive-behavioral therapy as well as therapy involving traumatic brain injuries. I work with Ethan Womack on a weekly basis, and I've gotten to know him well over the last two years. They called me in to assist in the interview."

Wolf nodded. "Yes, I heard."

The doctor nodded, flicking a glance at MacLean.

"I'll cut to the chase. Ethan's not speaking," MacLean said. "Because he wants to speak to you." He raised his eyebrows and nodded. "He says it's his mission that he speak to you, and only you."

"Okay."

Tennimen shifted in his chair, looking uncomfortable, but not nearly as uneasy as DA White, who stood and began pacing at the back of the office.

"Ethan suffered a horrific fall when he was a child," Tennimen said. "He fell down a flight of concrete stairs, cracking his head open. He had depressed skull fractures, meaning the bone pushed into his brain, causing extensive damage: intracerebral hematoma, subdural hematoma. The arachnoid membrane—"

"Hey, Doc, now you have my brain bleeding."

Everyone looked at MacLean.

"What?"

"Doctor Tennimen," DA White said, "I think what our eloquent sheriff means to say is, can you please stick to using layman's terms?" He looked at Wolf. "This is to give you a little background before you go in there, okay, Detective? Please, continue, Doctor."

"Ethan Womack suffered ... severe brain injury when he was four years old. For years, he was set back considerably, mentally and physically. Eventually, however, his neuroplasticity ... his, er, brain compensated. Meaning, the parts that weren't damaged took over, and the parts that were damaged died.

"For instance, growing up after the injury, Ethan Womack had very good motor skills, but lacked those of communication. He could throw and catch almost immediately after his recovery, but his speech abilities tumbled backward. Like before the accident, he was athletic in certain sports, such as basketball, but when it came to spelling his name, it took three years for him to remember the order of the letters. He could not, and still cannot, recognize a tune. Cannot sing."

"But he likes shooting guns," MacLean said.

"Yes. His father used to shoot with Ethan and his older brother on their family land. That's something he's continued to be passionate about."

MacLean nodded.

"His social skills are lacking. He went to the local public school and was put in the special-education program, where he was one of two kids. Growing up, he had no friends except his older brother, Paul Womack.

"Paul was fiercely protective of his little brother, and from what I can gather, used to beat up anyone who'd insult or make fun of him. As for Ethan Womack as an adult, I can tell you that as a thirty-nine-year-old he's much the same as a child. He's gentle. He's kind."

"He was charged with aggravated assault," MacLean said. "Isn't that how you two hooked up?"

Tennimen nodded. "Ethan's mother had just died from ovarian cancer and, according to the other employees at the gun shop, the other man had egged him on. Making fun of his mother in a sexual way. As far as I'm concerned, the other man was a monster and deserved what he got."

MacLean pulled the corners of his mouth down. "Can't argue with that."

"Where was I?" Tennimen looked flustered. "Despite the charges brought against him, and despite his outward appearance of being ... dangerous, he—"

"You mean, the fifty-caliber rifle he drives around with in his car? Or the 1911? Or the bulletproof clothing he wears? Or the arsenal he has in his backyard? The armor-piercing rounds?"

Tennimen's face boiled red. "That arsenal was inherited from his father, who also passed away within the last five years. Another thing he inherited from his father was an obsession about self-protection. I think the accident somehow enhanced that obsession in him."

MacLean nodded, keeping the skeptical look.

"May I continue?"

"Yes, Doctor, please." White's eyes flashed at MacLean.

"One thing we've been working on, too, is his trust in strangers. He's overly trusting. He's been duped by email scams twice. His employer at T 'n' T Guns has to monitor him when he's on the computer. If you were to approach him on the street and tell him you have a present for him, and that you'd like him to come with you, you'd have him hooked." The doctor snapped his fingers. "Simple as that.

"On the opposite side of the coin, he's terrified of social situations with multiple people involved. Which is a strange dichotomy and one we're trying to work through. It's interesting from a medical point of view. It seems that if he's expected to engage, he's terrified. Whereas if somebody engages *with* him, it's like the social-anxiety switch isn't flipped."

"Unless we're trying to interview him about his involvement in a murder," MacLean said. "Then he gets all the social anxiety in the world, because he's not talking."

Tennimen held up his hand, conceding the point. "It's not an exact science. Clearly he has a special need to speak to Detective Wolf, here, and he's subject to moods and emotions like the rest of us. I'm just telling you what I know."

The doctor's face turned red and he seemed through talking.

"Thank you, Doctor," Wolf said. "That information will definitely help."

"You're welcome."

"Well?" MacLean clapped and stood, which made Tennimen close his eyes.

The sheriff and district attorney stared at one another for a beat.

White rubbed his face, then gave a nod like he was authorizing a nuclear detonation. "Let's go."

CHAPTER 50

"WHY DID you come to Rocky Points, Ethan?"

"I was on a mission for my brother. He says you guys were in the army together."

Wolf bristled at his usage of the present tense when describing Paul. "And what exactly was the mission?"

"To go to Rocky Points and find you. And to deliver Paul's cellphone, 'cause he put a movie on it for you to watch."

Leaning forward in his chair, he was wide-eyed and answering without hesitation. Ethan Womack's social-anxiety switch was in the off position.

"We looked at your work computer and saw you did some Google searches on me, Ethan."

"Yes."

"And why did you do that?"

"I was working that day. I wanted intel. My brother always says that not gathering enough intel is a sure way to a failed mission."

Wolf nodded. "And then what? After work that day, what did you do?"

"I drove up to Colorado."

"Okay. And you came to Rocky Points, right?"

"Yes."

Wolf could feel MacLean's impatience seeping through the one-way glass. This exchange was too laborious, and to get a full picture of what was happening in this man's mind was going to take three hours at this rate.

Intensity burned behind Ethan's eyes. He was excited to be here.

He's gifted with a gun because he always wanted to be like us. He loves to act the part.

Wolf straightened in his chair and let his eyebrows slide down. "I want you to give me a full debriefing, soldier."

Ethan's eyes flashed. "Yes, sir."

"Proceed."

"I ... I came into Rocky Points and checked into the Edelweiss Hotel. I went to your house, but you weren't home. Nobody answered your door. And then I saw a lady and her kid there, and I didn't want to bother them, so I left."

"You knew where I worked. Why didn't you come to see me at the Sheriff's Department?"

Ethan blinked rapidly. "I ... I ..."

"You what, soldier?" He kept his tone just shy of drill sergeant.

"I was afraid."

"Afraid to come in to talk to me?"

Ethan looked down and nodded.

Wolf dialed down the drill-sergeant routine. "Okay. What happened next?"

"I watched you."

"You watched me?"

"I was ... gathering intel."

"And then what?"

"I did that for the first day. And also the second day. I followed you in my truck, trying to talk to you. But I was scared."

Wolf nodded for him to continue.

"And a man approached me. Told me he knew what I was

doing. That I was following David Wolf and he was going to tell on me. I told him, no, I was on a mission to talk to you. I showed him the cellphone and he took it. And he watched the video and—"

"Did you watch the video?" Wolf asked.

Ethan shook his head. "No, sir. Paul ordered me not to watch it, sir. No matter what."

"Proceed."

"He watched the video. And he started asking me questions about my mission, and I talked to him for a long time."

"What did this man look like?"

"He had red hair and muscles. He was the guy in the shack."

Wolf nodded. "Did he use his name?"

Ethan looked up at the ceiling, then back at Wolf. "Greg."

"What happened after you met him?"

"He had a friend, the other man in the shack. The one who shot me." His eyes glazed over.

"Ethan."

No response.

Wolf sensed that Ethan was back in the shack.

"Soldier!"

Ethan blinked. "Yes, sir."

"What happened that day? The day you met Greg. I want a full debriefing."

"Yes, sir. Greg took my phone. He took my car keys. He and his friend told me they were going to help me set a meeting with David Wolf and that I should come with them.

"I slept in their house. They had cows everywhere. I stayed there for a day and they asked me questions about my life and my head.

"We shot guns and talked more, and they said that they were planning a meeting with David Wolf. With you. And then when it was nighttime we drove out to a dirt road with my truck and their truck. They drove my truck. They told me it was a confusing drive and they needed to. When we got there, a storm was coming in. There was lightning."

Ethan blinked and looked down at the table.

"Go on, Ethan. Got where? Where did you stop?"

"We stopped on the dark dirt road in the trees. One of them walked away. They were on radios with each other. And a car came and they put up my truck's hood and made me stand next to it. They said you were coming and I needed to wait, and they went into the trees. But it wasn't you who pulled over. It was two other men. Greg and the man with the white beard came out and shot one of them and hit the other one in the head. Then I started crying."

Ethan began to weep.

"It's okay, Ethan. It's over now. You're just telling me what happened."

Ethan nodded. "Greg put handcuffs on me and pulled me to the other car. He put my hands on it. He gave me a phone and told me to hold it. Then he took the phone and threw it in the woods. They all had rubber gloves on, so I thought they were trying to make me look bad, because since I didn't have gloves on I could be leaving fingerprints and be blamed for what they were doing. I told them that, and they laughed at me."

Wolf nodded. "And then what?"

"They picked up the dead man off the side of the road and put him inside the trunk. And they pushed the car off the edge of the road. Then they put the other man into their pickup and they put handcuffs on me. I rode in the truck cab with the man who'd got hit. The white-bearded one drove my truck and we followed him up into the mountains to the shack.

"They put me inside and chained me to the table. And they took off the other man's clothes and put him on the straw." He looked at Wolf. "Your friend. My friend."

Wolf nodded. "And then what, Ethan?"

"And then the man with the white beard shot me." He stared

into the past. "But they took the chains off me. They scared me so bad. I just wanted them to stop. I got up and escaped, and saw my truck was there. I … I …" Clenching his eyes, Ethan bared his teeth and put a hand to his head. "I shot them. Because they were going to kill me. And they were going to kill you, and the girl. Greg was hitting you. They shot me."

"Your tournament rifle was inside your truck," Wolf said.

Ethan nodded. "I took it out of the case and shot the man with the beard. Greg got hit, too."

"Yeah," he said, deciding Ethan had a way with understatements.

Ethan stopped talking now and sat rigidly, staring at the wall.

"Is that all, soldier?"

"Yes, sir."

They sat in silence for a beat.

The door opened and Tennimen walked inside. "Hello, Ethan."

"Hello."

"You did a great job. Thank you."

Ethan nodded, clearly confused as to how Tennimen could know anything about what had just transpired.

"Can I see you for a second?" Wolf asked.

"Uh … yes, of course."

Wolf led the doctor out into the observation room, where MacLean and DA White were standing with folded arms.

When the door clicked shut MacLean said, "Good job with the military angle to get him talking."

Tennimen looked at DA White. "You're not going to recommend prosecution of this fellow, are you? Clearly he's been manipulated from the very beginning."

White shook his head. "There's no way I'm recommending prosecution."

"Good," Tennimen said.

"Did you see the Paul Womack video?" Wolf asked the doctor.

"No. What video?"

"Why?" White asked.

"Ethan Womack doesn't know his brother's dead yet."

Tennimen nodded. "I'll break the news to him later today. I'd prefer to tell him in a different environment."

Wolf looked at MacLean. "Did you see Paul's body?"

"Yes, I did."

"Where was it?"

"Back of the house."

"Where exactly?"

"Halfway between the shed and the back door. Lying in the dirt. Why?"

Wolf left out the door.

"Hey." MacLean followed him into the squad room. "Hey, where are you going?"

Wolf's boots chirped on the clean floor as he swerved through the desks. "New Mexico."

CHAPTER 51

A HAIRDRYER BREEZE skimmed over Wolf's skin, carrying the sharp scent of sagebrush and bunchgrass. A hawk circled in the contrail-streaked sky, screeching at two smaller birds attacking it.

Two shooting berms cast long afternoon shadows in the distance. Behind them, rolling hills butted up against taller, pine-covered mountains overlooking Taos, miles to the southeast.

Buzzing flies had led Wolf to the exact spot between the outside shack and the back door to the Womack house, and now he stared down at a large maroon stain on the otherwise tan-colored ground.

The lowering sun scorched the back of his neck and he longed for a cool Rocky Points breeze.

Slinging the shovel off his shoulder, he stabbed it into the earth. Pulling up a wedge-shaped chunk of the red-tinged soil, he placed it in a plastic lawn bag.

Sometimes endings are messy.

With that thought in mind, he continued cleaning up Paul Womack's ending.

"I pushed him."

Wolf was startled by the non-sequitur coming out of Paul Womack's mouth. The man had just succumbed to some sort of psychotic episode and shot and killed a mother and her child in front of dozens of other women and children.

The mother was dead and the child needed immediate medical attention if she was going to live. Chambers was in the hut, tending to the girl's wounds, and the rest of them had disarmed Paul and brought him outside.

Wolf had wrestled Paul to the ground and now sat on his chest, pinning his arms to his sides with his knees.

"Here," PFC Chan said, handing him a zip-tie.

"I pushed him. I pushed him."

The ranting coming out of his former-best friend's mouth was smothered by the crescendo of chaos behind him. Women were shrieking at the top of their lungs and pushing out of the hut. Children cried, clutching tightly to their mothers and ducking away from the soldiers as if they were demons.

"I'm gonna flip him over and put on the zip-tie," he said to Chan. "Help me!"

Chan snapped out of his shell-shocked daze and knelt at the ready.

Wolf's whole body shook, and with it his voice. "Ready?"

"Yeah."

Without any resistance, Paul rolled over onto his stomach and put his hands behind him.

Wolf stood him up, gripped his shoulders, and turned him around.

Paul's eyes were wide, unblinking. An animal on the hunt.

"I pushed him," Paul said.

"What are you talking about?" Wolf grabbed him by the edges of his flak jacket and shook him. "What are you talking about, Paul? Wake the fuck up!"

His voice was a whisper, only for Wolf. "I pushed him."

Wolf shook his head. "I don't understand, Paul. Who did you push?"

Paul's eyes shimmered and he looked up. Clenching them shut, tears cascaded down his cheeks.

"Get him out of here," Wolf said.

CHAPTER 52

WOLF SAT BEHIND HIS DESK, welcoming the soft leather seat's cradling embrace. His legs ached from standing the past three hours at Pat Xander's funeral reception. He suspected it was a hangover from all the hiking four days previously—another reminder that his body didn't recover like the old days and he wasn't in as good shape as he'd thought.

"Overall a good service," Rachette said, plopping down on Wolf's pleather office couch like he'd just run a marathon.

Charlotte sat down next to him and leaned back into the cushions. "Too many frickin' funerals in this town. Maybe we should move to Chicago or Detroit. Somewhere safe to raise this child." She looked over at her husband's vacant gaze and put a hand on his cheek. "Sorry, baby. I'm just bone tired. You're right. It was a great service."

There was a knock at Wolf's door and Lorber ducked inside. "Hey, bunch of us are going to Goggs tonight to throw some back. You know, unwind all this tension. You guys in?"

Pale-faced and with his bandaged left hand hoisted in the air, Rachette locked eyes with the medical examiner. "Hell, yeah."

Charlotte gave a sidelong glance at her husband, concern

creasing her forehead. She nodded at Lorber. "I'll drive whoever can fit in my car."

Lorber stepped inside and folded his arms. "Why?" He raised an eyebrow. "Are you not going to be drinking or something?"

"No, I'm not."

Wolf met Rachette's gaze and smiled, hoping the dual scabs on his lips didn't split open again.

"And why not?" Lorber asked.

Charlotte and Lorber had a staring war until he surrendered and looked away. "Fine."

"I'm pregnant. Didn't you figure that out, like, days ago?"

"You are?"

"Shut up."

"Well, yeah. I knew. But you never officially told me. So ... I didn't want to say anything, you know. The golden rule is to never ask if a woman is pregnant, right? I mean, that's putting your foot in your mouth right there."

She frowned. "No. You're talking about if you think a woman looks like she's pregnant, but really she's gained weight. Are you saying I gained weight?"

Lorber's eyes popped wide behind his John Lennons.

"Oh, honey, no," Rachette rubbed her knee. "You look great. Hot as ever."

"But you're gonna be a fat ass." A female voice came from the doorway and Patterson peeked inside. "It's inevitable. Hi." She knocked. "Can I come in?"

They ushered her inside, their tones suggesting she'd been silly for asking ... everyone but Lorber, who shuffled aside without opening his mouth.

"Hi." Just like the rest of them, Patterson was still dressed in black from the funeral. She'd left the reception early, citing her screaming child as the reason.

"How's it going?" Wolf asked.

"Good, thanks." She held her bandaged left hand close to her body and in the other dangled a manila folder. Patting it against her leg, she stepped toward Wolf's desk.

"Hey, yeah. What's up?" Rachette asked. "Can't keep away from the station? You miss this place, don't you?"

She narrowed her eyes at her former partner.

"What's that?" Rachette pointed at the folder. "You gonna submit your résumé for the open detective spot?"

"Uh ... yeah, right." There was a flash in her eye, and frustration crumpled her forehead. "You know what? I'm sorry. I'll just—"

"No, please," Wolf said, beckoning her closer. "What's up?"

Keeping her eyes on the floor, she walked over and slapped the folder in front of him.

Wolf ignored it, studying her face. "Rachette's right, isn't he?"

She raised her chin and stared out the window over his head.

Everyone leaned toward her. The air vent clicked on. In the silence, it sounded as loud as a hydroelectric dam turbine.

"Yes, he is."

"Knew it," Rachette said.

Charlotte slapped him on the shoulder.

Wolf narrowed his eyes. "You quit once. Why would I hire you again?"

"Because I made a mistake. And perhaps, because of recent events, you could ..." She swallowed. "... perhaps consider doing me a favor."

"You're saying that because you saved our asses, I should do you a favor."

"Yes, that's the general idea."

"But you quit. Now you're unreliable."

She snorted. "Oh, I think we've established I'm reliable."

If it weren't for her, Rachette and Wolf would've been sitting in the ground right now and they all knew it. As they all contemplated that fact, the silence took over again.

"You'd be demoted," he said.

"That's where the favor would come in."

He blinked.

"I'd be hired back at my old position."

"At the same rank." Wolf raised his eyebrows.

"Yes. You could call my year away an extended leave. A sabbatical of sorts."

He nodded and swiveled his chair to study the bookshelves. "So the favor is not to hire you back. Which would already be a mighty big favor."

"No. I'm the best candidate, that's just a fact. To rehire me is good judgment on your part."

He failed to suppress a smile.

She jumped at the crack in his serious expression. "The favor is the sergeant thing."

"But you quit." Wolf raised his voice a few decibels higher than he'd meant to.

The words made Patterson shut her eyes.

He was trying to get her to think. She didn't really want the job, did she? "You quit the department for a valid reason. One that nobody judges you for." He locked eyes with Lorber.

The ME dropped his gaze to the floor.

Wolf gestured out the window toward her office building poking through the trees in the distance. "You have a huge office overlooking the valley."

"A sick car," Rachette offered. "Or, it used to be. Sorry, go on …"

Wolf nodded. "A great salary. A schedule that allows you to see more of your son."

A tear fell down her cheek, and he shut his mouth, realizing that each of his words drove a dagger deeper into her heart. Why, however, was the ten-million-dollar question.

"I made a mistake," she said. "I let my emotions take over, and instead of working out my issues with the department, like I should've, I freaked out and quit." She turned to Lorber. "I let down the department. I let down the people who counted on me."

Lorber looked up from his shoes with shimmering eyes.

"I won't quit again." Her words were directed straight at the ME. Turning in place, she looked at Charlotte, then Rachette, and finally landed her glare on Wolf. "I won't quit again."

The temperature rose with the heat in her voice, and Wolf wondered whether electric sparks were going to shoot out of her eyes.

When the vent kicked off he heard himself blink.

He scraped the manila folder into the trashcan next to his desk.

"I want you to seek someone to talk to."

Her face dropped.

"If I hire you."

"Yes. Of course. I will. You're right."

He sucked in a deep breath, then nodded. "Okay, you're hired."

"Yesss!" Charlotte jumped up.

"All right!" Lorber punched the ceiling accidently, sending flecks of tile to the ground, then wrapped his tree-branch arms around Patterson.

"Ow, my ribs!"

"Sorry."

"Thank you, sir." Patterson's eyes were flowing freely now.

Joining in the group hug, Charlotte began to cry too.

"My God, easy." Rachette leaned back on the couch and pulled his feet up. "Watch the finger."

When the celebration had dissipated, Wolf clasped Patterson's hand. He said nothing, but thought that he'd just recommissioned the best detective he'd ever met. That, and that she owed him for keeping his mouth shut about illegal cellphone-tracking software. But that favor could be pulled another time.

"Thank you," she said.

Wolf smiled. "Welcome back."

"All right." Rachette held up his hands. "It's four fifteen. My pain pills are wearing off, so what say we hit the bar early?"

Patterson checked her watch. "I could do one. I'll buy."

"Sir? You coming?" Rachette asked.

He nodded. "I'll be there in a bit. I just have a few things to finish up."

"Hey, Patterson. You're buying?" Rachette asked, following them out.

"Yeah."

"Wait up. Stop."

She turned around. "What?"

He stepped close. "I'm going to ask you one more time. Okay?"

She frowned.

"Are you buying?"

"Yes, Tom. I'm buying."

"Pinkie-swear?"

She closed her eyes and sucked in a deep breath through her nose. "Ah, shit."

Rachette smiled at Wolf, gave him a thumbs-up and followed her out the door.

CHAPTER 53

WOLF DROVE up the steep hill to his ranch headgate. Passing through, the terrain flattened and the scene rose in his windshield. Deep green grass covered the flat expanse of land in front of the house. Behind it, scorched trees littered the mountainside from the explosion and resulting fire some years back. Between them, countless pine saplings competed to be the next-generation forest.

Lauren's Audi sat in the carport, reflecting the orange sunset behind him. As he rolled forward, Ella came running around the house and fell on the grass.

He leaned into the windshield and was relieved to see her pop back up and continue running.

He wondered why she was moving so fast, then realized she was coming to meet him. Maybe she would jabber his ear off about something amazing that had happened to her—like the time a pine cone had fallen from a tree and hit her on the head.

He was excited to find out.

Lauren sat on the front porch with a glass of red wine and a bottle of Newcastle beer in front of her, and she raised the drinks into the air.

He smiled wide, thinking he'd be hard-pressed to be welcomed home with a better greeting.

The SUV rocked to a stop next to Lauren's and he got out onto the gravel.

"Dave!" Ella hugged him and then backed away. "You'll never guess what happened."

"A pine cone fell on your head?"

She frowned. "No ... but a momma deer came behind the house with three of her baby deers." She popped her eyebrows high and nodded.

"That is awesome."

"Yeah. I'm gonna go see if they're still back there." She ran in between the cars to the rear of the house.

"Please stay up here where we can see you, honey!" Lauren yelled.

"I know! I know!"

This time of day, you kept your children close in the mountains. Wildcats were most active during the twilight hours.

Lauren stepped off the porch with their drinks and walked to him. She smiled and glowed by the light of the blazing sky. Not that her lightly freckled, tanned skin needed any help. Walking on bare feet through the flower-speckled grass, she wore a pair of sweatpants and an MC Escher drawing-hands long-sleeved shirt.

Wolf took the frosted beer from her outstretched hand. He kissed her first and then they clinked their drinks. The bottle was cold, and felt good on his scabbed lips. He took a long swill and it warmed his insides.

He followed her back to the front deck. "Wow, look at this." A plate sat on the table with an array of crackers, meats, and cheeses. "What's going on here?"

She shrugged. "Just thought I'd make a little something."

"Beer Goggles has nothing on this place."

After running an errand in town he'd foregone beers at the bar and was glad for it.

"Dig in. There's mozzarella, salami, and ham."

"And my favorite crackers with the sesame seeds on them," he said, stacking one inch-high and shoving it in his mouth.

She watched him with rapt attention.

"Thank you," he said, lifting his beer. "Wow."

She smiled, looking relieved.

"Everything okay?" he asked, not used to so much pointed attention.

"Take a seat. Relax," she said.

He shot her a suspicious look and sat down. Maybe she felt bad about the Baron thing. Maybe she'd nothing to feel bad about concerning that matter and he should shut up about things that were beyond his comprehension.

Ella came pattering around the front of the house and began doing as many cartwheels in a row as she could manage without falling over.

His body and mind were still exhausted from the past weekend's events and today's funeral, but as he sagged into the springy metal chair, he felt his insides recharging. Like he'd plugged into an outlet by coming home with these two girls by his side.

Birds chirped and flitted through the meadow, and an elk ate grass at the edge of the woods a few hundred yards away.

This was their own personal happy hour.

His legs and back relaxed in the oversized seat cushions. They were Lauren's chairs she'd brought with her when she'd moved in last summer.

That got him thinking about the old wooden chairs in the barn, waiting in a corner, collecting spider webs, ready to dish out splinters to the next person who touched them.

Why were those old chairs still sitting in there? He could've chopped them up for kindling over the winter, but he'd kept them.

He knew the answer, and that's what tightened his chest right now. Because he was saving them, just in case. Because this happy hour was just that—happiness that felt like it had a ticking timer.

Four evenings ago, he'd brushed shoulders with death more than once. He'd resigned himself to dying. More than that, he'd expected it. He'd held his final breath, felt warm blood on his face, and never expected to take another. And yet now he lived. Coming out of the ordeal, he felt an underlying impatience with any of the bullshit, petty pursuits of the normal lives of the living.

He stared at Lauren's beautiful face.

"What?" she asked, looking unnerved.

He put down his beer. "I'll be right back."

"Where are you going?"

"I forgot something in the car." He stood up and hesitated at the sight of Lauren and Ella exchanging a glance. He narrowed his eyes with the dawning realization that he wasn't privy to some important information. "What's going on?"

Lauren swallowed and shook her head, then took a sip of wine.

"Okay ... I'll be right back."

Eyeing the seven-year-old and her mother, Wolf walked off the wooden deck, kicked through the grass, and opened the hatch of his SUV.

The backpack sat inside, still damp from the hike days ago. He needed to properly wash all the clothing along with the bag itself, and then let the pack air outside for a few days. As he unzipped it, the Fabian stench that billowed out told him burning all of it would be a better option.

He fished inside and pulled out the tiny box. Its velvet cover was wet and the hinge squeaked as he opened it. The ring was like an explosion inside.

The certainty he'd felt only seconds ago wavered.

She'd already turned him down once. What's to say she wouldn't do it again?

He stared at the mesmerizing sparkle of the diamond. Why

did he even like the idea of getting married? He'd failed at it the first time around. But something primal inside of him wanted Lauren, and Ella, for his own. Because without the marriage they were in stasis. People got married because they wanted to commit, so they could get on with building the rest of their lives together. Because they loved one another.

"What's that?" Ella materialized out of another dimension next to him.

He snapped the box closed and shoved it in his pocket. "Nothing."

"Are those wind chimes?" She reached into the back and pulled them out by the top rope. The beetle-kill pine tubes clapped together, sounding like an octopus playing a xylophone.

"Oh! This is awesome! Are these ours?"

Wolf smiled. It was impossible not to. "Yeah."

She dangled the wind chimes in one hand and a fluttering piece of paper in the other.

"What's that?" Wolf gestured to the paper.

"Oh ... yeah, it's a drawing I did for you." She handed it to him.

He'd seen Ella Coulter draw with crayons and colored pencils before, and every time he'd been struck by the raw talent that came out of her right hand. He was sure some of the art hanging off their refrigerator could've found a place in a gallery.

But this picture was something beyond that, and looking at it made his breath catch.

The drawing was his house standing in a green meadow at the foot of a pine-covered mountain. The sky was orange, just like tonight. Lauren was there, on the front deck, and just like tonight she wore a dark shirt and gray pants with bare feet. Ella's outfit in the picture matched the blue jeans and red sweatshirt she wore now. Wolf was between them. As if posing for a photo, they all stood holding hands and smiling.

He opened his mouth, then closed it when he noticed the

food on the patio table, his bottle of beer, and Lauren's glass of wine, all of it drawn in detail.

"This is great, Ella. This is really great."

Ella smiled and nodded proudly.

"She wrote a note on the back." Lauren had walked over to watch and stood in the grass with crossed arms.

"Turn it over and read it," Ella said.

He flipped it over and read the sentence.

It read: Will you marry us?

He lowered the sheet of paper and looked at them.

Lauren stepped forward. "I ... I knew you probably didn't want to ask me again, seeing that I said no once. And I'm sorry, I ... I thought this was a cute idea ... but now I'm freaking out. This puts so much pressure on you. I thought—"

"Yes." He said. "Of course I'll marry you guys."

"Yay!" Ella ran up and hugged him, and the wind chimes clanked against his legs.

Lauren stood smiling with tears running down her cheeks.

"Come here," he said.

She did and he pulled out the ring from his pocket.

"You had the ring in your pocket?" She exhaled and sagged, looking like the mountains had been lifted off her back.

He opened the box and plucked out the ring.

She held out her hand and he slipped it on.

"I drew the ring, too." Ella pointed at the piece of paper.

"You did?"

Sure enough, she'd drawn a golden ring with a tiny blue diamond on Lauren's left hand.

"That's mighty confident of you two," Wolf said, pulling Lauren into a hug.

Lauren smiled. "You know the old adage: it's hard to say no to a seven-year-old."

"Impossible," he said. "And, of course, I would never want to."

Ella hopped in the grass, testing the timbre of all eight tubes colliding with the clapper at once.

"Oh, yeah." Wolf bared his teeth. "Fabian was right. Those are great-sounding."

"I've always wanted to marry you," she said with a sober expression.

He looked back down at her and nodded.

"I'm sorry I said no before."

"You don't have to apologize about that." He tucked a strand of her hair behind her ear. "But you do have to kiss me."

ACKNOWLEDGMENTS

Thank you so much for reading Dark Mountain. I hope you enjoyed the story, and if you did, thank you for taking a few moments to leave a review. As an independent author, exposure is everything, and positive reviews help so much to get that exposure. I'd greatly appreciate your support if you chose to do so.

I love interacting with readers so please feel free to email me at jeff@jeffcarson.co so I can thank you personally. Otherwise, thanks for your support via other means, such as sharing the books with your friends/family/book clubs/the weird guy who wears tight women's yoga pants next door, or anyone else you think might be interested in reading the David Wolf series. Thanks again for spending time in Wolf's world.

Would you like to know about future David Wolf books the moment they are published? You can visit my blog and sign up for the New Release Newsletter at this link – http://www.jeffcarson.co/p/newsletter.html.

As a gift for signing up you'll receive a complimentary copy of Gut Decision—A David Wolf Short Story, which is a harrowing tale that takes place years ago during David Wolf's first days in the Sluice County Sheriff's Department.

"DANG IT, are they coming out of the sea? There's another one of them. Hey! You there!"

Special Agent Kristen Luke watched with detached interest as a Seattle field-office special agent—she'd forgotten his name already—raised a hand and marched away from the shore toward two people with buckets near the water's edge.

"Shit!" The agent splashed through the edge of the tidal pool and kicked off the water.

A horn blasted somewhere out in the Puget Sound, revealing the presence of a cargo ship in the thick fog hugging the silvery water.

Luke brought her eyes back down to a twenty-one-armed starfish at her feet. Its red appendages moved imperceptibly.

"Luke!"

She turned toward the crowd of suits and white-clad forensic techs milling near a tent.

Swain stood further up the beach, waving his hand overhead.

She stepped through the rocky, wet sand toward her partner and past the scene. Wafts of human feces and decay tickled her nose, tinging foul the salty, rain-drenched air.

She kept her eyes on Swain as far as the high-tide mark, then concentrated on stepping over the driftwood.

She reached him and squeezed his arm. "I'm sorry, Jake."

Swain looked at her. His electric-blue eyes had lost their spark and threatened to spill tears down his stubbled cheeks. "Let's go. I wanna see him."

Her partner had been sitting in the car for the past ten minutes, gathering his wits. Now he led the way with sure steps.

They stopped at the crime-scene tape manned by an agent with a clipboard.

"We're from Snohomish," Swain said.

"Names?"

"Special Agents Kristen Luke and Jake Swain."

The agent scribbled on the clipboard and whistled over his shoulder toward the tent. "Hunt! The Snohomish agents!"

Inside the tent, a squat man clad in white rose from a kneeling position. His eyes were hidden behind glasses reflecting harsh lights.

A single raindrop slapped Luke's ear, and a breeze brought in a blast of drizzle. Months ago, she would have flinched and made a snarky comment about the persistence of the crappy weather. Now she zipped up her FBI jacket and flipped up the hood like she was scratching her nose.

"Hey. Special Agent Keith Hunt." Hunt put out a rubber-gloved hand and pantomimed shaking. "Geez, here comes the rain again. News this morning said forty-two days straight."

Swain stared the special agent down.

"Sorry. Come on. Follow me close."

They ducked under the tape, Swain first, Luke second.

Hunt slowed and turned. His eyes were brown and big, eyebrows creased in concern. "I take it you two knew Special Agent Hooper well?"

Swain grunted while Luke nodded.

In truth, Luke hadn't known Hooper well, not as friends like

Swain had. She'd seen the man around the office plenty, but he was the kind who seemed to shut off when she was close by. She was an extremely attractive woman—she was intelligent enough to know that—and the brains of many men closed down when she came into the room. Then there were those whose hormones went hyperactive. Both were annoying.

A few months ago, she'd discovered that if she spoke about the Seahawks, Hooper's eyes would light up and he'd talk her out of the coffee room, but she rarely had much to say about football so that tactic had been short-lived.

Hunt lowered his eyes and continued, giving a wide berth to a row of plastic evidence tents. "Footprints. Just the two joggers who found the body this morning. Other than that, looks like he took quite a swim with the high tide. Sorry ... he was lifted and moved with the high tide. Washed up."

"Got it," Luke said, eyeing her partner.

Swain pushed six foot four, and with the lip scar could come off intimidating, but he ignored their conversation, eyes glued to the body on the beach.

Hunt walked another few paces and stopped just outside the tent. "Here, please."

For the first time, Luke allowed herself to stare at Hooper's corpse. He was face down, displaying an exit wound at the back of his head. Luke studied the sand, saw tiny tracks leading to and from his skull, and knew crabs would have been dining when Hooper was discovered that morning.

"First responder's footprints here." Hunt pointed in the sand. "Seattle PD came first. Saw the FBI badge in his pocket and gave us a call." Hunt shrugged like the rest was history they all knew, which they did. The Seattle field office had called Snohomish minutes later, and now, after an hour of biblical Thursday-morning rush-hour traffic, here they were.

One arm of Hooper's FBI jacket had come loose and was wadded next to his side. His right arm was partially submerged in the sand. So was part of his face. The visible part pointed toward them, displaying a hollowed-out eye socket. Luke's tenure in the Pacific Northwest had yielded one other dead body on the beach and she'd seen what crabs could do to a human corpse in quick fashion.

"Crabs got to him before we could," Hunt said, looking like he regretted saying it as he eyed Swain. "Uh ... single shot to the face. Exit wound out the back of the skull. No other injuries as far as we can tell. We were just going to turn over the body." He looked at them, as if for permission.

Swain closed his eyes and nodded. "Go ahead."

Hunt rejoined his team inside and assumed his earlier position. "One, two, three."

Hooper's body was stiff and turned over like a door opening.

Swain watched with an unflinching gaze.

"Careful," Hunt said, scrambling around to the other side and helping ease the body down.

Black sand caked Hooper's face. The exposed flesh was contorted, frozen sideways as if it were a picture taken a millisecond after being clocked by a boxing glove. Kelp hung off his fed-blue suit and tie and more sand clung to the fabric. A crab scurried away and a forensic worker slapped it under the edge of the tent.

Luke pulled her eyes from the gruesome sight and looked toward a second tent erected a short distance down the beach.

Swain followed her gaze.

"You two want to go see the other guy?" Hunt asked.

"Yes, please," Swain said.

"Okay, back with me."

They followed Hunt back out the way they'd come and ducked under the tape.

Another agent ushered them to the asphalt path that ran along the beach.

Swain took the lead again, his muscular legs striding fast.

Their boss, Supervisory Special Agent Dale Earnshaw, strode toward them with equal purpose. His arms bounced outward at his sides, a side-effect of the muscles underneath his rain coat.

"Did you see him?" Earnshaw asked. He talked to Swain, not Luke, so she deferred to her partner again.

"Yeah."

Earnshaw nodded at Luke, and she felt energized by the basic acknowledgment. It had been eleven months since she'd made the long drive from Colorado, and she still felt like the newbie when it came to the Snohomish County FO.

Earnshaw's shaved head glistened with rain, and she realized she was the only one with a hood on. She considered pulling it down and letting the clouds spit on her face but, then again, men were stupid when it came to stuff like that.

"What's happening here?" Swain asked, gesturing to the tent.

"Follow me."

There were fewer personnel at the second scene, though the tent was erected at the same angle to block the elements, and the same harsh light poured out onto the sand. More driftwood littered the beach here.

The SSA said something to a CSI and ducked under the tape. The CSI nodded them through and told them to wait.

One of the forensic techs inside the tent saw them and came out. "Hello. I'm Smith."

"Luke."

"Swain."

The tech nodded at Earnshaw. "Come this way, please."

They stepped carefully to the exterior of the tent. "Stop here, please."

Luke shuffled next to Earnshaw to get a look. She was the shortest and felt like a kid at a concert, so she stepped up onto a sturdy log.

The body lay on its back, the head toward the water and tilted back so that the face was obscured.

"Can't see shit," Swain said.

"He was shot once in the chest," Smith said. "Here. Jones!"

The photographer walked over.

"Can you show those photos again?"

Jones seemed to know the drill and was already pushing buttons. Leaving the strap around his neck, he turned the viewer toward them.

Earnshaw backed away and turned to Luke. "Go ahead."

He put a hand on the top of her ass and pushed her closer so that she fell off the log. A couple of inches down and he'd have scored third base. Could have been a mistake.

Breathing through the semi-grope afterthoughts, she eyed the screen and saw an Asian face staring back at her. Or rather its eaten-out eye-sockets. The head tilted back because the sand had been eroded from underneath it.

"Please show the tattoo," Earnshaw said.

The photographer scrolled through a dozen photos showing the body from all angles and stopped at a blue ink mark.

"Chung Do," Swain said, eyeing Luke. "You see that?"

They all looked at her.

She leaned closer and looked at the symbol. A dagger stabbed through a globe—representing the vicious goal of Chung Do, a gang dealing in human trafficking, guns, and drugs, in that order. The group had arrived from Hong Kong ten years earlier. And just like other Asian gangs she'd come across over the years, human life was far down on the list of sick stuff they cared about.

"Yep," she said. "He's still holding his gun."

The photographer pushed a few buttons and showed them a closeup shot of the handgun held loosely in the dead man's hand. The handle was inlaid with a circled star.

"Norinco," Luke said, recognizing the Chinese make.

"Yes," Smith said. "You know your firearms. Norinco CF-98. Nine mil."

Luke ignored the praise. They'd all recognized that model on sight. She was the only one who'd voiced the thought. The guy was attracted to her and kissing her ass. Damn, she was an egotistical bitch if she did say so herself.

She eyed the beach. Six men with metal detectors swept the shore near Hooper's corpse. "Have they checked down here with those detectors yet?"

"Not yet. They just started a few minutes ago, as far as I know."

"Why?" Earnshaw asked.

"I was just thinking that these two were most likely closer to one another last night. I could be wrong, of course, but we have two people shot on the same beach. And I'm just a Colorado girl, so check me if I'm wrong, but it looks like Hooper was pulled out by the tide. That direction, toward the mouth of the Puget Sound. This man didn't move. Clearly the high tide came up to this guy's head, and that's why it's tilted back like that, but no higher. His gun's lying half on his palm, half on the sand."

"Yes," Smith said with a hint of a smile.

"Isn't it more likely that the gun was buried here by the wave action while Hooper was brought down the beach and deposited?" she asked. "Metal heavier than water and all?"

Smith sucked in a breath and let it out. "Well, if you're gonna put it like that."

"Get them down here, damn it," Earnshaw said.

Smith plucked his radio off his belt and made a call.

Twenty minutes later, three techs found Hooper's Sig Sauer P226. One round was missing from the magazine. Five minutes after that they found one of his spent cartridges.

They stood nearer the Chung Do gangbanger's body now, but far back on the asphalt path and away from the action. The rain had died down to a floating mist, and two news helicopters hovered overhead, taking advantage of the break in the weather for a glimpse of the action. Forensic teams at either scene scrambled to wrap up their work before an even higher late-morning tide rolled in.

"You're a good agent, you know that?" Swain said, eyeing the water.

A cargo ship slipped by, heavy with multicolored containers stacked impossibly high on its decks. Luke pondered the height of the rolling wave splitting off the vessel's bow. "Thanks."

"So what are you thinking?"

"Guy with a gunshot in his heart shot a guy with a gunshot in his head," she said.

"Meaning ..."

"Meaning it's two kill shots at the same time." She looked at Swain. "Right?"

"What are you saying?"

She shrugged. "I don't know."

"Hooper could have shot the guy in the chest. Guy drops on his back. Shoots Hooper with his dying breath."

"Couldn't have been any other way."

"So you're wondering why Hooper shot this gangbanger."

She was headed down the wrong path fast. "No. I'm saying clearly this guy pulled a gun on Hooper, and Hooper had to defend himself. I guess I'm just wondering why was he here in the first place."

They stood in silence for a beat.

"Well?" she asked. "Do you know?"

"No."

"So what? This guy's an informant? Hooper met him and things went south?"

Someone yelled down the beach and they both turned.

Earnshaw had a phone pressed to his ear and waved his free hand over his head.

They walked down the pathway toward the SSA, watching him finish a conversation and pocket his cell.

"What's up?" Swain asked.

"There's something going on." Earnshaw put his hands on his hips. His FBI jacket split open, revealing a beefy chest and the butt of his gun sticking out of his shoulder holster.

"Something besides one of our own getting murdered by a Chung Do on this beach?" Swain asked.

"Yes."

... Go to Amazon.com to get the next suspense-packed David Wolf Adventure today!

Made in the USA
Lexington, KY
27 October 2018